THE VINDICATED QUEEN

THE VINDICATED QUEEN

WHITNEY O MCGRUDER

THE VINDICATED QUEEN

This book is a work of fiction. Names, characters, places, and incidents are the product of the author's imagination or are used fictitiously. Any resemblance to actual events, locales, or persons, living or dead, is coincidental.

Cover Design: Naimly A (naimlyarts@gmail.com)
Editing: Travis McGruder (witandtravesty.com)
Map Design: Whitney McGruder
Book Design and Typesetting: Enchanted Ink Publishing

The text type was set in Adobe Caslon Pro

ISBN: 979-8-9999793-0-8 (E-book)
ISBN: 978-1-7355064-9-4 (Paperback)
ISBN: 979-8-9999793-1-5 (Hardcover)

Thank you for your support of the author's rights.

WWW.WITANDTRAVESTY.COM

*If you've ever sought to know
who you are beyond societal roles,
this book is dedicated to you.*

You get to be whoever you want to be.

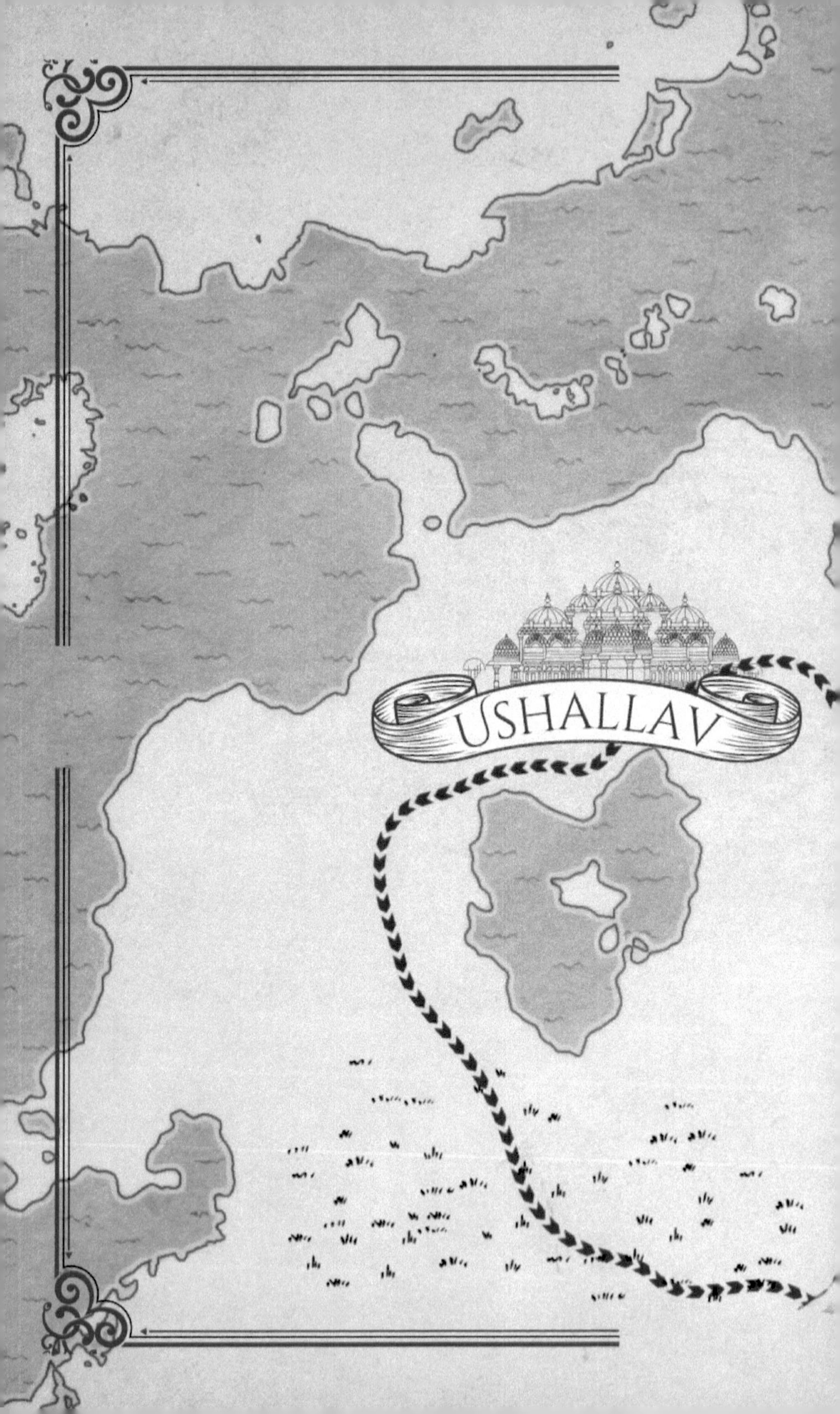

USHALLAV

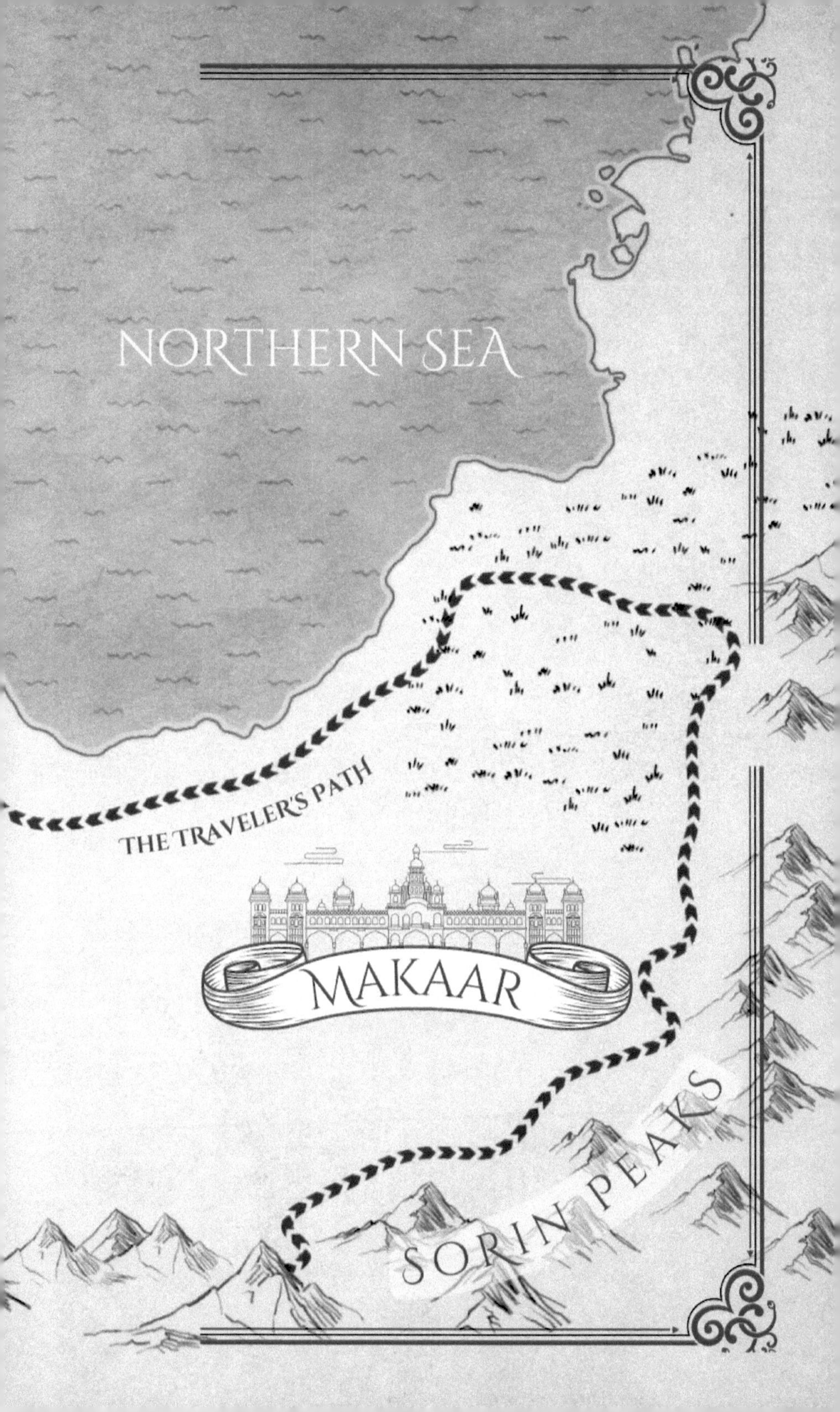

NORTHERN SEA
THE TRAVELER'S PATH
MAKAAR
SORIN PEAKS

BOOKS WRITTEN
BY WHITNEY MCGRUDER

The Destiny Seeker duology

Destiny Seeker: The Messenger

Destiny Seeker: The Defender

Ushallav's Queen duology

The Throwaway Queen

The Vindicated Queen

CHAPTER
ONE

When I nudged my son awake, I could tell that he sensed me coming. My 5-year-old, Devraj, stirred and rubbed his eyes.

"Are we going to see Papa?" he whispered.

"Yes, love. He won't let the carriage go without you."

I knew he would cry for a bit and go back to bed instead of rising with the sun to play, so I dressed him in some thicker, comfortable trousers and tucked his favorite blanket under my arm.

One of my handmaidens, Dipa, was already bent over and talking softly with 2-year-old Sanjana in her little bed. She didn't seem ready to wake up. If I was being honest, I wished I could stay in bed a little longer. I've equally wanted this day to pass quickly and never wanted it to come.

Heavy is the head that wears the crown? How about heavy is the head that signs up for a life of co-parenting?

Pari held a sleepy, bedheaded Sanjana while Ziya helped me wrap a long cotton cloth around my shoulders, torso, and waist so Sanjana was bound to me in a comfortable cocoon.

"Mama, I'm tired," said Devraj.

"I know."

"Can you carry me like Sanjana?" He raised his arms, ready for me to lift him up. With a half-awake brain, I leaned down and pulled him up and found a place for him on my right hip. The wrap holding Sanjana secure to my back also provided a cushion for Devraj on my side.

After completing their task of dutifully coaxing us out of bed and ensuring we looked somewhat presentable, my handmaidens filed outside the room. Dipa gave me a soft, encouraging smile. I smiled back.

So long as we're not the last ones at the carriages, we'll call this a win.

We shuffled quietly through the halls. Beyond the line of pillars, the sun greeted us across a wide expanse of ocean. There was a slight shiver in the air because of the early hour but it wouldn't last for long. The Ushallav sun would soon warm us to the bone.

Our little entourage reached the edge of the palace and we saw a line of carriages filing their way toward the gates.

I first made eye contact with Queen Einora. She

blinked sleepily before waving us over and smiling at us. It earned Damir's attention. I smiled briskly and nodded as we closed the distance between us.

"Good morning," I murmured. "Sanjana wasn't ready to wake up. But she didn't want to miss your departure."

"Oh, look at those cheeks," Einora cooed. I turned my back toward the royals so they could see the little princess. Einora brushed her pointer finger across Sanjana's serene, drooly face.

Einora was already fitted into her travel dress—something she would melt in if she wore it on this side of the continent but would suit her the closer they traveled toward the mountains. She still looked radiant and cheerful without her court makeup and her simple blond plait.

Devraj went to his father's legs and clung to his trousers.

"I'm here, Papa."

Damir smiled down at our half-awake firstborn. Our little prince.

"Let's look at the horses," Damir suggested, reaching out for Devraj's small hand. Our son grasped a few of Damir's fingers. As they approached the four horses hitched to the royal carriage, Damir picked up his son and held him close. He began to whisper and point at the horses while Devraj waved at the horses.

It almost felt wrong to watch them. This was Damir's last few moments here in Ushallav with his children before returning home and facing his court and his kingdom. With Einora—without me.

I let Einora and Sanjana distract me from my pangs of guilt.

You haven't done anything wrong, I thought to myself, almost sternly—trying to slap away the last dregs of sleep from my face.

As grown adults, we'd all made our decisions. We'd done the best with what we had. And for now, the best thing was to have the kids with me…for a time. Not forever. But I didn't even want to think about my moment with the children when one of us was in a carriage and the others stayed behind.

Damir is a good father. That man was practically born to be one—not just out of duty, but there was something in him. There was something in the way he smiled as he watched Devraj touch the gentle long nose of a horse.

I knew Einora was a great mother. The way Devraj didn't shy from her presence convinced me that she tenderly stepped in on my behalf while I was in hiding and in healing and in mourning.

What about me? Maybe it was the feeling in my stomach—am I sick or hungry?—or the T-shaped soreness across my shoulders and down my back.

I sensed this recognition flooding through me. Damir would go home with his wife and their shared child, and I would be here with two mournful children. I would pick up the pieces—gladly. If it meant that I got to connect with my kids and show them their second home, I would endure the bitter feelings.

Eventually, father and son rejoined us by the carriage doors. Einora already hugged me and kissed both my cheeks. I know we'd see each other soon—for festivals and birthdays no doubt—and I could admit that I would miss her. Through all of this, she became my friend; someone I could unflinchingly trust with my kids if it ever came to it.

Devraj creased his father's tunic and shirt as his tiny fists held on tight. He somehow let go after Damir whispered something in his ear, gave his cheek a kiss, and set him down. Damir reached for Sanjana and Devraj clung to my skirts.

I asked Devraj about the horses he met while Damir just held Sanjana and swayed and rocked her—held her close and placed one hand on the back of her head. If he said anything, I didn't hear.

His eyes rimmed with tears. My lips scrunched in an attempt to hold back my own emotions. I wasn't sure why I wanted to mask my feelings—not in front of the people I cared about most.

We made this decision together, and yet we both looked like we regretted it and what was to come. The guilt and grief crept up my neck like an allergic rash.

"It's only for a short time," Damir said, breaking the silence. "They're going to love spending their summer here with all their cousins."

"Thank you for trusting me," I replied. "Please send a report as soon as you make it back safely."

"Of course."

"Damir?"

"Yes?"

I paused. We'd hardly spoken to each other since our divorce. If we conversed, it was only to figure out how to raise our kids—the heirs to his kingdom—together and apart.

Who would educate them, and where? How long would they stay in one country? How old would they need to be before moving them more long-term to the country they would one day rule and protect?

The questions made my head spin. There was hardly any room to talk about us and how we felt about it all.

Talking about their futures felt a lot easier than thinking about my own. What was I going to do next? What was left for me on the other end of this tearful goodbye?

"Have a safe trip, Damir. Goodbye."

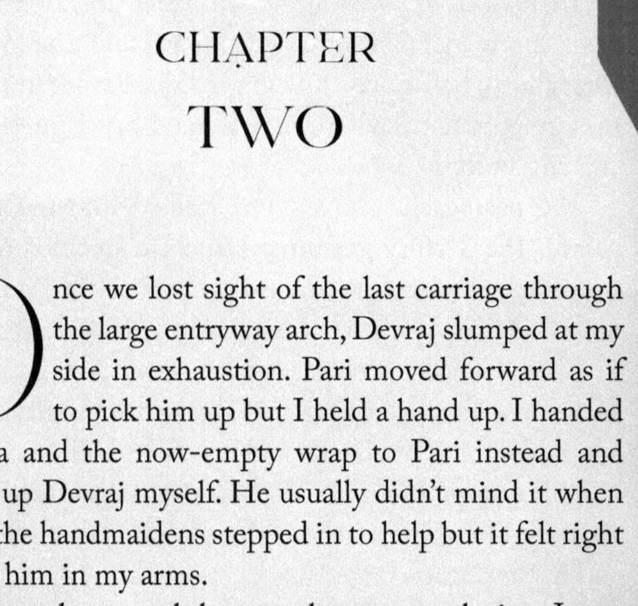

Once we lost sight of the last carriage through the large entryway arch, Devraj slumped at my side in exhaustion. Pari moved forward as if to pick him up but I held a hand up. I handed Sanjana and the now-empty wrap to Pari instead and picked up Devraj myself. He usually didn't mind it when any of the handmaidens stepped in to help but it felt right to take him in my arms.

I forgot how much he grew between each time I carried him. I shifted his weight slightly as he clung to my neck. He cried on and off as we watched the carriages depart, then resorted to sniffling and rubbing his eyes.

"Why does he have to go away?" he blubbered into my neck.

"He's returning to Makaar. The people need him to make decisions and lead them." I didn't want to linger on the accusation that he was "going away."

"Why do I have to stay here?" Devraj dared to add. His little hands grip my clothing like a small human appealing to a goddess.

"Devraj, you are very lucky to have two homes," I sighed. "You get to stay at this home and then after your birthday, you'll get to visit your other home."

Instead of answering, he squirmed in my arms and gave in to exhaustion. I gave Pari and the others a weary look before continuing inside. I wanted to leave this guilt outside where it belonged but I guess it was coming with us.

We passed the stables and walked into my family's palace. The 3-story gleaming structure shielded our eyes from the morning sun. The early risers nodded politely at me as we filed up the staircase toward the kid's room.

They needed rest. I needed training. Once I saw Sanjana and Devraj sleeping soundly in their beds, I could begin wrapping my hands and wrists with cloth.

"I'll stay with them," Dipa insisted. I nodded appreciatively. She shifted her weight and relaxed on a sleeping pad in the corner.

Dipa, Pari, and Ziya had served me diligently as my handmaidens for several months. They were a gift from King Ray, my brother. I lost Swaran, Gamani, Maliha, and Neha years ago thanks to the treachery of another handmaiden, Leela.

Sometimes, I looked at my new handmaidens and they seemed so far away. What did it mean to serve a queen who had no country to lead? Did they worry that their lives would end grimly because of me?

Dipa seemed unaware of my inner struggle and settled into a sleep that would allow her to catch up on rest but remain diligent should the children stir. Pari covered her fellow handmaiden in a blanket and a smile tugged at Dipa's lips.

Handmaidens choose to take on the role. They serve their queen in various ways: physical protection, spies, and caretakers for the queen's children. My mother's handmaidens were musclebound aunties who kept me safe; kept me humble.

Perhaps with time, I could form another bond with my handmaidens that would bless my children. Make the goddess Abhijita proud.

Pari and Ziya led the way toward the training facility. Back down the stairs we went. The natural sunlight shone through the open archways that lined the back of the palace. It was one of my favorite places to be. You could see the glittering Northern Sea and the skies beyond.

The morning sun warmed our backs as we descended the stairs and turned left. One door lead to the infirmary and the other to our family training facility.

After changing into wrapped trousers and a fitted blouse, I got a look of myself in the mirror that stretched across an entire wall. I watched myself braid my waist-length hair and smoothed the pleats in my dhoti. I hadn't really looked at myself truly since coming home. I wasn't sure I was ready for what I would see.

Thanks to Pari's recommendation, I was regularly using oils and lotions to keep my skin healthy and bright. But beyond the shimmer and shine, I saw a mother of two children. I saw a divorced queen. I saw a woman with deep brown skin, dark brown eyes, and black hair, who flexed and stretched a body blessed with curves, muscles, and skill.

What am I doing? I thought to myself. Would I just practice my hand-to-hand combat and run simulated drills until my kids grew up to run Damir's kingdom? What am I doing here and what am I going to do?

I blinked a bit and cleared my throat. Pari and Ziya were already running laps around the track barefoot to warm up and I soon joined them.

Nearly three weeks ago, we put quill to paper and declared divorce. I was no longer queen of Makaar, nor Damir's wife. That was Einora's job now. And I knew she'd do a great job. I was still responsible for raising my children, Sanjana and Devraj, so they could one day rule the southern country.

My strides grew wider as I put far too much gusto into a simple warmup exercise.

I wasn't angry.

I wasn't mad at Damir or Einora. None of this was their fault. This was all planned out behind the curtains by Leela. The rest of us did what was right for the children and our people. Damir spent nearly a year believing I perished at the hands of assassins, and sought out a new companion and mother for Devraj. Einora filled that role, and I could not be angry that she did so while I was gone.

Could I focus my wrath on Leela? Sure. But, she wouldn't live to see sunlight again. And hating her wouldn't bring back my handmaidens.

Considering the unprecedented situation handed to us, we all handled it rather maturely and selflessly. Even the people who disliked me in Makaar dared to call me a hero for every step I took for the good of two nations.

So why was I the one consoling the children and made to feel like the villain?

Devraj was just a child. He always had big feelings in such a small body. He wasn't angry at me; he was confused by what was happening. A little prince usually has everything figured out for him, and right now, there was a perfume of uncertainty in the air.

Like mother, like son, I supposed.

"My lady?"

Something spasmed in my ankle and I tumbled to the porous ground. Pari and Ziya rushed to my side.

"Are you all right, my queen?" Ziya asked. Concern spread across her face. "You pushed yourself too hard."

I groaned, more out of frustration than pain. "No. But I will be."

As I got up, a messenger hailed us from the entry way. She handed a note to Ziya before making her leave.

Ziya inspected it briefly before handing it to me.

"It's your brother's seal."

Good. I'd been expecting this. I had sort of avoided my brother, King Ray, since we arrived. So of course, now that my ex-husband was gone, it was time to figure out, well, everything.

THREE

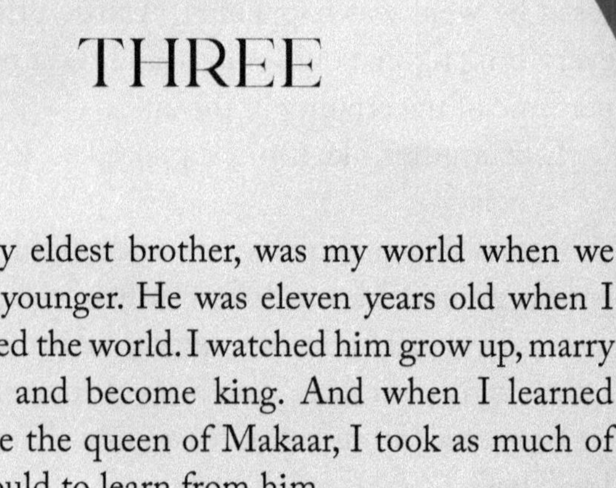

Ray, my eldest brother, was my world when we were younger. He was eleven years old when I entered the world. I watched him grow up, marry Tejal, and become king. And when I learned that I would be the queen of Makaar, I took as much of his time as I could to learn from him.

Part of why I wanted to be a good queen was because I wanted to create a brighter future with Damir—parallel to my brother. I used to daydream about a more peaceful future where our kingdoms could coexist in harmony. We could finally put the disputes, the wars, and the distrust behind us because I would be the bridge.

And I was the bridge…until I wasn't.

As I walked to Ray's private offices, I almost reverted to my teenage self. Would I be reprimanded for divorcing my husband? Would I be punished for not fighting hard enough for my marriage and my role as mediator? I had this power in my hands and I relinquished it.

And another scarier thought came to mind: Was I really necessary in these peacemaking plans anymore? Had I already served my purpose? Am I just reduced to my role as co-parent to the Makaar heirs?

I arched my back, moving my elbows back and forth to stretch the stiff muscles in my upper back and shoulders.

I didn't have to knock; a guard immediately saluted and opened the door for me. As I strolled in, I saw Ray sitting cross-legged on a cushion before a low table. The lunch spread on the 6-foot table looked inviting. He looked up and smiled before ushering me to sit.

Why did he look so nervous? The way he used his napkin to wipe away some curry from his sharply styled goatee and fingers told me this wasn't just going to be a pleasant lunch break with the king.

"Anjali, thank you for coming," he greeted. "Please eat. Tejal and the kids already ate so what's left is fair game."

I smiled at his generosity and the gorgeous smells. I dipped some naan into lamb saag once I made myself comfortable in the seat across from my brother.

"Am I in trouble?" I asked with a nervous laugh. Might as well get this out of the way to calm my nerves.

Ray echoed my nervous chuckle and shook his head no. "Well, I may be biased but when it comes to you, sis, it seems like you're always in trouble even when you're innocent."

If he was referring to our childhood, then he was reminding me of the many times my younger brother,

Harshad, and I would get into trouble and Ray would cover for us. Our big brother—our king.

I looked into Ray's face. He wasn't wearing his formal crown, but he still wore a circlet with tiny sapphires—it reminded me of the color of the sun touching water. Wrinkles formed around his eyes and forehead and it looked like his hair was thinking about graying soon.

"You look stressed," we said, nearly simultaneously. Then we laughed.

"You seem to be wearing your stress well," I said.

"Have compassion on a man who's getting close to his 40th birthday," Ray chuckled. "You know as well as I do that being a parent and a ruler is not easy. And I wanted to talk to you because I'm worried about you."

"Worried how?" I practically squeaked. I carried this conflicting feeling of wanting help and not wanting it. It was as if I wanted someone to see me and what I just went through but I also wanted to be invisible. Would it kill the rest of the world to let me figure my shit out in peace?

We ate a bit in silence before Ray stopped eating and looked at me.

"I know that you're already navigating a new situation with you and King Damir but I didn't want to keep you in the dark about…my part in all of this."

If he didn't clarify immediately, I would vomit.

"You deserve to know. Just hear me out first," he began. "Maybe this was me being your over-protective brother but I corresponded with your handmaidens before you officially married Damir and moved to Makaar."

He saw my gaze sharpen and continued, "I merely

asked them to reach out to me if things got bad. I wasn't sure if you would be open with me about life in Makaar, especially since things were tense between our countries before your wedding. I hoped they would inform me if they were treating you and my nephew less than deserved. And Leela was the only one who actually corresponded with me. And what she said gave me pause.

"I didn't want to 'wake up Zayant' over her reports, but I wanted to help you. I'll admit, with every moment they took you for granted, being cold and standoffish, my pride stepped in. Leela at the time had my trust and I told her to intervene on your behalf. This was when you were pregnant with Sanjana.

"Know that I didn't order her to kill anyone. If anything, I hoped that if she intervened it would be because you already stood your ground and needed backup—that's the handmaiden's role after all."

I had to interject. "Ray, why did you do that?" I sputtered. Damir's court didn't really respect me. And now it sounded like Ray didn't fully trust in my abilities. What was happening?

"You're my younger sister, Anji," Ray insisted. "You were a great queen. You are a great queen. No matter what, I still see you as a queen. I just know what it's like to want allies and someone to rely on. I wanted to be there for you but I didn't want to push you. Everything about your marriage and divorce are unprecedented, and I thought I could protect you. I failed you.

"When I heard about the attempt on your life—on unborn Sanjana's life…those were dark times. I almost made some decisions that I'm glad I didn't make. Now that we know more that Leela was mostly operating on her own, it doesn't make me feel better.

"In short, I take some responsibility for what Leela did. I didn't ask her to be violent or vengeful but I can't help feeling I put her on that path."

After swallowing down a lump of nausea, I asked, "Why are you telling me this? What am I supposed to do with this revelation?"

Ray held my gaze as he answered, "Based on what little information we've gathered, Leela hired help. She didn't sabotage your carriage alone. She went to great lengths to protect those identities. In the past few months, I've been working with my spies to learn more.

"We suspect that there's a deeper thread to their actions. Based on how Leela acted when she returned to your court, the running theory is that they might not approve of our ongoing positive relations with Makaar. We haven't received any formal complaints, and it's probably because their dissent is mostly unpopular. But they might get braver with time.

"I am doing everything I can to sort this out with my court and my resources. I don't want you to have to deal with all of this again—you already have so much on your shoulders. But it's also not fair to keep you in the dark about something that put you in such an unjust situation."

I stewed for a few minutes. I mulled over this additional layer on my past.

Weeks ago, I rode my carriage and revisited the place where I almost died. I didn't make a scene. I thought that meant that I had officially put this behind me. I thought it meant that all I had to do was find someone to remarry—

maybe someone of royalty so I could still be queen—and just move forward with my life.

Strong arms wrapped around me. I realized that in my dark thoughts, my brother was at my side and pulling me in for a hug. It was like I had just knocked over an expensive vase and he was telling me that it wasn't my fault or it was just a vase. Always covering for me.

I put my arms around him and hugged his back to show I was okay with the hug. But I felt so heavy and on the brink of tears. Maybe I was the broken thing, and his arms were holding the pieces together.

"You and your children are absolutely safe here," he spoke softly. "Leave the security and worrying to me. But if you want to do your own intel—much like how you discovered the truth behind Leela's motives—I'll leave that choice to you. Maybe it'll help or maybe it won't. Ignorance got us in this mess, and ignorance won't rescue us."

I wasn't sure what he meant by "we" when I was the divorced queen here, but I nodded in his shoulder.

"Who else knows?"

"You, me, and a very short list of investigators. And they only know what is absolutely necessary for their task."

"Should we tell Damir?"

A pause.

"What do you think?"

"Well, if we learn that Leela hired Makaarians, then it becomes his business, correct? What if her reach went beyond our countries and across the continent?"

I had to wonder what about my marriage to Makaar's king drove Leela and her team to end the lives of my innocent handmaidens and the guards who protected me. I almost died as a result, too.

"That's what I was thinking."

By this point, my brother let me go and he just sat on the floor next to me.

"I don't want to push you, but I want to share what resources I have to help you during this time," he continued. "Maybe you don't always want to talk to me because I'm the king and because I have no idea what this all must feel like for you.

"Just know that I have a few counselors on hand you could talk to. Especially in the past couple of decades, I've needed someone—someone who isn't our father. They listen to me and are strictly forbidden from sharing anything about our conversations with anyone else. It might be nice to unload whatever is on your mind and know it won't offend or upset anyone."

We Ushallavi are a wise people. There are devout servants of the gods who can connect us with the immortal. Others used bones, or cards to divine counsel for anyone on how to confront their problems.

This counselor role was very new to us. Rather than connected to gods or fate, I understood they were more like our sorcerers—linking the divine with the sciences.

At this point, I would welcome any of these people to help me detangle my life. My fears. My dread that I didn't know was there until I named it.

"No offense, Ray, but you're right that I need to talk to someone else. Do you have any particular recommendations? This feels bigger than you, me, and everyone else."

CHAPTER
FOUR

My brother said he knew just the person I should talk to…" I should've been so surprised when I immediately recognized the recommended counselor.

"What, not what you were expecting?"

Sauntering into the room was none other than my childhood friend Gurpreet.

"Well, no. Not exactly. It's still good to see you."

I embraced them and we laughed. We hadn't seen each other since they visited me after Devraj was born. They clapped a hand on my back and held me out at arm's length.

"You're not dressed up for your appointment? No family jewels?"

"I didn't think that was important," I smiled at my friend's wry humor. "Are you going to withhold your good advice because I'm not dressed for a ball?"

"I don't know. I always seem to feel much better when I'm wearing an expensive outfit," Gurpreet answered. I've never seen them ever wear something drabby, ill-fitted, or unflattering. Honestly, I was surprised they didn't wear their usual liquid gold makeup to accentuate their lips and eyes.

For our appointment, they looked like all business. They wore a black, masculine jacket with beautiful, bold embroidery at the cuffs and hems that touched the knees. The buttons fastened up to their neck which contrasted with a set of pearl necklaces. I noticed that their cream-colored trousers matched the embroidery nicely. Their hair fell in shaggy curls at the base of their neck.

"If only we were reuniting under better circumstances, right?" I offered weakly. "I was meaning to visit you at the sanctuary soon."

"That's all right. And these are very suitable circumstances. We're healthy, alive. I get to meet Sanjana a lot sooner than expected. That sounds good to me."

My jaw slackened a bit, at a loss for words.

Gurpreet was one of my oldest friends. The only reason they didn't come with me to Makaar was due to their recent promotion as the Hand of Abhijita—running the sanctuary was a pretty busy gig. I was half worried that I wouldn't get a moment of their time once I returned home—I supposed I didn't need to worry after all.

"Forgive me. I'm not my usual self," was all I could muster. A tear trickled down my cheek. Gurpreet's eyes flickered with concern.

Why did I feel so embarrassed? I knew I was allowed to cry. I dabbed the sadness and frustration away.

Gurpreet and I used to share all kinds of things together. I didn't know where to start in that moment. I married Damir and moved to Makaar; Gurpreet became the most eligible dating partner in Ushallav and a top spiritual guide for Abhijita's worshippers. Ever since, we've led very different lives. Not that it was bad but what would they know about what I was going through?

What mattered was that even though Gurpreet looked a little surprised at my vulnerable tears, they listened. They didn't crack a joke; they wanted to help.

"I'm sure with your status in the court, you know what happened, right?" I asked. Gurpreet often knew more than my handmaidens did—they had a way of knowing pertinent information first.

"I know what your brother knows," Gurpreet acknowledged. "But I haven't seen a thing through your eyes. And that's more important to me right now. My friend is hurting and I want to stop the hurt however I can, Abhijita willing."

I looked down at my lap and the hands that lay there palms up.

"Why don't you start from the beginning—catch me up. You can tell me anything."

So, I nodded and took a breath. While I would've preferred to speak along the court bridge that pulls the outside air, sun, and water to the senses, I felt relieved that we were in my newly designated office where I could be my most vulnerable, transparent, and raw.

I told the story and they wrote. The story began all the way at the ambush—losing my entire entourage, being rescued by the Gavril people, raising Sanjana in the forest, thinking I would come home a survivor or hero, and learning that Damir remarried someone else. I explained the frustration and betrayal. We went through what I learned about Leela and why she was the one who planned this violence and animosity between two countries trying to reconcile.

Rolling my eyes, I explained why I divorced Damir.

"I keep thinking it was so stupid." The words tasted bitter on my tongue. "I was queen first. I didn't do anything wrong. That role—that right—belonged to me. And I just gave it to Einora."

"Well then, go undo that," Gurpreet quipped, grabbing yet another sheet of parchment paper. I gasped before they added, "You were married, then you weren't, so just go marry him again. It's not impossible if that's what you want."

My guts twisted.

"Well, no." I shook my head. "I mean—"

"I'm not trying to speak over you. I'm simply reminding you currently have the power to do whatever you want to do. If you want to go over there and reconcile with Damir, you know your brother would order a carriage and off you'd fly.

"You are not powerless. And honey, you're not stupid. I don't have stupid friends. So why do you believe that?"

Gurpreet's good at what they do. At the moment, I wished we were speaking in the sparring room so I could get a quick jab in but this wasn't exactly the environment for upper cuts.

After taking a deep breath and squaring my shoulders, I filled the silence.

"This isn't really about Damir or even Makaar right now. Damir hurt me by marrying someone else but he didn't mean to cause harm or betrayal. He needed to move on, and Devraj at the time needed a parent to care for him. I think Damir and I were in love and made a great team but that…that feels like a lifetime ago. So no, I'm not going to fight over a man who has already moved on from the relationship."

"Thank the gods," Gurpreet muttered—in that way that is supposed to be subtle but absolutely easy to hear. "What? You can and will do better. And besides, you and I know that healing takes time.

"I'm not going to tell you what to do but maybe keep your distance from Makaar and the bad memories it holds until it doesn't hurt to think about even being there."

"I can't wait to hear more about where you picked up all this wisdom on courting," I asked with a mischievous grin.

"That was an obvious subject-changer, Anj. But this session is all about you," Gurpreet answered, still jotting down notes. "We can gossip about my exploits after your appointment is up."

"Well, you gave me your advice. What more is there?"

Gurpreet leaned back from their writing position and rested on their elbows.

"You talked a lot about what happened and how you felt about those things. That's honestly really good. Even the most transparent Ushallavi has a hard time really expressing how they feel.

"All throughout our friendship, you had this one thing to look forward to: your betrothed marriage to Damir. And hey, now that you're divorced, I don't like him anymore. I don't care that you were the better person and chose to have a second chance at life. He still should've seen the powerful woman that you are and taken you back immediately. But that's for another appointment. For now, why not have something new to work towards? Again, you can do anything, so what do you want to do?"

I wanted to roll my eyes and explain how I couldn't just do anything because rules and laws and expectations still exist. But I pondered their words, "second chance at life."

"You really think I can do anything?"

"It's certainly a better place to start than assuming there's nothing you can do. That's a bad starting point for any negotiation."

I nodded, gesturing at Gurpeet's writing. "What's all this?"

They handed over several sheets of parchment with their hurried scrawl still drying. "You and I both know that you tend to keep a lot of thoughts in your head. I took the liberty of writing everything down so you don't have to. You can do whatever you want with this, but this is the story you chose to tell me."

I shuffled through the parchment so I could see the pages upon pages covered in ink. My story.

"We got through all that and you've hardly smudged your makeup with tears. I think we more than deserve some dessert."

I scoffed-laughed, knowing that we didn't care about our appearances *quite* like that. But trust Gurpreet to dig us out of an emotional moment with a joke.

They got to their feet and pulled me up, knowing that I didn't need it but still appreciated it.

A second chance at life, huh? If I could have anything, I would want to hopefully find someone who would want to go on that journey with me—and see what unfolds. I have my family, my friends, my children, and my hand-maidens. Was it so wrong to want a romantic partner too? Damir and I were duty-bound. I wanted something, something deeper than that.

I wasn't sure how long it'd take to calm my anger about what had happened to me but I felt something in me say that I and my children were finally safe enough to…I don't know? Figure out what happens next.

"I don't know if you have to report anything to anyone," I paused to give Gurpreet a knowing look, "but if anyone asks about what I'm doing next or how I'm going to spend my time in Ushallav, can you—?"

"Tell them to back off in a professional way? Anything for you, friend."

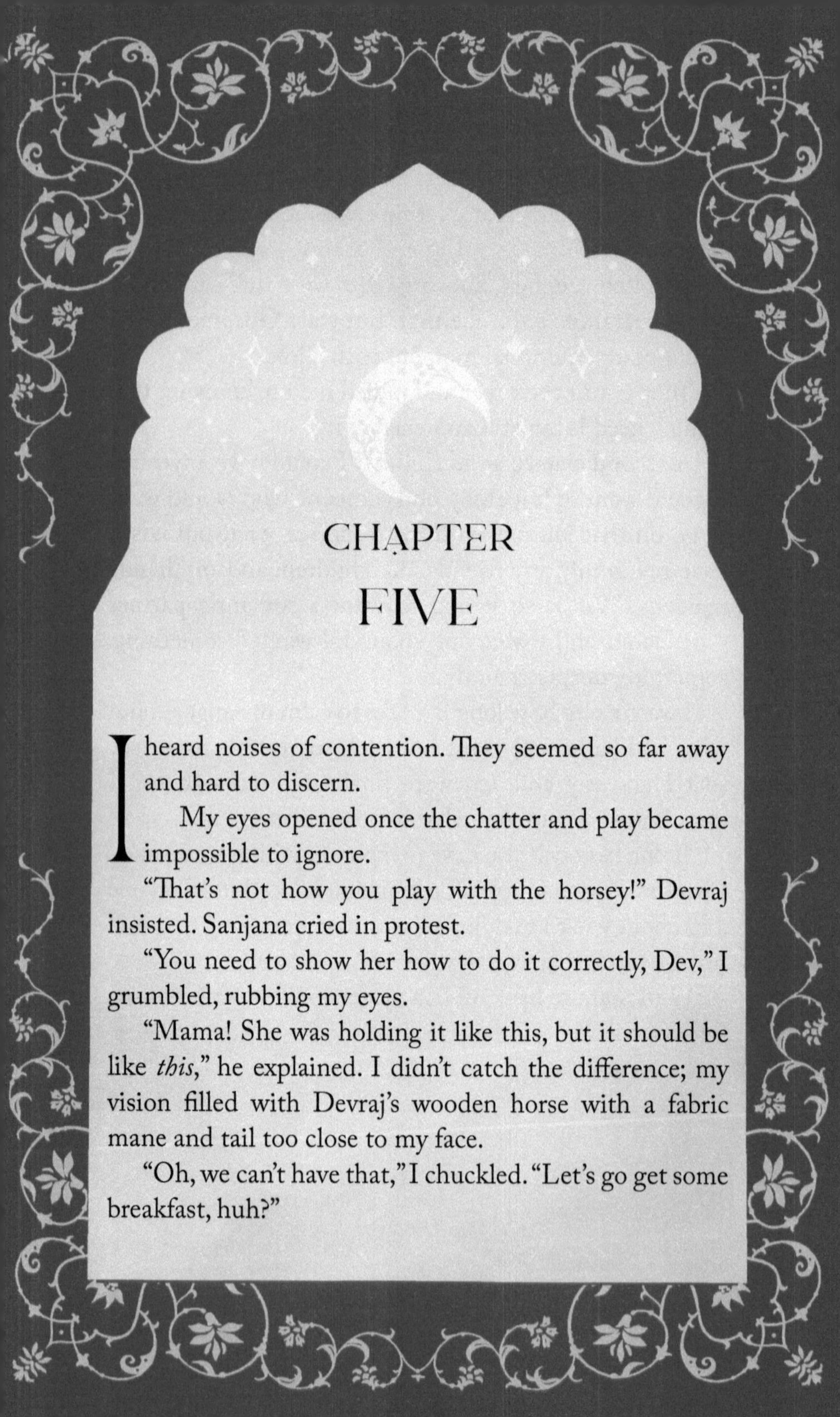

CHAPTER

FIVE

I heard noises of contention. They seemed so far away and hard to discern.

My eyes opened once the chatter and play became impossible to ignore.

"That's not how you play with the horsey!" Devraj insisted. Sanjana cried in protest.

"You need to show her how to do it correctly, Dev," I grumbled, rubbing my eyes.

"Mama! She was holding it like this, but it should be like *this*," he explained. I didn't catch the difference; my vision filled with Devraj's wooden horse with a fabric mane and tail too close to my face.

"Oh, we can't have that," I chuckled. "Let's go get some breakfast, huh?"

Once we were presentable but comfortable, we shuffled our way to breakfast. The rest of the day and the faces of those passing by would unravel in a blur; like I never actually shook the sleep from my eyes.

Sometimes, it felt like the days just slipped through my hands. I took the children to meals, and they didn't mind if we arrived after everyone already mingled and ate. It meant we had the low tables and plush seats to ourselves. They were punctual to play dates with their cousins and we practiced our Makaarian every day without fail.

Sometimes, the handmaidens would escort the children to their activities; if they offered to help, I let them. I still carried a guilt that refused to feel resolved. I don't have much else to do around here besides raising my children. And everyone in this palace is poised to play their part in supporting me.

The handmaidens were only doing their jobs; so why did it feel bad? Maybe because only queens had handmaidens to carry the burdens of parenthood, and I wasn't really busy with queenly duties. They weren't exactly expected to carry *everything*.

I wanted to look into Leela but the thought of returning to that world, of reviewing details, researching, and keeping a keen eye over my shoulder felt so impossible. I swore to myself that I would get to it eventually. But the hours would slip by as the sun slipped under the horizon, and soon it was time to close my eyes and sleep.

I slept through the mornings but never felt fully rested. I was surrounded by my children, my family, my native language, my favorite foods, and a world where I supposedly fit in perfectly. And yet, I couldn't enjoy it—not without knowing that I had quite possibly made the biggest mistake of my life, though it felt so mature and correct at the time.

Damir didn't feel like the right person to be with. The person he married died in a tragic assassination attempt. He didn't know the woman who emerged from the forest.

I still don't know who she is. If she knows what she wants, why isn't she doing anything about it? Where's her spark? Where does she belong?

Why won't she do something??

Sitting frozen on my bed, I stared across the room at the mirror. To a stranger or acquaintance, I looked appropriate and fine. I looked like I was ready to do some work. Behind my eyes, I could see someone trying to break out.

I already knew I was holding myself back—from discovering the truth behind Leela's true intentions, training with my handmaidens, or finding a husband. I've been here for how many days now—and I haven't even made a list of potential candidates?

"What is wrong with me?" my reflection asked.

***

"What's going through your mind, beta?"

"What do you mean?"

My mother, the former queen of Ushallav paused from dishing up some snacks for Sanjana and Devraj and gave me a knowing look.

"I, like many people here, have given you some space. Why haven't you come to talk to me yet?"

"Talk, talk, talk, Mama," I sighed, exasperated. "I feel like I do so much talking and no *doing*. I'm doing nothing, and I'm starting to feel like nothing."

"Beta—"

"It's how I feel. Is that what you want to hear? Hm?"

Maan doesn't speak for a moment and I don't know what to do with that dark space. I shouldn't have snapped.

"I'm worried about you. You're carrying a lot. I don't like to see you so upset."

As we spoke, Devraj and Sanjana were eating pieces of fruit and looking up at me. Really? Mom wanted to ask her questions during snack time?

"I'm not sure this is the best time," I replied, gesturing around. If she wanted honesty, she should've known that I didn't want to talk about my problems around the children.

"Mama, it's okay." Devraj held out a tiny, sticky hand. I smiled and did my best to school my emotions.

"You're right, baby," I replied. "Mama needed the reminder. It looks like your cousins are here for some lunch, too. Why don't you go see them?"

He smiled and peeled off to talk to one of Ray's younger children.

I felt angry that my problems felt too wild and abstract enough for the usual solutions and advice I could expect from my mother. What's the point of sharing my grief if no one knew how to help me?

"I've never been divorced before. I'm taking it one day at a time," I explained to my mother in low tones. "And with everyone watching and waiting to see what I do next, it makes me feel like a fool. Whatever misstep I take will be seen by everyone, including my own children."

Sanjana sat in my lap and ran her fingers along mine. She admired the jewelry but lingered on the curve of my fingers and nails. Ever since she was born, she'd witnessed me at my lowest. Her presence has always centered me. I hope to forever return that favor.

"Anjali, I know this might not solve everything, but why not start small? Leela left a dark cloud over you ever since she cruelly tricked and betrayed you—even tricked your father and I. Maybe replacing her and finding a new handmaiden will help."

I stared off into space, looking at a piece of decoration beyond my mother's concerned expression.

"Maybe," was all I could muster. I kept staring into space as my mother's demeanor changed.

"I'm sure visiting Gurpreet would raise your spirits. You haven't seen the sanctuary since the wedding. They could help you find a new suitable handmaiden. You could have another person to help you. It's been so long since I've visited the sanctuary myself…"

Thoughts bounced on the inside of my skull. Even though I knew Leela was no longer in my life, her actions still left a scar on me. Maybe this idea would be more than a distraction; maybe I could finally bury Leela for good. I wanted to live my life instead of mourning what it could've or should've been.

"Do you think Gurpreet is available or up for this?"

Maan brightened, unconcerned. "I'm sure they would make an exception for one of their closest friends."

"But what about Sanjana and Devraj?"

I had to ask. The last time I trained and chose my own handmaidens, I was still just a fiancé and not a mother of two. How did this work?

"They don't need to be glued to your hip, Anji," *maan* smiled. "Your other handmaidens and family members can take turns. Of course, the children may need to visit a few times so your newest handmaiden can bond with them and you can determine who will serve them well."

There was a glimmer in Mother's eyes. She looked pleased and determined, and I felt pleased and determined, too. My mother is my mother after all; no matter how old her children get, she was there to love them.

I gave a small smile. I wanted to know where my future would take me; and this felt like the best way to leave my past firmly in the past.

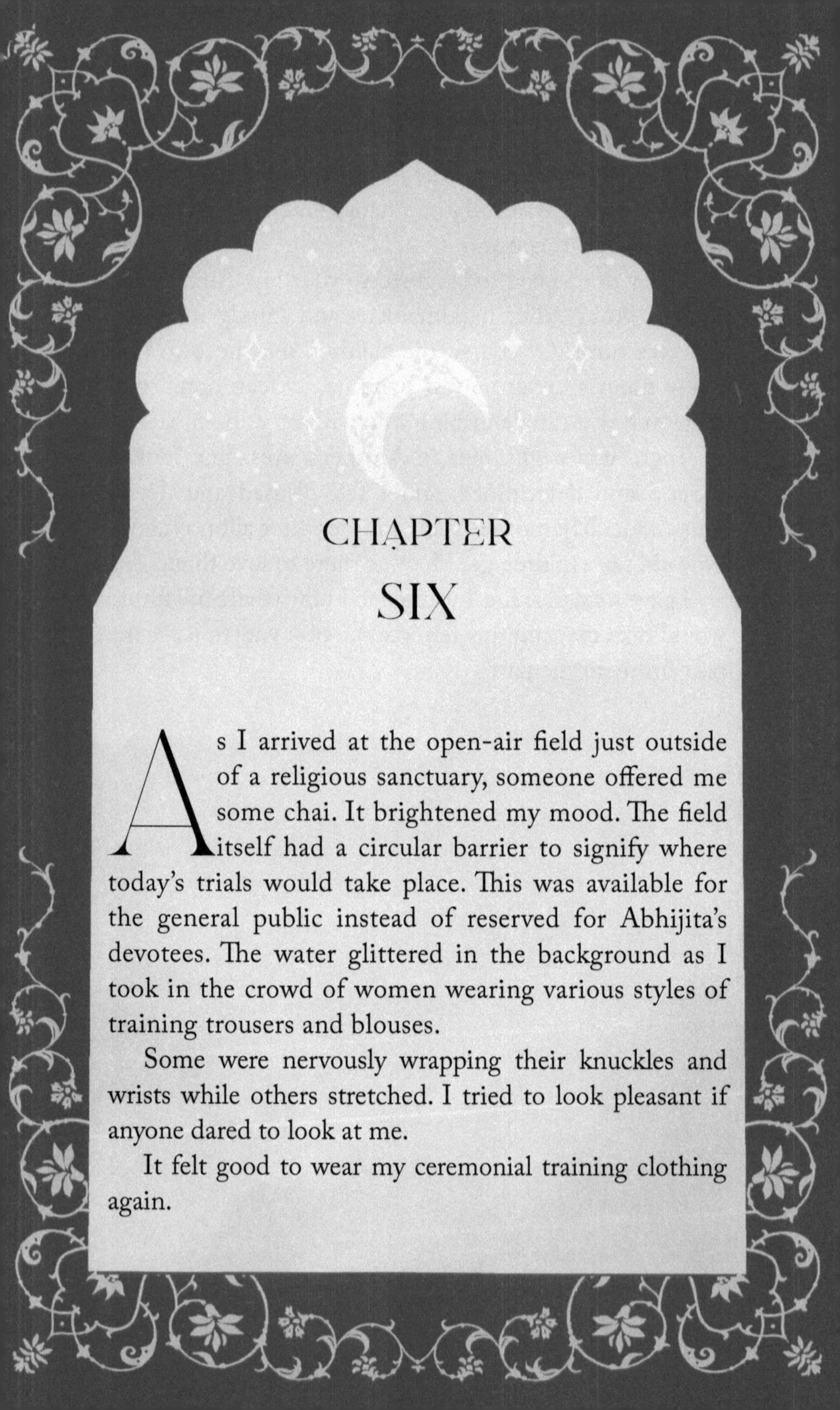

CHAPTER
SIX

As I arrived at the open-air field just outside of a religious sanctuary, someone offered me some chai. It brightened my mood. The field itself had a circular barrier to signify where today's trials would take place. This was available for the general public instead of reserved for Abhijita's devotees. The water glittered in the background as I took in the crowd of women wearing various styles of training trousers and blouses.

Some were nervously wrapping their knuckles and wrists while others stretched. I tried to look pleasant if anyone dared to look at me.

It felt good to wear my ceremonial training clothing again.

On a normal training day, it didn't matter what happened to my clothes—they'd get dirty or torn. But on rare occasions like this, I wore something a bit finer. My handmaidens helped wrap me in a long, ivory silk fabric around my waist as well as around my legs to create trousers—a dhoti. As a teen, I learned how to tuck my skirts in a similar fashion if I ever needed to defend myself or needed easier movement. I wore a matching blouse with one strap over my left shoulder that exposed my stomach and back. My long tresses were in a tight braid that ended at my navel.

Upon looking at me, there wasn't much indication that I was royalty—the only clues were in my stance and proud gaze as I looked over the small sea of women who could potentially join my household as a handmaiden.

Gods, I hoped this would be easier than finding a new husband.

As I flicked a stray thread from my dhoti, I remembered back to when I first tested and selected my handmaidens a decade ago. At that time, my mother's handmaidens helped raise me and my siblings—like older sisters or aunties. It meant something more when I got to train with women my age and pick the ones who were strong and soft enough to join me in Makaar to continue our traditions.

I smiled slightly—remembering the time I looked at the warrior women sitting with me in the carriage on our way to our new home. I blinked away the startling, contrasting memory of seeing their broken bodies in a similar carriage—defending me bravely against figures in black, pierced by black arrows.

Shaking my head felt like I was shaking the memory loose and away. Leela wouldn't dominate this day. She was dead, and today I would be one step closer to replacing her.

This was also an opportunity to bond with my new handmaidens—the ones my parents sent to me when I returned from my time with the Gavril people. Our meeting wasn't easy; at the time, I wasn't sure who to trust and who could carry me when I fell.

If I couldn't put these sad memories away, I was going to drop into a set of push ups or yoga.

I tried not to smirk or show a glimmer of amusement as Gurpreet took their spot next to me. They planted their feet in a shoulder-wide stance, holding their arms behind their back. Their presence encouraged a hush to fall over the crowd.

"Welcome. The Sanctuary of Abhijita invites her strongest to train their bodies and spirits—whether it is in the service of one or the service of our community. Today, Queen Anjali steps forward and wishes to test you and call one of you to her ranks. Show her the gifts our mighty goddess Abhijita has planted within you."

My friend did their best to look intimidating—in all the ways. I was well aware of their ability to cause the women around them to either be afraid or attracted to them. Their bleached hair was shorn short, although I could tell they were purposefully letting it tangle into wisps around their face and the back of their neck.

We somewhat matched in style but not in color—Gurpreet donned trousers that were so dark and blue the material almost looked black. Their chest, arms, and legs

were wrapped in deep-blue cotton. The tight wraps made them look deceptively thin and petite.

Their slight tenor voice rang throughout the crowd of fifty or so candidates, and an audience—some older people, mostly parents or guardians, sat at the edges of the painted circle to watch.

"Today, we're testing your bravery and your wit. All of you will have your chance to defend the queen. You may use any means necessary to prevent me from landing a blow. We end the moment I draw blood or Queen Anjali signals for me to stop."

A murmur went through the crowd. I nodded in approval; Gurpreet and I had trained together and talked about this days before. I was tired of being stuck in bed. I felt ready.

To Gurpreet's right stood five attendants. Everyone looked politely towards them as Gurpreet explained that the attendants would help each woman know when they could enter the middle circle and when they had to leave. They would have minutes to make an impression while I planned to defend myself for several hours as Gurpreet would strike—and they promised not to make it easy for anyone.

An attendant struck a bell the size of a man's skull with a soft mallet and we began.

***

Gurpreet extended a fist toward my left cheek. For the sake of the exam, I could only block, duck, and guard. When I got particularly frustrated, I at least batted their blows away. The poor hopeful candidate couldn't wedge herself between us—even when I took several steps away. Gurpreet would just close the space with their large steps and box the woman out. She huffed and bowed slightly when the bell rang and announced the end of her examination.

With each bell toll, Gurpreet would extend a fist—not as a punch but as a nudge. It was a way for us to touch hands and recognize that we were sparring and giving each other our best skills and top energy.

No matter where I would go or stay, Gurpreet promised they wouldn't send me away with the wrong handmaiden.

At the thirty-minute mark, we danced this dance again with 15 handmaiden hopefuls. I was tired, sure, but with slight breaks every 10 minutes, I was feeling hopeful. It felt like someone in this crowd would impress me; I already had a few standouts in mind.

The sixteenth candidate came in like a rainstorm—powerful and beautiful. Some candidates arrived with blunted weapons to show their expertise—this one came unarmed but just as lethal.

As Gurpreet took a step and swooped in with a kick, the candidate immediately stood before me and blocked it with her shin. She wore some light protective armor and I heard it take the full brunt of Gurpreet's strength.

For the first time, I could actually watch this woman fight—because she didn't let Gurpreet get an inch closer to me. If I wasn't so close, I might've missed their slightly frustrated grunt.

This woman only fought beside me for two minutes but it felt like a lifetime. She looked close in age to me and was one of the sturdiest fighters I'd ever seen. Like a vision of Abhijita herself. Her arms and legs were powerful and quick despite her being larger and wider than the other candidates.

She fought like this was already her job.

"To my left," she urged and I remembered my role. Her voice was slightly higher than I imagined but to the point. She was trying to tell me where to go.

"Got it," I huffed as I ducked and slid slightly behind her to the left. I evaded a twirling kick in time had I not been gobsmacked by this woman's impressive show.

With her continued communication, we could work in tandem. When the bell tolled, I could tell Gurpreet and I were grateful for the interruption; a moment to catch our breath.

Gurpreet stretched and gave the candidate a slight bow and prepared for her 17th opponent.

"Thank you," the candidate breathed out in mixed exhaustion and exhilaration. I could finally see her face as she smiled, slightly bumped my bicep with her fist, and ran to the outer edge of the circle. By the time she reached the attendants for their scoring and analysis, I was already dancing with my new defender.

CHAPTER
SEVEN

Applause and cheering rippled through the supportive onlookers once the last participant finished her sparring match with Gurpreet. Their attendants brought us towels and water as a few others escorted everyone inside the sanctuary to wash up and eat. My parents and my children would join us, and I looked forward to chatting together.

Gurpreet did their best not to look like they had sparred against fifty people in one day. But something told me they'd be up with the rest of us for morning training and would not use this as an excuse to sleep in. I gave them a rueful smile as they patted their face dry.

"I'm thinking out of all the participants, you were by far the most impressive. You could make this easy for me and just take the job," I teased.

"Look," Gurpreet said between breaths, "I like you. I like your kids. I like your family. But I love my space more."

"It's not out of divine admiration for Abhijita?" I wasn't sure if I was allowed to tease about that. Being a follower of Abhijita was one of the few things Gurpreet was serious about.

"She knows me well and guides me well. And we both know that I'm not fit to be a muscle-bound nanny for the royal kiddos. Besides, Janitra got your attention. I expected as much."

"Who? What?"

Gurpreet jutted their jaw towards her—the sixteenth fighter. She smiled cheerfully and joined some other participants who filed through the double-door entrance to the sanctuary.

"She definitely stood out, yes. But I can think of several others who did a good job, too."

"See? I'm off the hook yet again," Gurpreet grinned triumphantly. They rubbed the small towel through their hair, sending the ends in all directions.

"For someone who regularly rejects the palace lifestyle, you seem well suited to it," I smirked. "I think you'd enjoy the glamor and the drama more than me. And the attention."

I earned a chuckle from my friend as we stretched and joined everyone inside.

I gestured to my waist. Under some gauze and medicinal cream was a thin slash. It wasn't the worst wound but the attendants wouldn't let it fester.

"By the way, I'd say this is a personal record. You usually get me three times. Are you going soft?"

"Have you considered that you've gotten stronger since we last went toe-to-toe?" Gurpreet called over their shoulder while reapplying lotion to their arms.

"That's one way of putting it," I muttered. They hadn't gone soft; I'd become harder.

***

Gurpreet beat me to the dining area by a long while. It was no easy feat, washing and perfuming my hair or getting a toddler to wear their shoes. Dipa, Pari, and Ziya had brought Devraj and Sanjana so they could watch me spar. My handmaidens said they didn't watch everyone but still wrote out their impressions and gave them to Gurpreet's staff.

As I combed Devraj's hair and listened to him recount about his day at the palace, I wondered what my three remaining handmaidens thought. I smiled politely at the trio as we filed out of our guest quarters towards the gorgeous smells that invited us down the hall.

Maybe Gurpreet could help me sort these awkward feelings between me and my handmaidens. I learned from my mother and my grandmother—every woman who raised me—that handmaidens were blessed by our goddess, Abhijita, to help us raise our families and serve our people. They were her arms, her eyes, her femininity, her wisdom. If there was ever a template for a queen—it was Abhijita.

My parents chose these three handmaidens for me. I didn't watch them spar against Gurpreet. I didn't measure them against the other qualified women. Would I have chosen differently? I didn't think it would affect me so much until I returned to this place.

To their credit: the children seemed very comfortable around my trio, and these warrior women kept us alive when I needed them most.

I made a mental note to have a heart-to-heart with them. My role as queen without a throne was fairly un-conventional—just like the circumstances of how they came into my life. Like Damir and I, my handmaidens were doing their best.

My entourage and I had reserved seats next to Gur-preet. We sat criss-cross at a table that had a good view of the entire room. The circular room was guarded by larger-than-life statues of Abhijita in various poses and forms. Looking around, one could see that her statues covered a wide range of emotions—the many sides and facets of our goddess. For special occasions like today, each statue was decorated with flowers.

My favorite was practically locking eyes with me across the echoey atmosphere. The relief gazed at me with an expression that surprisingly brought me comfort. She carried a vase with her muscular arms on one shoulder and laid her other hand over her breast. Her soft gaze and lips always gave me a sense of gentle pride.

I always believed her to be a goddess who doted and thought fondly of her daughters. She was like my own mother—a person I admired and could never be disap-pointed in me. Even when I felt like a royal fuck-up.

I dished up some food for the children, knowing that I would likely have free-reign over their untouched food.

"Mama, can I play with Sanjana?" Devraj asked halfway through mealtime. I took the opportunity to hold his face and wipe stray berry juice from his upper lip.

"She still needs to clear her plate," I insisted.

"I'm full, Mama!" she insisted.

"You can go play after you finish your rice," I replied. "Look, Gurpreet is eating all their rice and look how strong they are."

Gurpreet expertly turned away from someone they were conversing with and flexed their arms at the three of us. The golden armband on their upper arm glistened as they showed off.

Devraj laughed with a mouthful of food and flexed his arms back.

"Looking good, little man," Gurpreet complimented. "Are you gonna arm wrestle me later?"

"No way!" Devraj giggled.

"Should I arm wrestle your mom?" my friend challenged.

"Yeah!"

"Wrestle!" Sanjana tried to echo.

I laughed at her enthusiasm. I studied her expressions to see if she was catching interest—even if she was too young to understand why we were hosting such a boisterous party.

Something in me hoped that she wanted to be a part of this world. If I needed extra training to be queen in Makaar, how much more would I need to prepare her to grow up there? I had to wonder how much she remembered of her time surviving with me—fighting for our lives for years. While Damir and Devraj thought we died by an assassin's hand, we traveled with the Gavril people—waiting to be strong enough to emerge and live to tell our tales.

My little girl was already strong. She didn't need to train and spar with anyone to show me that. I hugged her closer and longer than she expected. She ate her last bite of rice and squirmed away to go play. They joined the other eager and rosy-cheeked children to release their boundless energy.

As they toddled off, I caught someone's eyes. Janitra, if I remembered her name correctly. She had made quick friends with those lounging with her on the pillow-covered ground. She gave me a subtle nod before focusing her attention on someone sitting to her left.

My mother found me after making her rounds to greet our guests.

"I can tell you're working instead of relaxing," she gently teased.

"I'm just thinking," I replied, shrugging.

"Let the others eat in peace, at least. The exam for today has ended, has it not?"

I smiled and nestled my head against hers. Our jewelry jangled and twinkled as she hugged me from the side.

We were both wearing newly commissioned anarkali suits that allowed us to sit comfortably. She matched her eye makeup with the light turquoise silks of her dress and trousers. She emulated our seas well. Her black and silver hair fell into gentle waves around her face.

I leaned into the theme and wore a pearl and gold suit.

It was my best attempt to shine even though I felt like I was still earning back my light and luster.

"How are you doing?" Mom asked gently.

"Maybe sit with me for a bit?" It was an answer and a request.

"I don't have anything better to do." She settled next to me and rubbed my back reassuringly. "Good form today, by the way. They don't make these trials any easier. Is that a knot here? I need a massage just from watching you today."

She could've given me a back or shoulder rub anywhere and she'd find something that a masseuse ought to attend to.

"My trio definitely live up to my expectations—but Leela still found her way back into my life. What if I… don't pick the right person? What if I pick yet another Leela?"

Mom sighed but didn't stop rubbing my upper back. "Anji, my girl. Leela knew what we wanted to see and performed well. I can tell that these women are here for the right reason. Maybe I'm right or maybe I'm wrong. But I believe enough in myself to know that if I'm wrong, I'll figure out how to eventually get things right.

"Leela underestimated you, and Abhijita gave you the strength to strike her down and protect yourself and your children—including little Gregori."

She referred to the night I saved my step-son from being abducted—or worse—by my assassin.

"You've been tested by the gods more than anyone I know, Anji. But not everyone is trying to spar with you. Not everyone is designed to harm you. Everyone in this room is here for you. Those women are trying to prove just how much they want to be your handmaiden. See this night as a blessing and be blessed, my girl."

"If you insist, Mother," I sighed, half-assured.

CHAPTER

EIGHT

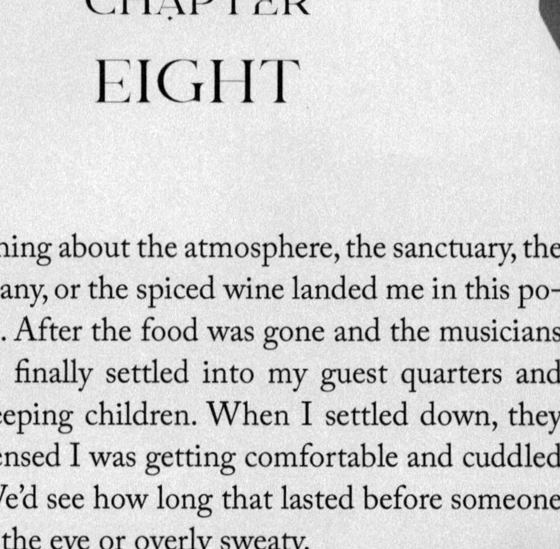

Something about the atmosphere, the sanctuary, the company, or the spiced wine landed me in this position. After the food was gone and the musicians left, I finally settled into my guest quarters and found my sleeping children. When I settled down, they half-asleep sensed I was getting comfortable and cuddled at my side. We'd see how long that lasted before someone got poked in the eye or overly sweaty.

But at that moment, I looked up at the ceiling and felt that spark. I wanted to be in love. I wanted love. There had to be someone out there who would love me deeper than my royal title. Someone had to see me as something more than a leader with an agenda or as *the* agenda.

For once in my life, I just wanted to live for myself. Just for a moment. My eyes watered at the thought, the dream.

Growing up, I knew who I'd marry. I was trained and prepared. I didn't have to wonder who I'd marry or what my future would look like. I didn't know how much that took up space in my heart until I lost nearly everything.

Some part of me wondered: was anyone even up for the task—able and willing? It was one thing to marry a rich, young, royal woman. It was another to marry someone co-parenting with the neighboring king.

Would this always feel this painful? Why did it feel impossible to imagine myself happy—alone or married? I sighed, ashamed of where my mind was going.

"Don't. Stop," I murmured aloud. I begged myself not to think such unfair things. I wouldn't know my options or my chances unless I tried. And watching the vigor and strength in fifty potential handmaidens showed me that plenty of people wanted the position to support me and my family. Maybe there was someone out there willing to fill the space in my heart.

As if sensing my distressing line of thinking, Sanjana gripped my clothes tighter and nestled closer before letting out a calm sigh.

***

I groaned in both palms after setting the parchment back on my desk. Who talked me into dating and courting again? "Oh right, me," I grumbled to no one in particular as I sipped my chai.

Almost as if they were waiting for the right moment, my mother and father prepared and presented a list of potential suitors. It was only days after the initial festivities at the sanctuary, yet they were all too prepared when I finally opened up to them about my experience and asked for their help. I tried not to roll my eyes too far into my skull when I learned that the list was already approved by Ray.

I told myself out loud, "They're just trying to help you and weed all the bad options out. They're not picking anyone for you. You get to choose."

"Mama, are you drawing?" Devraj practically yelled. Whenever they spent time with me in my office, we liked to lay on the floor and cushions with parchment and graphite and draw together. Devraj already drew several simple portraits of his father. Sometimes they were holding hands with a Devraj self portrait or riding creatures that he insisted were ponies.

"I'm working on a project, Dev," I answered. I held up the list so my kids could see it. "I want to find a new person to join our family."

"A new day-den?" Sanjana tried. I knew she meant "handmaiden."

"Well, we are looking for a new handmaiden but I'm also looking for another special person."

I looked into their shining eyes and down at the list and sighed.

"When you go to live with your papa, who will live here with me?" I asked. "Your papa has Einora and Gregori. I want someone special like papa to live here with me."

"We could just live with Papa and…Mama Einora," Devraj suggested, slightly deflated. His tiny brows furrowed like he was trying to read a word he hadn't learned yet. He looked like he was trying to sound it out and waited for help.

"Devraj, Sanjana. You two are so very very lucky. You have me, Papa, Einora, Gregori—"

"And Grandpa and Grandma?" Devraj smiled.

"Yes! And all your aunties, uncles, and cousins, and Dipa, Pari, and Ziya. Look at how big our family is. You have two homes. I hope to find someone who will join our family, since Papa and Einora and Gregori are living in Makaar and I must stay here."

I smiled sadly as I hugged him close and he clung tightly back. This was a lot for a young child to grasp. Sanjana joined in on the hug, which crumpled my list a bit.

"Hey, gentle," I urged with a laugh. "Okay, so here's my list. Maybe you can help with Mama's project?"

"Yeah!"

I went through the list and talked about the people on the list—in terms I could explain to a 3- and 5-year-old.

I already crossed out a few names, specifically nobility with connections to the family—men I already didn't like and couldn't understand why they made the approved list. And after consulting with Ziya, who was pretty good at reading people, we agreed that they weren't worth pursuing.

According to Ziya's findings many of them were intimidated—by me, the kids, and the overall situation before me. Well, except for one candidate. I heard that he seemed a little too confident in his abilities to "handle" me.

I could readily beat him in an arm wrestling match, I thought as I added three extra strikes through his name.

As I pointed to the names that weren't crossed out, I hoped that my kids could see that Damir was a good man. He was just not my husband anymore. And I wanted that kind of love back in my life. Sooner rather than later, I hoped.

Sanjana gleefully helped me cross out names that Devraj didn't seem excited about. Mostly because she got to use my stick of charcoal and mark my paper instead of the papers scattered around reserved for her creativity.

I had to hope that I could find someone who would be a good father, be a politically sound fit, and the person I was clearly meant to be with.

All I knew at that moment was that I wasn't going to get married just to get another divorce or be in a loveless relationship. This time, we would do things right—my way.

"Thank you for helping me," I smiled. "I knew I could count on you."

"We crossed out a lot of names," Devraj observed.

"That's because this person has to be very special," I replied.

"How will you know, Mama?" Devraj asked.

"Mama, I'm thirsty," Sanjana interrupted.

"Are you thirsty, too?"

"Yes!" Devraj sprang to his feet. "Can I pour the water?"

"Let me help," I urged. Once the water made it mostly into their small cups, I returned to Devraj's question as I looked at the list. "I think we'll have a special feeling in our hearts. Like, if they go away, it really hurts. We feel better when they're with us all the time."

I couldn't help but feel deflated when Devraj clutched his tunic over his chest.

"You're thinking about Papa, aren't you?" I comforted.

"My heart hurts a lot," he answered.

"You get to stay in this home for a few months and then you'll go visit him."

"But I want you to come with me," he insisted. His eyes prickled with tears. Sanjana hugged him, seeing a need to comfort.

"Yes, he's sad, Sanjana. That's such a good hug," I affirmed. "Dev, I want to be honest with you because I know this is hard. Papa and I aren't married anymore. He is still your papa but he is not my husband. We decided he needs to live in Makaar with Einora. It's not easy or fun but I'm okay."

As I talked, my kids cuddled close on my lap. I pulled my dupatta around my shoulders and my kids so we were encased in a glittery cocoon of jade green silk.

"I still have you and Sanjana. I want to have a new husband. But only someone who is just as good at being a father as Papa. I will be patient and maybe someday that will happen. But as for me going to Makaar, it hurts my heart. But maybe we can talk about it when it's time to see your papa again, okay?"

I felt Devraj nod but I heard a sniffle and he started to cry. I felt like a great statue of Abhijita carrying rainwater and the salt of crashing waves.

"I know," I murmured. Sanjana didn't cry and cry like Devraj but she whimpered in solidarity.

"I know," I kept repeating. "This is tough. I'm here."

CHAPTER

NINE

After Sanjana and Devraj settled in their puddle of pillows in the corner for their naps, I could reexamine the leftover names. We'd crossed out a lot of names that represented Ushallavi nobility—I wasn't too displeased with that. The remaining names were fairly interesting.

I gazed at five of the potential matches, all of which would send me far, far north. Across the lapping waves and ocean miles lay the Haneul, Calfuray, Fumanya, and Elpídio kingdoms. And I was looking at a list of men who weren't anywhere on my parents' list when establishing my future. Things had been so tense between Ushallav and Makaar that everyone hoped the marriage would show good faith and goodwill—that the time of war was truly and firmly behind us.

Now that we had put that fear to rest, perhaps one of these princes could be the political match that would put my talents to use. After all, things were still relatively peaceful in our corner of the world all things considered. Maybe we could reconnect with our northern neighbors.

I bit my bottom lip in thought. I couldn't remember the last time I met any of these men. Were they friendly or handsome? Would any of them be a good partner? Were they worth the extensive travel to and from their kingdom and Damir's?

And another question gurgled in my guts: did I want a political match? I immediately started thinking about how these matches would serve Ray or my parents or my kids or my ex-husband…I had to wonder which choice would serve me.

Maybe I could fall in love with one or any of them. Maybe I needed the space from everyone to be somewhere new that I could use to reinvent myself. Maybe this could be a good thing for everyone—including me.

With an anxious knot in my gut—what's the worst that could happen?—I called for a translator and began drafting some letters.

There was a whisper of excitement—eagerness?—in my chest as I handed my sealed letters to my messenger and watched them turn on their heel and begin their task. Soon, I'd hear back from these five strangers. I even asked Ziya, the artistic handmaiden of my team, to sketch my portrait and copy it. Maybe I'd get more promising responses if they knew of my goddess-given beauty and features. I certainly hoped they would respond before I changed my mind and remained a recluse for the foreseeable future.

I sheepishly opened up to Mother about the letters while I posed for Ziya's sketches. In response, she gushed, "We could host a party in their honor! The perfect excuse to show our guests a good time and you can intermingle—do your thing." She clapped her hands together, already plotting the details.

I warmed up to the idea. Even if I didn't find any of them to be a good match, it'd be an excuse to rekindle some relations swathed in cobwebs.

"I'm pretty sure they're younger than you—but not too much. I can't remember the last time I visited the northern kingdoms."

Mom's face settled into a nostalgic, wistful glance at nothing in particular. I wasn't sure if she was describing the kingdom or a certain someone. Her marriage to my father was more or less political—marriages in my family always are—but I knew they fell in love before the week-long wedding celebration. But I wondered if she ever imagined herself the queen of another distant land.

"Well, I should have more than enough time to brush up on my history before anyone responds or deigns to visit us."

"You haven't lost your touch," Mother smiled charmingly. "I was going to say the same thing."

"I know it's too much to ask to…wait before sharing this vinformation," I said, hooking my arm in hers, "But thank you. Thanks for being here with me."

"The walls have Eyes," Mother replied, glancing at the painted Eyes that decorated her palace. "But I can't control the other eyes around here. But I think everyone is excited for you."

"Well, I better be off to the sanctuary," I sighed, putting a pin in this conversation. "Thank you again for taking the kids."

Mother looked at Sanjana and Devraj with all the warmth and pride a grandmother can muster. "We're happy they're both here. They're so good—despite it all."

I didn't want to open up another avenue of chatter. My day was very, very full.

As I put on my sandals, my *maan* squeezed my arm.

"You made a good choice, Anji," she smiled. I didn't have to tell her that today I would announce my official choice for the new handmaiden—she didn't even know the woman I was prepared to introduce to our family. I appreciated the warmth all the more.

We hugged, bowed quickly, and I finally strode to my carriage.

She called after me, "Maybe it could be a party for your birthday? It might line up nicely!"

"Love you," I called over my shoulder.

As I got into the carriage, I noticed something glinting in the sunlight in my peripheral. I turned slightly away from the open-air carriage and to my left.

I watched as a man drove his own carriage away from the palace. By the looks of his plain but clean wooden wagon and horses, I guessed he was a merchant. Not one I recognized while growing up—but I guessed that he was a new favorite based on the way his cart seemed half empty.

I squinted to get a better look. What was half-exposed to the sun like that?

For a moment, the driver glanced over his shoulder and caught me staring. And he…winked at me? Not only did he look my age but he was someone I didn't mind staring at.

His black, somewhat shaggy hair was slick back and graced his shoulders. A goatee rimmed his grin as he arched a brow and nodded at me before continuing on his way. His tunic suited him well—especially since the mint green sleeves were rolled up to his elbows.

Maybe he was being polite. I am who I am, I mused. But I smiled to myself as I found my seat in my carriage and arranged myself into the visage of grace and beauty as my carriage driver pulled us forward fast enough to go alongside the merchant. He politely gestured for us to go first, giving us an opportunity to exchange polite stares before going our separate ways.

I couldn't stop thinking about that gentle, was-he-interested-or-just-polite expression all the way to the Sanctuary of Abhijita.

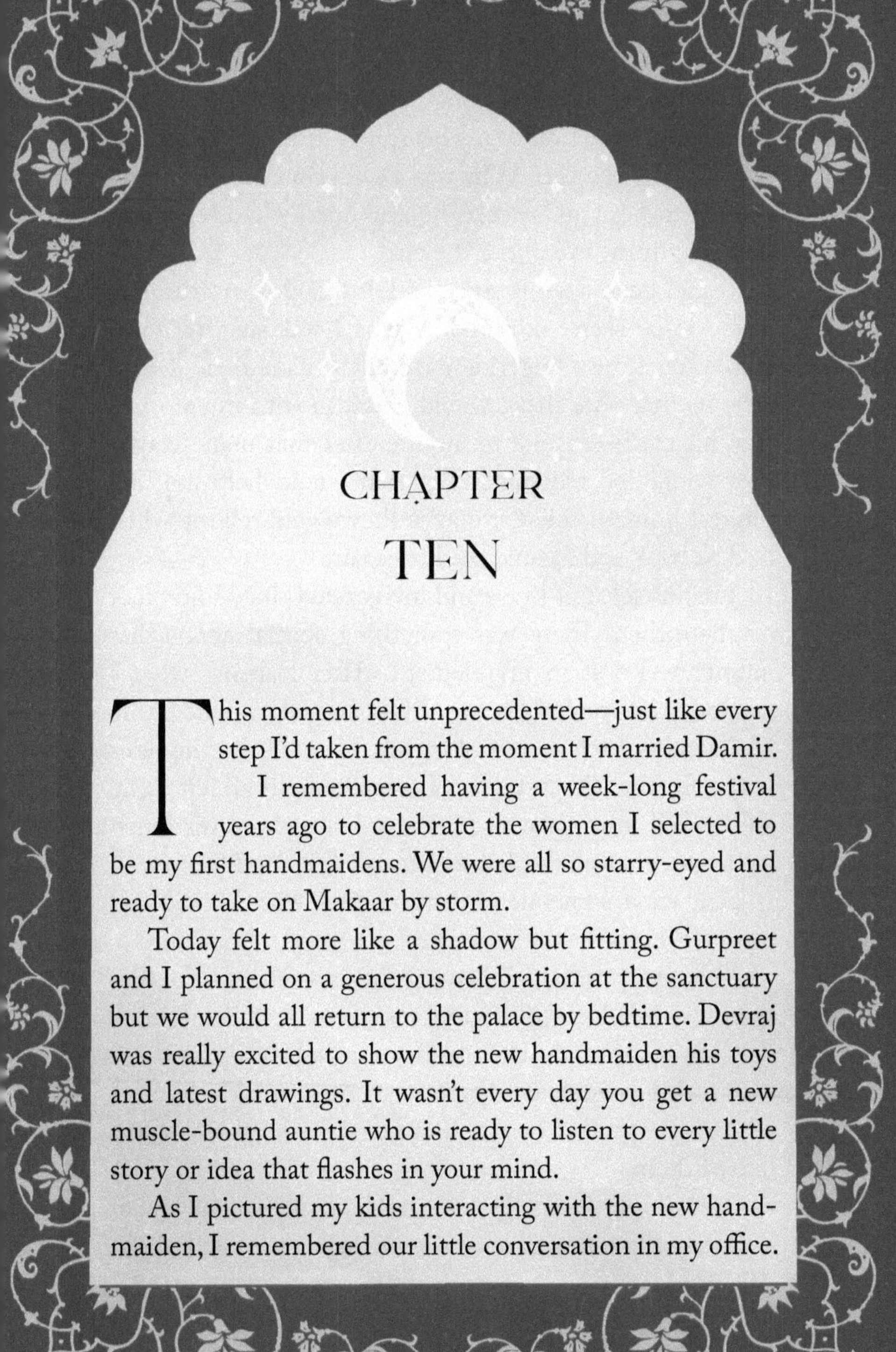

CHAPTER

TEN

This moment felt unprecedented—just like every step I'd taken from the moment I married Damir.

I remembered having a week-long festival years ago to celebrate the women I selected to be my first handmaidens. We were all so starry-eyed and ready to take on Makaar by storm.

Today felt more like a shadow but fitting. Gurpreet and I planned on a generous celebration at the sanctuary but we would all return to the palace by bedtime. Devraj was really excited to show the new handmaiden his toys and latest drawings. It wasn't every day you get a new muscle-bound auntie who is ready to listen to every little story or idea that flashes in your mind.

As I pictured my kids interacting with the new handmaiden, I remembered our little conversation in my office.

How I talked about wanting to find someone to fill the husband-shaped hole in my heart. My mind drifted to the man driving the cart. Why was I so curious about him? I wanted to hear his voice as he explained whatever it was that caught my eye under the tarp.

It had been a while since I'd felt this way. A crush? A desire to be seen—admired. Maybe I was starving for a gentle touch or a lingering gaze but I made mental note after mental note that I would check in with my mother, Ray, his staff—anyone to inquire after that man. Maybe they could tell me something that would help me lose interest immediately. Or maybe they would tell me when he'd be back and I could see him again.

I hadn't felt this brave and invigorated since I first met my betrothed. There was something special about that moment—I was in my element. After learning what I needed to know about being a ruler and taking care of the Makaarians, I felt so sure of myself. I knew I was the right queen for the job, and when I met Damir, it all felt right. We locked into place and lived in bliss—however much we could—before our family became fractured forever.

And now someone else was ruling with Damir and raising their new son in peace.

This handsome man driving the cart felt like the first reminder of what self-assuredness could feel like. I could see him again and just introduce myself. We could see where things took us. There were many times where I felt brave—guided by Abhijita herself. And this felt like one of them.

I let people see the genuine smile on my face as one of my assistants offers to open the carriage door and I alight the small steps to the ground. Gurpreet and my current handmaidens stood in a line, waiting for me.

Gurpreet nodded in greeting. "You're in a pleasant mood."

They arched a brow. Since I last saw them, they had dyed their shaggy, jagged curls a dark maroon and even colored their eyebrows to match. One eyebrow had a diagonal cut through it—stylistic as opposed to the real scars on their arms and back.

Sometimes Gurpreet dressed for tradition or comfort when formally conducting her work. But for informal visits, Gurpreet experimented with cuts, color, patterns, and textures. Today, Gurpreet graced us with a very low V-cut blouse that showed off their recent arm and collarbone tattoos. Their silk, shiny trousers matched their septum ring that twinkled in the sun.

I always liked Gurpreet from the moment I met them. It's not easy making friends as a princess. There was always a royal family, sometimes several protective handmaidens, and the politics interfering with friendship. Gurpreet was one friend I had made when they first let me train with the other women to start building my muscle and learning about Abhijita. They trained with me, laughed with me, and helped me sharpen my wit and sense of humor.

Now that I was walking into the sanctuary and reminiscing, I remembered how Gurpreet was going to spend part of their holiday with me before I was nearly assassinated. I even put my hand over my stomach as if taken to that moment. I remembered sitting in the carriage and going over my itinerary built around giving birth to Sanjana, eating all my favorite foods, speaking

Ushallavi, and having as many visitors as possible, re-kindling past friendships.

As the colors around me dimmed, I remembered how the arrows killed Swaran. And then the carriage over-turned and we ran for our lives. And then Gamani, Neha, and Maliha dropped to the ground. And then I dove as deeply as I could into the dense forest until I was sure no one and nothing could find me.

I blinked away that moment. The colors in my vision reverted to their natural vividness. The hitched breathing and sense of dread never left me but I kept my smile and greeted the warriors around me.

You're safe, Anjali, I thought to myself. I breathed fully and blinked away would-be tears. *You couldn't be safer at this moment. Leela can't hurt you or haunt you here.*

As soon as we went through the double doors, a com-forting crush of voices and laughter echoed through the chamber and into my ears. This was a huge reason why this sanctuary was truly a sanctuary. The warmth, the laughter…it made it easy to smile and forget my troubles. I almost felt like they were melting off of me—down my spine, past my elbow, off my fingertips, and dripping on the floor.

The attendants were truly dressed to impress even though my handmaiden choice was already pretty ob-vious. This was also an opportunity to celebrate all the women who trained, make new friends, beat their per-sonal records, or might even pursue different work in or out of the sanctuary.

We all walked through and made the rounds, greeting the women who approached me. That was the first hour. I spent the next hour snacking while my handmaidens and I touched up our clothing, jewelry, hair, and makeup.

"You should still wear the crown," Dipa insisted. She held a box out so I could take the crown. The lid was hinged back so I could see my crown perched sweetly in the velvet and silk. I hadn't really looked at it since I left it in Makaar years ago. If I brought it with me on that fateful trip to Ushallav, it would've been lost to the forest. I mean, why would I bring it? I was going home to have a baby—not hold court.

And when I returned home and learned that I was swiftly replaced with Einora, I didn't think there was much point to wearing the damn thing. Where was my kingdom? Who were my people?

I had commissioned this crown from two artisans. A symbol of my new life with Damir, since one artisan worked with the Makaarian nobility and the other for my family. The crown sparkled in earnest, like it begged to gleam for everyone to see.

"I'm not sure about that. Did you bring it here as a surprise?" I replied.

"Well, we sort of always have it on hand for big occasions. It looks beautiful on you—and it's yours. We made sure it would match tonight's gown," Pari explained. Sitting in my chair, I looked around at Gurpreet and my handmaidens in various states of glam. They looked at me with a mixture of hope, encouragement, and sadness.

I walked away from Makaar for many reasons—some of which I hadn't let myself sit and unpack. But this night was about us. No politics, no drama. Just an excuse to celebrate our new handmaiden and look gorgeous.

I gave a little smile—the kind I give when it's past Devraj's bedtime but I allow him to pick out another story to read. I also feigned a humble blush as I put a fingertip to my lower lip and scrunched my shoulders a bit.

"I might have to take part of it off for the dancing but I think we can make it work. It does suit my gown well."

I was already dressed in my Anarkali suit—an embroidered dress with long sleeves and a bell-shaped skirt that went to my calves. Trousers peaked out from underneath. I chose to go for a teal for the pants and an off-white dress with pink and gold embroidery. I was initially going to braid my hair and apply hair gems but decided to let the tresses unfurl down my back.

Pari grinned proudly and unabashedly as she gingerly lifted the crown from the box. Dipa helped position it on my head and weave my hair around the parts of the crown that actually touched my head. She locked it into place and made quick work.

I held up a somewhat large hand mirror to my face so I could watch my transformation. I actually had to extend my arm so I could fit the whole look in the glass.

The main part of the crown haloed my head with jewel-encrusted points that pointed up and away from my head. A smaller headband actually rested on my head to help create the illusion of a nine-point sun haloing me.

The gems were various shades of blue that reminded me of the ocean always just outside my palace windows and the blue sky that hung over the Makaarian mountains. Three chains of jewelry laid over my hair—starting from either temple and my hair part to meet at the center of my forehead. There was a jeweled depiction of a sun between my brows with little stars dangling and twinkling at the top of my nose.

More dangling gems hung from the left and right, just above my ears, with eye motifs that purposefully harkened to our tradition of the Eyes painted in our palaces to look for danger and know when to provide protection.

Overall, I knew it was very lavish—so much so that I really only wore it for special occasions. But my royal spine and core snapped into place like it was natural. My posture adjusted appropriately and I lifted my chin in approval.

Dipa, Pari, and Ziya gathered around and they smiled and gasped in delight. I could see their excitement through the mirror.

"This was a great idea," I admitted out loud. "This party is just as much for you as it is for me. You helped me get to this point. So please go enjoy yourselves tonight."

Gurpreet, who only added more glitter to their chest, neck, eyelids, and lips, smiled at our merry band.

"Well, I'm glad it didn't take long to convince you. You look gorgeous. Now, let's go eat!"

There was a moment of silence as the musicians ended their song and the attendants fell into hushed tones, though the excitement only increased. I could feel it in the air.

The drummers began an intoxicating rhythm to welcome me and my entourage more formally to the circular room with high domed ceiling. I took in a blur of sparkling jewelry, flashing smiles, raised glasses, fire dancing in sconces, and hundreds of wide bowls full of food. It felt only right to step and sway my hips with the beat as the other instruments and vocalists joined in.

They were singing about Abhijita—one of her many tales of triumph put to song. I flashed a smile and held my head high as the crowds parted to let the five of us through. We made it to our table slowly because it felt right to dance our way there—a warrior in the crowd would shimmy, or arch her arms in a graceful pose, or kick up her feet and we'd echo them back to the crowd. My crown twinkled and shook like a great chandelier—much like the ones that decorated my old castle.

After dancing from one end of the room to the other, we made it to a large, curved table decorated for us. And whether it was planned or not, my new handmaiden was there waiting for us.

I took Janitra by the hand and plucked her from the crowd and lifted our arms to the ceiling. The music and cheers swelled as I did so. This felt oh-so-right. I have handmaidens, I'm with my people, and I'm wearing my crown. And had I secured a babysitter for my children that evening so I could celebrate with Ziya, Pari, and Dipa and give them the night off they truly deserved.

Still holding Janitra's hand in the air, I twirled her around so she could show off her whole look. Everyone was wearing various shades of cream or blush pink, and Janitra's blush pink gown fit that perfectly.

The bust of her gown was essentially fabric that crisscrossed over her chest and joined at the back of her neck to show off her thick, muscular arms. There was a diamond shaped hole stitched over her stomach to reveal her pierced belly button. The skirt flared out from her hips. With two long slits over the front of her thighs, the twirl revealed her deep brown skin and fabulous heels. Her raven brown hair was crafted into a braided bun at the top of her head to make room for the large bell-shaped earrings dangling from her earlobes.

After we completed the twirl, the musicians and I began a small chant of Janitra's name, finishing the last verse by adding her name to Abhijita's song—a charming way to anticipate her forthcoming victories and feats of strength and beauty.

As we sat down, we laughed and caught our breaths. The song ended, we cheered for the energetic musicians, and then we all dug into our feast.

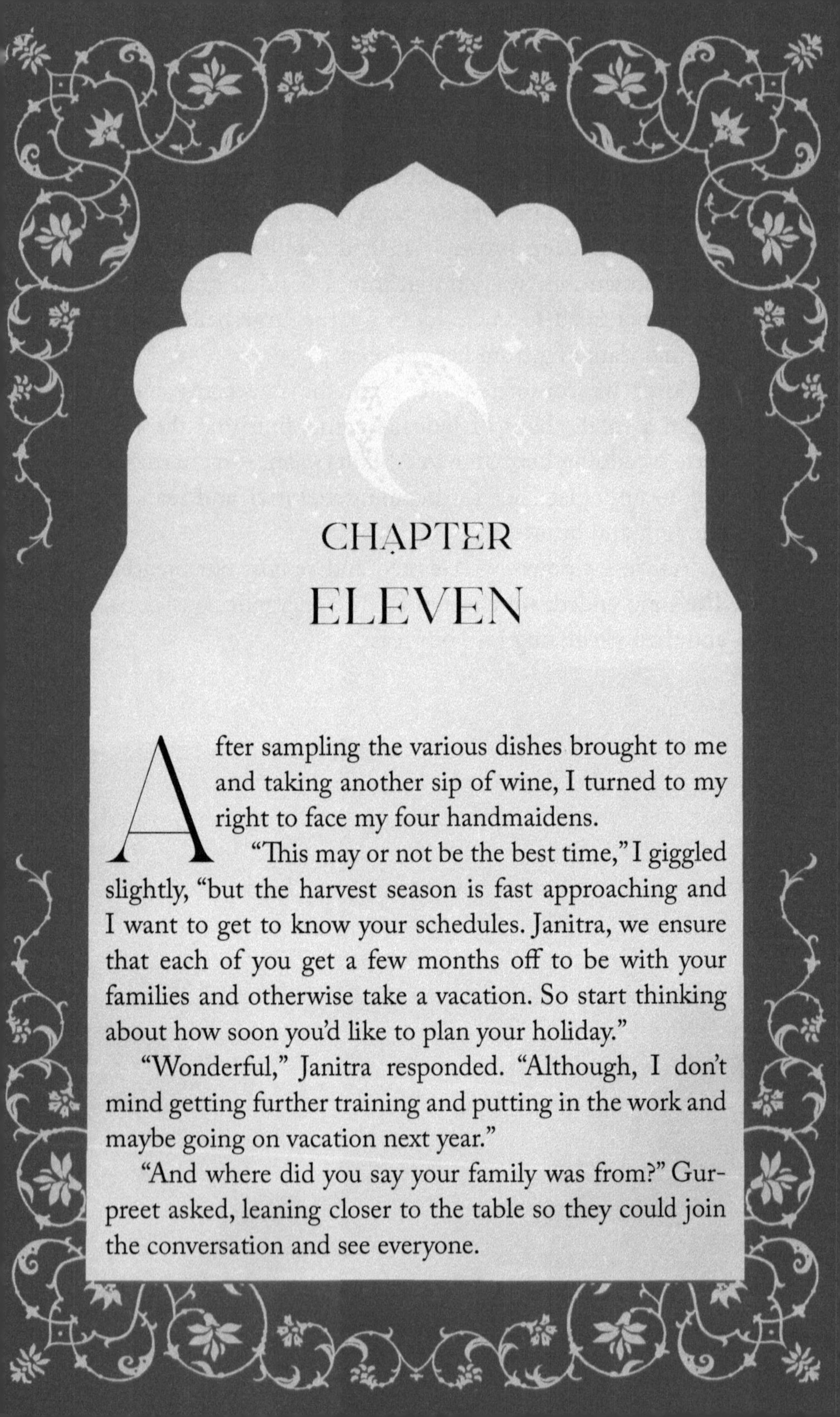

CHAPTER
ELEVEN

After sampling the various dishes brought to me and taking another sip of wine, I turned to my right to face my four handmaidens.

"This may or not be the best time," I giggled slightly, "but the harvest season is fast approaching and I want to get to know your schedules. Janitra, we ensure that each of you get a few months off to be with your families and otherwise take a vacation. So start thinking about how soon you'd like to plan your holiday."

"Wonderful," Janitra responded. "Although, I don't mind getting further training and putting in the work and maybe going on vacation next year."

"And where did you say your family was from?" Gurpreet asked, leaning closer to the table so they could join the conversation and see everyone.

I was partially confused—she was Ushallavi, so where else would she be from? But Janitra quickly responded,

"Well actually, my parents are living in Makaar right now. I traveled here as soon as I heard word that Anjali was looking for another handmaiden."

"You're from Makaar?" I said it like a question and a statement. My lips turned up into a smile, intrigued.

"Well, we moved there when I was around 14 years old," Janitra explained. "Both of my parents are Ushallavi but we moved to Makaar for work. It's been…well, you know what it's like there."

I and the other handmaidens gave each other glances, unsure of what to say. We knew what she meant but I personally wasn't sure I had enough alcohol in me to start saying how I really felt about my previous life in Makaar.

"It's a beautiful place but they haven't quite discovered what we're really like," I said, finding my footing in the middle. "And to be fair, it might not be that much easier for a Makaarian to set up shop here. Old wounds take time to heal, and all that. I admire your parents for likely being some of the first people to make the move. Do you think they will return to Ushallav at some point?"

"Maybe," Janitra mused. "I think they like it there. They don't seem to be in any rush."

I took a hearty swig from my goblet.

"You mentioned that you spoke Makaarian," I said, veering the conversation onto a better course. Janitra nodded and smiled.

"The language was fairly easy to pick up. I actually started to brush up on my reading and spelling if it meant I could get this position."

Gurpreet swallowed some food before piping up, "You'll be pretty popular once we take the royal heirs back to Makaar. Less work for our queen." Gurpreet gestured toward me with their head.

That's true. The handmaidens learned Makaarian quickly but their preparation only took them so far. If a Makaarian noble tried to make a snide joke, they would often wrinkle their noses and look at each other. It was like they knew from inflection that it was unkind but that was as far as they could go. But in their native language, they could fling something sharp and witty in return.

If Janitra lived in Makaar—longer than me and my children—her guidance could really help all of us. I imagined that Sanjana and Devraj wouldn't lag behind in their studies now that they had someone besides me to practice with. Janitra knew the real life use of the language and could help them understand more than just the written grammar rules.

Janitra must've lived there when things were far worse. Back when the outright fist fights and blatant name-calling were expected—considered mild, even. I was looking at a fellow survivor. Even if she wasn't with the version of me that fought through the forest, I felt like she would understand—more than most.

Maybe my stomach was full of good food, or maybe I was having one of those good gut feelings.

"So you came all this way for the trials," I said, trying to get out of my own head. "Did you make it the first time? Forgive me but I didn't quite recognize you."

In fact, I recognized many of them and marveled at their continued devotion to the craft. They either trained at the palace or attended the first trials when I was engaged and assembling my first team of handmaidens. Gurpreet, of course, knew everyone and helped me when remembering names.

"Well, I wanted to, if I'm being honest. But spending my youth in Makaar made it difficult to train and travel back. My parents also weren't sure I'd make the cut since I was so behind." Janitra bit her lip almost in embarrassment. Was she blushing?

"Clearly that didn't hold you back," I shrugged with a grin. She had held my attention since the moment she entered the ring. I couldn't help but imagine how things would be if my training facility on the castle grounds was open to the public. Would she have come? Would we have been friends? Could I have helped her and other immigrants to feel connected to home?

With my absence from the Makaar castle, my indoor training den was shuttered up. Who knew what they're doing with it now?

Janitra's story drew me back into the present.

"I trained a lot on my own. A neighbor of mine had a little Abhijita shrine and they let me train around it. I think they hoped it would bring good luck. Some people wanted to remember their traditions and what makes our people great—and others wanted to lean into their new lives in a new place. I think everyone got what they wanted by the time I left."

There was something sparkling in her eyes when she spoke, like her body was telling the parts of the story that words couldn't. I wondered what my eyes gave away when I spoke.

"I guess all roads lead back to the sanctuary," I answered, raising my glass. The rest of my table clinked their cups against mine, and a few women nearby caught on to the toast. "I can't wait for you to meet the kids. They're going to be so excited that you lived in Makaar. I bet they'll want to hear all about your adventures."

"Oh, Queen Anjali. Tell Janitra about our next big party. You were talking about something big while we were getting ready for tonight."

"I like the idea of going to lots of parties," Janitra grinned. "I know a really great florist—one of my neighbors when I was a kid. I bet they could really beautify the palace for whatever it is you're planning."

"Does he have long-ish wavy hair?" I said in-between chewing—mimicking the swoosh of the stranger's hair— the one I saw earlier in the day.

"No," Janitra drew out the word. "Who are you talking about?"

I definitely felt a blush bloom across my cheeks and neck. I swallowed and tried not to choke at the sight of Gurpreet's confused and intrigued face.

"Give us the details, Anji."

"Okay, try not to laugh too hard. But I saw this man leaving the palace just before I did. He seemed pleasant," I began. After a fire of intrigued blazed in Gurpreet's eyes, I added, "Fine, he was really handsome!"

Pari had a look of genuine delight and surprise on her face. It wasn't a mystery that I wasn't exactly doing well since being home, and I'd become fairly selective with whom I admit is easy on the eyes.

"So we're throwing a party for…him?" Ziya guessed before giggling with Dipa.

"Well, sort of," I began. "I've actually invited several princes from Elpídio, Hanuel, Fumanya, and Calfuray to come for a visit. I want to see if they're interested…"

"Interested in courting you?" Gurpreet finished. "Anji, any of them would count themselves lucky to get the invite, let alone get the opportunity. I hope you're inviting me because I absolutely want to help with the selection process. I've got connections and I can help you figure out whether they're not worth your time."

Why did I feel so shy all of a sudden? I felt like everyone in the room could see me blush and note my heart rate.

"Well, this could be pretty monumental for all of us if I make a *connection* with someone," I smiled at the word choice. "Well, I want this connection to be for love but it could be a boon for Ushallav as well. Things between us and Makaar are stable for the time being. We could spark something interesting with one of the northern princes."

"That's a long way from home," Janitra whistled. But she seemed excited by the prospect.

My smile faltered. "That's what I'm worried about," I conceded. "It might be too much distance, for the children, maybe even me. The way we divide our time is already complicated."

I zoned out for a moment, as if I could see my future playing out in the dancing candlelight and sconces.

"Finding a partner in Ushallav would be nice," I shrugged. "And maybe Gurpreet and their connections could help me figure out who this man with the wavy hair is. Preferably before my mother catches wind of this?

Gurpreet flashed a smug grin. "Say less. Say, could you describe that luscious hair for me again?"

They mirrored my drunken hand movements—a bit too dramatically and more embellished than necessary.

"Friends," I laughed. "I just want…love again. And I could use your help in finding it. Please help me avoid another disaster, okay?"

"Of course!"

"Ahh, true love."

"It's about damn time."

"Oh my days. How much time do we have to prepare?"

The words climbed over each other and we started yelling at each other to hear ourselves talk. We agreed to pause the party planning and man stalking once the musicians filled the hall with a jaunty tune. We brushed off the crumbs off our gowns and rose to our feet.

Everyone joined the dance floor as Janitra helped remove the delicate, tinkling halo above my head, leaving the rest of the head jewelry in place.

"I think you look ready to dance," Janitra smiled, holding out her hand. I took it and joined her.

CHAPTER

TWELVE

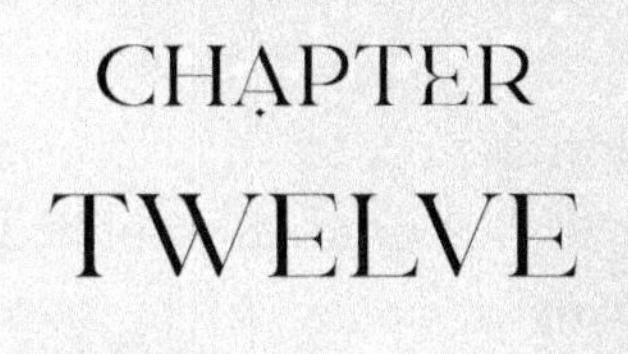

Sun rays pierced the corners of my vision before I truly woke up. I reached out and felt a cup at the side of my bed. With a quick sniff, I could tell it was something to quell the constant thudding in my head—a sign of a fun night.

I let out a cough-laugh and rose to a sitting position. "Mama!"

"Are you still sleeping?" Devraj asked incredulously. Judging by his wild hair and his incredulous eyebrows, I could tell that I really overslept.

"Come here," I conceded. They scrambled into my bed, already dressed in their play clothes.

"It's lunchtime!" my son informed me.

"Time for lunch?" I asked with exaggerated astonishment. "Then let me get dressed and we'll go together."

After slipping into a cropped blouse, trousers, and a long silk robe, I reached out my hands and let my kids take them.

My handmaidens and I exchanged knowing smiles as we sipped from our water glasses and helped ourselves to more lunch. The kids looked up at Janitra with awe.

"She's officially the newest handmaiden. Her name is Janitra. We'll show her the rest of the castle soon, won't we?"

They wiggled in their seats in response. Devraj was too shy to really speak but gradually inched closer. Sanjana couldn't stop staring in awe.

"Sanjana, eat your food. It's impolite to stare, honey."

"She's pretty," Sanjana mused in awe. She was still staring.

"Yes, she's very pretty. And she's trying to eat her food."

Janitra gave me a grateful glance as she focused on her plate.

Eventually, my parents and other extended family members arrived and took their places in the dining area. My kids left their seats and gleefully joined their cousins.

"Janitra," my mother greeted. "It's lovely to see you join us. Your fighting was truly remarkable."

"You're very kind, Your Majesty," Janitra inclined her head in a small bow. "I want to use my strength for the good of Ushallav. And this lamb saag is an added bonus. I haven't tasted anything like this since I moved to Makaar."

"We did hear about your story," my father chimed in with a warm smile.

He always did his best to not be incredibly imposing—knowing that his previous service as the king tended to unnerve people. To me, he was just a talented negotiator and gentle teacher. He had stepped down from the throne to let Ray lead.

I think he just wanted to rest from the fighting and enjoy the peaceful times with his grandchildren. He'd done his work—it didn't feel like I'd done mine yet.

"It's very noble that you trained and traveled all this way to prove your strength," Father continued. "Anji chose well."

He gave me a soft, encouraging smile before scooping more rice.

Janitra beamed at me. "Thank you. It's an honor. Truly."

Father spoke to me but didn't look up from his plate. "After your tour with Janitra, we'll be hosting a guest at the palace. He'll be meeting with Ray just before supper. Just thought you'd want early notice."

Mother looked from her husband to me.

"Who's this 'he'?" she questioned.

"Mother," I insisted. My eyes flickered to the decorations lining the upper walls. Eyes. I smirked at Father who still didn't look up. He must've caught wind that I wanted to learn more about this man with the cart.

"I didn't want to ruin the surprise," Father shrugged before returning to his food.

What brought this mysterious man back to the palace so soon? I counted myself fortunate that I would find out by the end of the day. Father must have thought highly of him if he was dropping this hint for me.

After I felt stuffed, I encouraged the kids to join me for a walk around the gardens. Soon enough, I felt a familiar flock of handmaidens catch up and match my stride. The time between lunch and just-before-supper went by quickly and slowly simultaneously.

"Should we come with you?" Dipa asked.

"Or we could watch the children," Ziya suggested. "Whichever is most suitable."

I bit my bottom lip in thought. Was this really a big deal? I made a split decision to, well, split the handmaidens.

"Janitra and Ziya can watch the children. Dipa and Pari will come with me," I instructed. The kids needed more time around Janitra. And I wanted eyes on this… endeavor of mine. Someone to ensure this was someone worth pursuing.

I remembered watching my mother open her heart to her handmaidens—my fierce aunties—and they were still lifelong friends. I wanted that. No better time to plant those seeds than to potentially help me meet this man and figure out what would come next. I had already had one wedding and the "riding off into the sunset" moment. What was I going to do after that?

Everyone nodded in unison, some hiding their amused grins better than others, and we went our separate paths.

I gathered myself, hoping that the cheer and joy I felt last night would return. I wanted to feel brave, bold, and undeniable.

Ray usually met the guests in the interior of the palace after they left their horses and transportation with attendants. He enjoyed a good stroll through the palace before stopping at his office or whichever suitable place he chose for his appointment.

I recalled a nice hallway to his office that had open-air views to the shores just past my home. It was very picturesque and a good place to disarm the more nervous or agitated visitors.

Perhaps if I met him at the entryway, I could intercept and get in a few words.

When we approached, I could hear voices echoing and knew my timing was correct. There was Ray's voice and… who was that? Ray was not speaking Ushallavi.

The two guards on either side of the entryway gave me puzzled expressions but they didn't stop me. Their gazes flicked from my trio to the walls straight ahead—our signal to pass through the curtains and into the threshold.

"Cladiu?" My voice carried through the room, confident that my guess was correct.

A man in leathers looked from Ray to me. I tried to read his expression. Shock—relief? He was a very hard man to read. Nonetheless, I smiled broadly and went to shake his hand. He took my hand before shaking my handmaidens' hands.

"It's so good to see you," I said. I had lost a lot of my Gavril language skills but that was one of the easier phrases to remember.

In formal, direct Makaarian, he replied. "Queen Anjali. You are here. Are you safe and healthy?"

It had been several months since I'd seen him. Claudiu and the rest of the Gavril people constantly moved with the seasons. They followed a traditional path around our continent said to be set by The Traveler. Not quite a god but more of a legend, The Traveler wanders, and so do Their followers.

I didn't care all that much to judge; but it was this traveler, Claudiu, who had found my half-alive body in the mountain forest when everyone else thought I was lost to assassins.

Those months ago, he had escorted me back home to Makaar and stayed quite some time to help me discover the person—or traitorous handmaiden—behind my near-demise.

And now he was here—at my home. Was he here to see…me? I stopped myself from making any assumptions.

Was Cladiu the "he" that my father had spoken of? I couldn't help but smile through my embarrassed blushing. Of all the people I expected to be here, Claudiu was dead last.

"My my, Her Majesty must have Eyes and ears," Ray said tersely through a thin, polite smile. "Care to join us?"

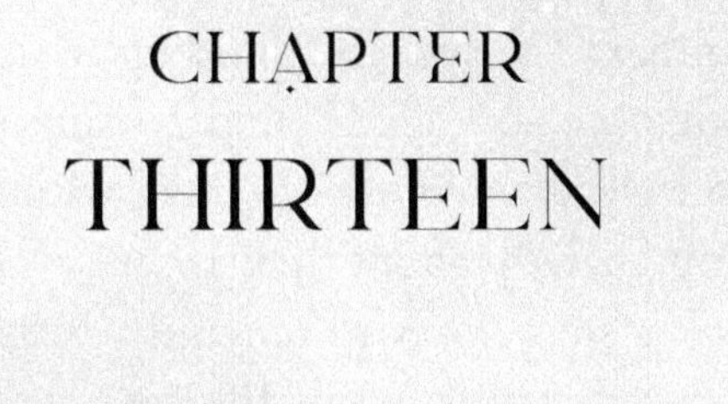

CHAPTER
THIRTEEN

I wasn't sure if the man with the cart was actually going to be here, so I accepted Ray's offer and my handmaidens trailed behind. They had met Claudiu before and they greeted him in polite Makaarian, the common language between us, while I took a step closer to Ray.

"Claudiu is my friend. Why did I have to hear from Father that he would be here?" I spoke Ushallavi in hushed tones.

"He told you?"

"Well, not exactly. Father mentioned that 'he' would be here meeting with you, and so here I am. Where was my invitation?"

"You're clearly surprised that he's here. Who were you expecting to be here today?"

"We'll talk about this later. For now, is this a private matter—should I leave? I can chat with Claudiu later."

My brother smiled and gave me a side-long glance. "*Very* thoughtful of you to ask. Honestly, I'd prefer you stay. Usually, when the Gavril people are passing through, they send someone to pay us a visit before they go on their way. If they have something important to share beyond traditional pleasantries, I don't mind having a bilingual sister on hand."

"Brokering peace and prosperity between peoples. Sounds familiar," I answered. Nodding to my brother, we changed our pace so Claudiu and I could switch places and let him walk shoulder-to-shoulder with Ray. The king began asking Claudiu about their recent cyclical journey.

Pari took a step closer to me and whispered, "Something tells me that this is not the man you expected to meet. What can we do to help?"

"He's a friend but not the man I spotted earlier," I clarified. "We can chat with him before he leaves with the others. I guess we'll have to learn more about the mystery man from Gurpreet's intel in time."

"He's a handsome friend," Pari whispered with a shrug and a small smile.

I looked straight on to see my brother and rescuer walking and talking. As I suspected, Ray took us to the hallway with the gorgeous view.

Claudiu came from a resilient people. From what I remembered, they traveled as a way to preserve tradition and serve the earth that Bhooma, our earth goddess, created. They had certainly served my country by saving me and Sanjana from assassins. They didn't even know me; they simply saw a stranger in dire need and rescued her.

For a moment, it was like I saw Claudiu in a new light. I wasn't sure if these feelings were real or a trick of the hallway's beautiful lighting. Could he be someone I could become closer with? He had lost his wife before he met me. I wondered if he finally remarried or if—there was something there for us.

I uncharacteristically and shyly looked through the archways and out to the ocean and hoped that Claudiu was looking at me instead of the view. Sure, it was sudden and not a part of my plans, but something in me encouraged me to try. He saved my life once; what wasn't romantic about that? It'd been some time since I felt this daring to try something–or someone–new.

The conversation remained professional and polite for about fifteen minutes before an attendant approached our group and whispered in my brother's ear. He politely listened before saying, "Well, Claudiu. Something has actually come up and I must attend to it right away. But you are in good hands with Anjali. I will return to you shortly."

"You're leaving?" I asked, somewhat shocked.

"Yes," smirked Ray. He gave a low, formal bow to Claudiu before adding, "We have guest quarters available for you and your companions. Feel free to eat dinner with us and stay as long as you see fit."

"Thank you," Claudiu murmured as he gave a less flourishing bow.

Ray practically sprinted away—leaving me, Claudiu, and my two handmaidens.

"I'm sorry, I'm confused," Claudiu said, turning to me. He gestured with his hands like he hoped I caught his meaning without having to clarify. Ray must've used some Makaarian that wasn't clear or literal enough, so I clarified,

"Ray must speak with someone else. You can talk with us now or I can walk with you to your quarters and you can rest. We also have food. Are you hungry?"

"Let's tell my companions about dinner," Claudiu nodded. "They'll be happy to hear about that."

This was an excuse to see who these other guests were. I couldn't help but check Claudiu's hands for rings to see if he wore a wedding band. Of course, just because he didn't wear any jewelry didn't answer that question—the Gavril people had traditions of their own that didn't always translate to ours.

"It's good to see you," I smiled. "How is everyone doing?"

"Well, we all completed the Path once more this year, although there is never really an end or beginning. But we all made it back to Ushallav in peace once more. How is Sanjana? And Dev-De—"

"My son Devraj? They're both growing so fast. Sanjana will be so happy to see you, too! I wonder if she remembers any of the songs you taught her."

Claudiu smiled at that, and it felt like a victory. He quickly excused himself as he ventured back to where a group of twenty waited for him in the dining hall. I waited for him where Ray initially welcomed him.

I didn't quite catch everything due to Claudiu's low, quick words but I knew when to wave and bow when he stopped talking and everyone gave appreciative waves. They seemed to recognize the queen, once hidden under sorrow and borrowed clothes that they'd traveled with.

Claudiu then returned to my side and explained, "They will prepare and meet us for dinner. They are happy to see you and look forward to eating food."

Maybe this was childish but I couldn't suppress my smile. I didn't notice anyone that acted like his partner or wife when he spoke. I wasn't sure if I was reading them correctly but it gave me some vigor in my step.

I clasped my hands behind my back and gestured with my left hand for my handmaidens to give us a bit of space. When their footfalls sounded noticeable further away, I gathered my courage.

"Claudiu, I know that you and your people are here to visit. But I wanted to know if you could stay a little longer."

Creases between his brows furrowed. "I don't think I can. Why do you ask for me to stay?"

"Well," I swallowed. "I value our friendship. I got to know you when your people took care of me and Sanjana. But I might want to know more. Do you want to stay and…learn more about me?"

I sighed. The language barrier was holding me back and I tried to not lose my nerve. How do I communicate that we're friends but we could potentially be more?

"Do your people court each other?" I asked.

It was then that Claudiu's forehead relaxed in realization. He stopped walking to face me, his face stone and forever unreadable.

"Are you asking me to court you? Here in Ushallav?"

"Yes. I want to court you and see…if we make a good match."

He sighed and took my hands into his. My heart fluttered—was this going to turn out in my favor?

"No, I cannot." No malice or disgust. Just factual and honest. "I am…see, you are beautiful but not beautiful like my late wife. I only see you as a friend—a very important friend. I cannot stay because I must follow the Traveler. I want to follow Their path. Your path is not my path. You can stay but I must walk."

I was stunned. And embarrassed. Stung, angry, offended. I just wanted to try, and I reached out to someone I was truly friends with. I wasn't proposing marriage; I just wanted to get to know him!

At first, I wanted to cry and then I found my breath and exhaled. I wasn't even fully attracted to him and he had flatly turned me down. He just turned down *me*—a former queen. But…he was allowed to do that, and I didn't need to take it personally.

Well, you can at least say you tried—even if it bruised the ego more than expected, I thought to myself.

I released my other arm so they hung limp at my sides. I quickly pulled out my diplomatic smile.

"Well, I'll admit that I'm sad that you cannot stay but thank you for explaining your feelings. I hope The Traveler helps you find what you're looking for."

My handmaidens played as though they were "catching up" with us and I felt their shock behind me. It felt as though we all needed a moment of privacy to let out a held breath.

"Let's all gather for dinner." My smile didn't falter for a second.

Later that evening, servants closed the curtains framing the open-air arches that surrounded our dining area so the setting sun wouldn't blind us. We ensured our guests sat wherever comfortable and mingled to be warm and polite.

Janitra must've read my expression because she leaned to my right ear. "What happened? Did you meet the cart guy?"

"I didn't. Instead, the Gavril people paid us a visit. I think my father got his 'he's' mixed up. Ray was actually meeting with Claudiu."

I gestured quickly with a nod in Claudiu's direction. Sanjana was initially shy around his tall, broad frame but soon fell into her old patterns of begging to ride on his shoulders or repeat words in his language I didn't know she still remembered. Devraj was speaking Makaarian to the other children and sometimes the other adults had to help translate.

"He's the one who protected you and Sanjana during the years we mourned you, right?"

I nodded. The way she phrased that felt so intimate; as if she attended a funeral for me while I recovered in the forests along The Traveler's Path.

Maybe she did.

"You're…clearly not talking to him."

I deflated a bit, my shoulders drooped.

"Did you ask him—?"

"And he rejected me," I said in the lowest whisper possible.

"Anji," my sister-in-law, Tejal, pipped up in a normal volume, "we were just talking about how handsome your friend has become since the last time he was here. Will he be staying a bit longer?"

I couldn't tell whether she was giving into her gossipy nature but I felt eyes and ears in my direction.

"You know as well as I do that the Gavril people are devoted to The Traveler. And I don't think someone like me could change that."

Tejal scooped more food with her hand and gave me a sympathetic shrug.

"His loss," Dipa murmured between bites. My heart panged a bit. I equally appreciated the vote of confidence and wanted to shrink under the table.

"Well, we can all respect a person who can speak honestly and plainly."

And I meant it; that trait was something we all championed in our culture. I still felt surprisingly discouraged. Hours ago, the thought of dating Claudiu hadn't existed in my head. Now, it felt like I'd lost him without a fighting chance.

Janitra murmured, "I bet the man with the cart will want to park it here and spend all his time courting you."

I gave her a sidelong glance and she gave me a wink.

"You think so?"

"He better. I may be biased but the least he can do is finally introduce himself."

I grinned as I brought my goblet to my lips. She gave my back a quick pat and Ziya squeezed my hand. Pari and Dipa gave me assured smiles as they kept eating.

I tended to the crushed self-esteem of the day—I'd find this man tomorrow.

CHAPTER
FOURTEEN

During my morning hours, I suddenly heard footsteps approaching.

"Your Majesty," greeted a messenger marked by the sash resting on their right shoulder and tied at the opposite hip. He held out a folded and sealed piece of parchment. I turned over the paper and recognized the seal.

"Thank you. Have a good day."

He bowed before leaving me and venturing down the hall. When left alone, I slipped a fingernail under the seal and unfolded the message.

Morning, Anji.

I found out a few details about your cart fellow. His name is Kavi and he was recently hired as an artist around the palace. He's the newest person to help with the upkeep of the Eyes so he must have a steady hand—if you catch my meaning. I think he works with metals, too. From the looks of it, he crafts jewelry. The locals seem to respect him and his work.

I personally don't know much about him, and you know how I know too much about everyone. To be honest, I wonder whether he's hiding something about his true nature or he's led a very plain life. Anyway, I look forward to meeting him in person and figuring out if this guy is your type. I just want to protect you and that heart you wear on your sleeve.

Speaking of which, I heard about Claudiu. I know you're desperate to be in love but he wasn't going to work. If you can't imagine being a follower of the Traveler with him or keeping him here in Ushallav, then just be friends. Unless you really want to embarrass yourself.

If you need your ass kicked in the training hall to get your head back in the game, you know where to find me.

I rolled my eyes at Gurpreet's tender words.

Kavi. It was a nice enough name. Kavi with the hair. I smiled to myself. Now that I knew he would occasionally work at the palace, I could find him here—or seek him out wherever he worked.

I folded up Gurpreet's message and tucked it away. There was a bit of mischief in the corner of my smile as I finished writing some letters headed to Makaar and got to my feet. I was hungry for food and a fated meeting.

<hr>

My handmaidens heard about what I learned earlier that day and helped me gather more information. Janitra confirmed that Kavi usually worked during the afternoon hours. Dipa shared word that he was halfway through his work and would be here for another week. Pari had learned where Kavi's workshop was in Ushallav. Ziya was fairly sure he was unmarried and available.

Ziya and Janitra joined me for this particular adventure. Within a few hours, they learned more from the staff about where we might find Kavi with the hair.

My plan was to casually walk past and feign surprise should we make eye contact. Somehow, I wanted to give the impression that I didn't send out my handmaidens and friends for intel, and that our meeting was purely coincidental. It was only a matter of making it happen.

We didn't really hide our mirth as we walked through the hallways and chatted and neared a quieter part of the palace. If our information was correct, Kavi should be working on some Eyes near our gardens. I daresay it was perfect. A quiet place for him to work and for me to interrupt him for a moment.

"Greetings, Your Majesty," came a soft voice from seemingly nowhere.

I looked around, puzzled. I could feel Ziya and Janitra tense behind me. It took a few heartbeats but I soon saw someone wave at us from across the garden. I had to look past some weeping fig trees to see what must be Kavi's workstation.

How could he see us from all the way over there?

"You caught me during my tea break. I hope I'm not disturbing your stroll."

Indeed, the man driving the cart was sitting on a crate with a cup and saucer. There was a wooden ladder propped against the wall, along with some buckets of paint, brushes, and a satchel which I guessed was either full of tools or his personal things.

"No disturbances here." I covered my open curiosity about his workstation by appraising his work in progress. After admiring the half-complete work, I said to him, "I've always wondered what went into the art of creating the Eyes. What is your role in the process?"

He rose to his feet and craned his neck to gaze upon the same artwork in progress.

"I make them aesthetically pleasing," he grinned, taking a sip. "A palace sorcerer is the one that takes it a step further and ensures they function properly. But I might argue that my job is more than just creating little murals."

"Sure," I conceded. "How else do they blend in with their surroundings and quietly do their work? I remember my father and mother telling me that the more intricate the design, the more worthy they are of the gods seeing through them."

We all looked up to his design. They reminded me of the design that I commissioned for the Makaar castle when I was initially crowned their queen. The typical pattern usually starts with an open eye with a pin-prick pupil but they're often decorated with the texture of wood, marble, or stone—depending on where they're located. Sometimes they're embellished with swirls, diamond shapes, or other symbols that show particular adoration for a particular god.

The few Eyes in the sanctuary often looked like the eye was peering through tall fields of flowers. This one looked like he was just about to add flecks of gold material to outline the design and represent sun rays.

"What does Her Majesty think of my work? Do you think they're worthy of the gods?"

I put a finger to my lip and squinted as if I was thinking much more deeply than necessary.

"I'm not much of an artist," I began, giving him a small smile, "but I'd say your work is rather lovely."

He smiled and dipped his chin—whether his humility was genuine or good-natured teasing, I wasn't sure.

I extended a hand. "I think you know who I am. I would very much like to know your name."

He took my hand as if to shake it but quickly gave it a kiss before answering, "I'm Kavi. It's a pleasure to finally meet you in person. Well, with a formal introduction. I believe it was you I saw the other day once I finished work for the day."

I made a little "hmm" sound like I didn't recognize him or hadn't fantasized about him at all since seeing him.

"Kavi, please allow me to introduce you to Janitra and Ziya. They are two of my handmaidens."

"I recognize you. Pleasure to meet you," Kavi said to Ziya. That made sense because she'd been seen with me since I returned to Ushallav. He turned to Janitra. "You must be new."

"Freshly initiated this week," she smiled, inclining her head.

"I hope I don't sound too informal but it does bring me and my family joy to see you here with your handmaidens once more," Kavi said to me. "My parents were particularly worried for you when you initially started your rule there. And then the worst happened. I think my mother will be particularly proud that I got to meet you today and could personally bear witness to your health and resilience."

My mouth formed some sort of grin that almost broke into a laugh. I was used to hearing the devotion my people have for my family. This was more of the light-hearted charm and I did my best to see this for what it was: an excuse to flirt with me.

"Yes, please let your parents know that we're all safe and happy here," I said, smiling knowingly. "But I don't want your chai to go cold on my account. We can leave you to your work."

"You're probably right." Kavi sighed. He had set his chai down at some point; it was long cold and forgotten on the crate. "I hope you have a great rest of your day. You're free to stop by again and check my progress. Maybe during my next chai break?"

"That's quite possible," I answered. "Or perhaps you could see me when you're done working for the day?"

He smiled broadly, clearly shocked. "Of course, my queen. I could give you the address to my shop. I make jewelry and do some repairs here and there."

"I would love that. One of our messengers can deliver your address to my office."

"Okay," Kavi let out a chuckle. "Wow, what an honor. The queen, coming to visit my shop. I'm blessed by the gods."

I'm not sure how long I stood there looking into his eyes but I took that as a sign that things would only get awkward if we stayed longer.

"Good day, Kavi," I breathed before turning towards the way we came and left him to his work.

Once we were out of the garden and reliably out of earshot, Ziya and Janitra leaned in close.

Ziya whispered, "I don't know what happened with Claudiu but this seemed much better. And he's very handsome."

Janitra murmured, "He gave me a weird look like he recognized me. As for looks, he seems fine."

"Not the type you usually fancy?" Ziya mused good-naturedly.

"No, not really. I usually fancy other women." At this, Janitra grinned broadly. "Don't worry, my queen. He's safe from me."

They slowed their steps and fell into place behind me as we passed more people. I held a neutral, pleasant expression on my face as people stopped to greet me before we continued in our separate directions.

We would continue to chat once we reunited with the rest of the handmaidens and brought them up to speed. But for now, I couldn't help but think about Janitra's statement. She didn't seem impressed with Kavi but at least admitted her bias. But I didn't want to discount it entirely.

If she continued to express discomfort around Kavi and his demeanor, I wanted to trust that. Especially if the others agreed with her. If the handmaidens picked up something off, I wasn't about to introduce him to the children.

In fact, it seemed like the wise, safe choice to wait a long time for any romantic partner to meet my children—even if everything went well.

Something deep down valued Janitra's opinions more than I expected. I wanted to be smart. But I also hoped that this, seeing Kavi again, could be the start of something truly wonderful for me.

After all, this felt like the one thing I was really doing for me—and the kids—without waiting for permission or weighing the political scales.

And long after I talked with the handmaidens and long after I put the children to bed, I lay staring up at the ceiling.

Abhijita, is this what you want for me? Am I doing this right?

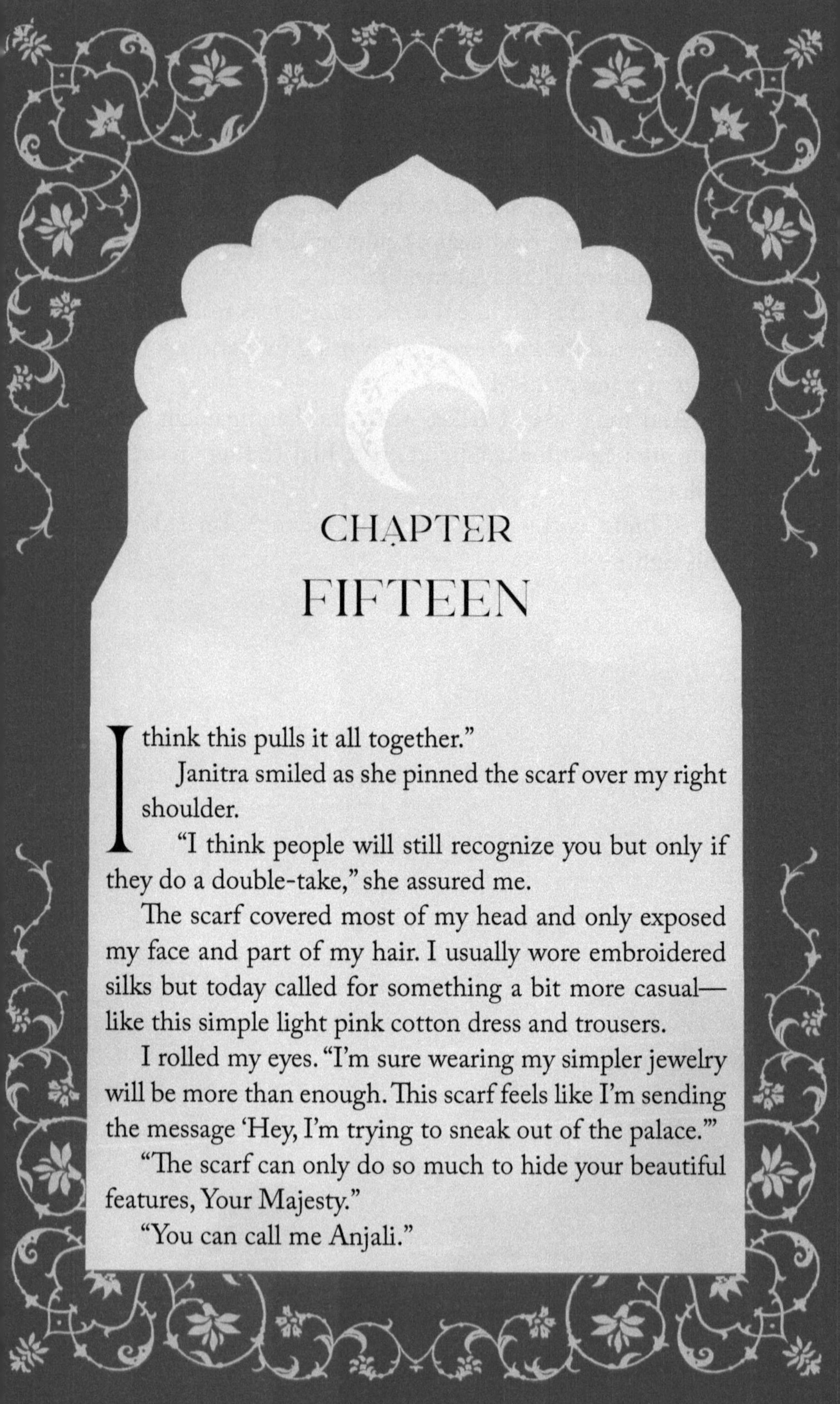

CHAPTER
FIFTEEN

I think this pulls it all together."

Janitra smiled as she pinned the scarf over my right shoulder.

"I think people will still recognize you but only if they do a double-take," she assured me.

The scarf covered most of my head and only exposed my face and part of my hair. I usually wore embroidered silks but today called for something a bit more casual—like this simple light pink cotton dress and trousers.

I rolled my eyes. "I'm sure wearing my simpler jewelry will be more than enough. This scarf feels like I'm sending the message 'Hey, I'm trying to sneak out of the palace.'"

"The scarf can only do so much to hide your beautiful features, Your Majesty."

"You can call me Anjali."

"I know," smiled Janitra—as if politely declining the suggestion, "As you requested, your carriage will take you halfway and then we can walk the rest of the way to Kavi's shop. And by design, we'll arrive during the slowest part of the workday."

"I hope this part of the job isn't too dull for you," I joked. "A lot of the tests are feats of strength. Not helping me go on a date."

Janitra put the finishing touches on her eye makeup. She went for a simpler look with kajal around her eyes and brassy earrings. Our goal was to appear as two friends out for a brief shopping trip. She smiled at her reflection and turned her gaze to me.

"My role is to support you," she shrugged. "Support your physical and mental wellbeing. So this sounds like a very appropriate use of my skills."

"Yes, true. Just tell me if something seems off about him," I replied. I hid some coins discreetly on my person and strapped on my sandals. "Let's go before I lose my nerve."

"Nervous, Your Majesty? That might be a good sign. You want this to go well."

I flashed a grimace in her direction and off we went.

About an hour later, we arrived at what I guessed was Kavi's workshop. I could tell because Janitra wouldn't stop waggling her eyebrows at me. It felt like we were teenagers sneaking out without parental permission.

As we passed under the canopy and through the doorway, a faint smell of incense flooded my nose.

I heard some shuffling in the back.

"What can I help you ladies find today?"

I waited for Kavi to look up. He was wiping some-thing off his hands with a dirty towel and didn't quite notice who we were. Maybe our disguises worked a little too well?

"We're just looking," I said softly. I turned to my left and began looking-but-not-looking at the jewelry on display. I did want to see his work, as if it would tell me something about his personality. Did he make things that followed the current trends or did he dare create some-thing with a more eclectic taste?

"Oh," came the soft reply.

I looked up and Kavi dropped the dirty towel and froze, looking at me. As if snapping out of a trance, he removed his work apron and smoothed his hair back.

"It's…you," he said, a bit bewildered.

"Good day," I answered. "You do know that you invited me, right?"

He chuckled shyly. "That's correct. Well, take a look around and let me know if you see anything you fancy."

He winked at me and retreated beyond a set of curtains.

Janitra gave me a knowing look and lightly hip bumped me before bending over to examine the wares.

"You're both so nervous," she mused. "It's adorable."

I looked at all the jewelry on the left side of the store. I saw a lot of familiar motifs—women in the palace loved this style. Sparkling stars, phases of the moon, and eyes. They were all popular symbols of all kinds of gods and goddesses. I marveled at some of the wooden earrings painted with small lines and dots. They seemed so small, like he used a paintbrush with a single hair to get the dots as tiny as possible.

As I crossed the store to the right side, Kavi emerged with significantly fewer smudges on his face and arms. He wore a tunic with the sleeves rolled up to the elbows and gleaming earrings in his left ear. His stance and facial expression reminded me of many a hero of Ushallavi legends or fables. The black necklace tight around his neck added to the charm.

I looked over my left shoulder and smiled at him. He had some coffee and fruit set out on the table next to a small scale.

"This is usually a dull hour for me so I tend to sneak in some food. Please." He gestured to the coffee cup closest to me.

"I was hoping to chat with you," I smiled. "I must admit, I don't know much about you." I sipped the coffee. It was…plainer than what I was used to. And it felt like the right thing for this moment.

"What's there to know?" Kavi shrugged. "I'm flattered but I'm just an artist. What interest could a queen have in me?"

For a moment, I flinched and turned around. Where did Janitra go? She was here one moment and then disappeared the next.

"She, uh, stepped outside for a moment," Kavi smiled politely. "I think she's just outside or nearby."

I was just so used to having someone at my side— whether it was my children or my handmaidens. We made very specific plans for how to arrive and how to leave. The middle part was all up to me. I had a feeling she would be right by my side if the situation really demanded her.

"Your jewelry is beautiful."

"Thank you."

"What inspired you to make jewelry—to be an artist?"

Kavi sat back in his chair deep in thought but it lasted as long as it took to savor a sip of his drink.

"It's hard to describe," he admitted. "After all, I don't make weapons, I'm not a farmer, and I don't have a family to raise. But when it comes to art, I almost feel like I'm not myself if I'm not making something. I almost feel like I'd turn inside out if I stopped. I guess the gods know how to inspire me. How else would I find myself in the palace and in your wondrous presence?"

"Ah, so you're a poet as well?" I smiled.

I found myself admiring Kavi and his words. I wondered what that felt like—to be so drawn to your destiny that it gripped you and wouldn't let go. A long time ago, I felt truly drawn to my role and destiny of ruling Makaar with Damir. And now, I was the furthest I could imagine from that path.

What was I drawn to now? What tugged at my heart so obviously and clearly? Of course, I was still a mother and that would never change. But what else? What was out there waiting for me—a craft, skill, or position that sang to me?

"You seem deep in thought," Kavi said. "What's on your mind?"

"Oh," I smiled as I sipped my drink. "I just admire your devotion to your craft. It suits you."

"If you stay a little bit longer, I can make some supper for you. You can let me know if cooking also suits me?"

Without thinking, I nodded. "I'd love that."

"Do you think your, uh, handmaiden, will join us?"

"I hope so," I replied. "We'll see."

After a bit of conversing, some people arrived to peruse Kavi's wares. I swiftly adjusted my scarf and ducked away and out of the gathering crowd.

I knew where to find him and when. I just needed to find Janitra first. And once I found her not too far off, she pointed her finger back toward Kavi's shop.

"This is officially a date. Go on! I'll be here when you're done, but this date is for you. Go enjoy yourself," she insisted. I laughed.

"Are you sure?"

"I can take care of myself. You got this, my queen."

After Kavi's meal for two, my handmaidens waited silently outside and took me back to the palace. Thanks to their swiftness and discretion, I was able to slip out of the palace for much of the afternoon and evening. They watched my children and ensured a very short list of people were aware of my intentions and location.

When it was just the five of us in my carriage, everyone started to chatter.

"So, have you already declared your undying love?"

"Oh, your mother won't know what to do once she hears that you went on a date!"

"Are those earrings from Kavi? Not too bad!"

"He seemed nice. Did he tell you about his family—is he single for good reasons or bad ones?"

I held up my hands in mock surrender.

"Let me explain myself," I chuckled. My handmaidens listened with various levels of intrigue and excitement in their eyes.

"It was nice. I like his artwork–and I don't think it's because I'm trying to be nice. His cooking wasn't so bad and it was nice talking to him. It was a very pleasant evening. What did you think, Janitra?"

My handmaiden smiled. "I knew Anjali could handle herself so I looked at a couple of other shops before she came out to find me."

I tilted my head in her direction.

"What? I know you're capable of handling yourself. Besides, I don't need to be the awkward third person on what was clearly meant to be a date."

"Who knows if this will even work out," I sighed.

"What do you mean?" Dipa practically sputtered. "You seem really happy."

I looked at my painted fingernails before folding my hands in my lap.

"I'm not used to dancing around someone, especially when I know how I feel about them. With Kavi, we didn't have to say it but I could feel it. I think he's too intimidated by me. I'm a queen after all. If we were to be together—however long or short that may be—that can change his life completely. I don't know if he's even considered the idea of parenting the future heirs of Makaar with me."

The women nodded thoughtfully.

"But he hasn't said that outright, so you can't assume just yet, my queen," came Pari's calm voice. "Try to be as unbiased as possible here."

"Besides, most mere mortals like us have to court several people before finding someone who fits and suits us," Janitra added.

"Some parents do choose their children's future spouses but many of us have that choice. And it's not easy," Ziya confirmed. "You have a difficult decision ahead of you, should you choose to marry again. Might as well have some ups and downs and some laughs along the way, right?"

My heart swelled with several emotions as I absorbed the council from these four capable women. This was probably why I wanted to find Janitra right away; I felt so much ease and confidence around her and my other handmaidens. I would've certainly found the courage to plan another meeting or date with Kavi if I knew one of them were in my peripherals.

"Is he coming to your birthday celebration?" Janitra reminded me.

"Yes! You could invite him and dance with him. It could be a perfect way to show him off in a public way if things are going well. And you can see how he operates under pressure." I could already see the wheels turning in Ziya's head.

"It's almost like he's auditioning for the role of your partner or spouse," Pari mused. "That sounds oddly familiar, right ladies?"

I laughed at her words. It did really sound like I was going to put Kavi through the ringer like all the other handmaiden hopefuls.

"Give that job to Gurpreet," Janitra snorted. "They'll sort him out swiftly and efficiently."

"Ah, leave the poor man alone."

"Do you think I could beat him in an arm wrestling match?"

"That reminds me—I need to write letters home and see if my sisters can make it to the party," Ziya added, and the other handmaidens chimed in about who they planned on inviting.

The coach filled with nonstop chatter and laughter. I leaned back, tired from the talking and mental load of extroverting. I felt like I'd really made the gods proud of me and all I did was show up at Kavi's establishment and try to strike up a conversation.

My handmaidens, my sisters. They were right. I didn't need to out-logic myself now. I could stand to be more blunt with him about what life was really like with me and see if he was up to that challenge. Maybe he would or maybe he wouldn't but I could at least say that I tried and had some fun along the way.

As my home came into view, a smile played on my lips. With all the excitement about Kavi, I had missed my time with the children. I promised them, in my head, that I would spend more time with them instead of relying on the handmaidens or grandma to play with them.

"You did great today, my queen," Janitra said, cutting through the rest of the chatter. She gave my hand a squeeze in triumph. "Kavi seems to really fancy you. I imagine things will become more fun once he realizes he has the chance of a lifetime to court someone like you."

"Thanks," I murmured. "I do think it's a good idea to invite him to the birthday party. I don't think I could move forward if he wasn't a good dancer."

The last part was a joke but it didn't quite earn the chuckle I was expecting from Janitra.

"What?"

"Aren't you also inviting all those northern princes to the party?"

"Yes," I winced slightly. She whistled low.

That was five men at least who would come with the expectation of talking or dancing with me. Or expanding our relationship into something much more romantic.

During my birthday week.

I couldn't tell whether excitement or anxiety bubbled in my stomach.

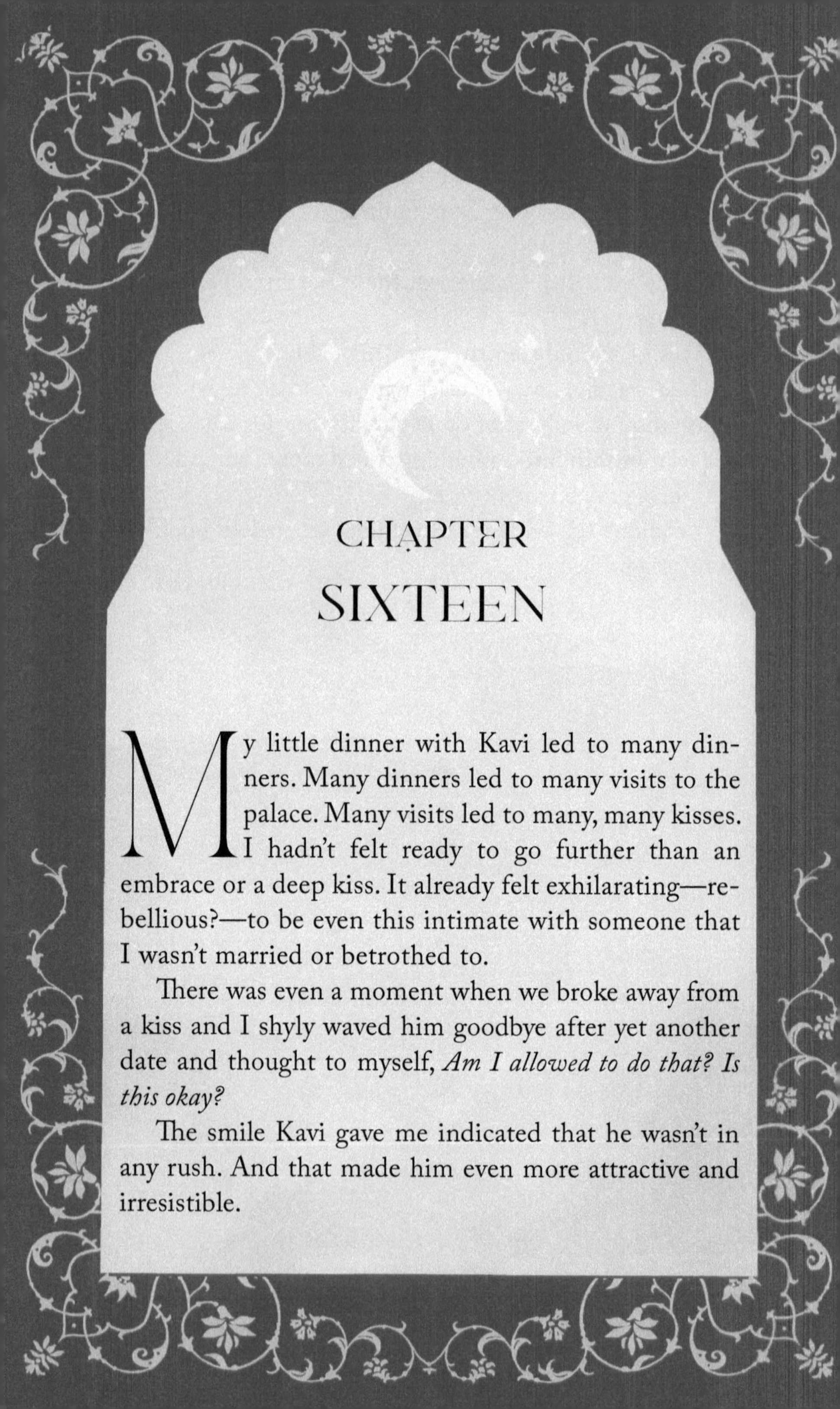

CHAPTER
SIXTEEN

My little dinner with Kavi led to many dinners. Many dinners led to many visits to the palace. Many visits led to many, many kisses. I hadn't felt ready to go further than an embrace or a deep kiss. It already felt exhilarating—rebellious?—to be even this intimate with someone that I wasn't married or betrothed to.

There was even a moment when we broke away from a kiss and I shyly waved him goodbye after yet another date and thought to myself, *Am I allowed to do that? Is this okay?*

The smile Kavi gave me indicated that he wasn't in any rush. And that made him even more attractive and irresistible.

I leaned a bit dramatically and sighed as I waved one last time before he drove his cart away. He was handsome, creative, smart, and charming. This felt like a good pace. We're just getting to know each other. Well, I'm getting to know him; he already knew a lot about me as a public figure. But somehow, it felt like there were things that I could share with him that felt like they were mine to share.

I learned how he became an apprentice to be an artist and jeweler. I learned that he came from a farming family, and they were so proud of him, if not a bit surprised, that he lived comfortably in the busier part of Ushallav. He had several siblings, and the mostly stayed on their family's land to continue that legacy.

With time, he did finally warm up to me and joked with me or teased me. I was worried he would remain intimidated by my status. But with our recurring meetings, I could see he was chipping away the public persona and finally seeing me, Anjali.

After a few weeks, I still hadn't introduced Sanjana and Devraj to Kavi. And he didn't really ask, either. This all felt exactly like what I wanted. I had all the time in the world to be a mother and someone's partner. Well, I wasn't sure if I was a partner or lover, of course, since we were taking things so slow.

But no one was complaining. If anything, Kavi and I had all the room and space we needed to discern each other and whether this would work. As Kavi disappeared from view, I knew I needed to fill him in on the rest of the guest list.

I sighed dreamily. I pictured him meeting the children before the party and dancing with them on his shoulders. It was easy to picture him becoming another father figure for Sanjana and Devraj—helping them in their studies and feeling more at home in their homeland.

Everything felt picturesque except for the gray cloud hanging over me. He already knew about the party but I needed to tell him about the full guest list, as well as the full intent for the party. I hoped that in all the understanding he had for me and my pacing, there would be just enough room to understand why these princes would be visiting Ushallav very soon.

My heart leaped for the umpteenth time; that seemed to happen every time Kavi's shop came into view. I always took care to approach Kavi's shop on foot to avoid as much celebrity fanfare as possible. So I gave a subtle wave and gestured for the carriage to create some distance. Ziya was in the carriage at the ready should I need her. Again, in my casual Ushallavi outfit, I strode into the shop. I waited until there was only a few minutes left before closing time.

Kavi wrapped some merchandise in a soft linen and handed it to another man with both hands. It wasn't until the man nodded and walked toward me that I caught Kavi's eye.

I waved shyly as I watched surprise, intrigue, and joy bloom across his features. I turned slightly to my right to observe Kavi's latest creations until I was certain that the patron left and hopefully didn't catch my features.

"Anjali! What a surprise," Kavi said. He used an excited hush that sounded like he was a teenager worried he'd get caught doing something bad or mischievous. With just a few steps, I was already in his arms.

"I wanted to see you." I finally revealed a basket that slung over my shoulder and hid behind my back. "I also brought some dinner."

"I wondered why you smelled so strongly of samosas," Kavi teased. After securing the entrance to his store, he turned to me. He held the basket by the bottom so I could lift the strap over my head. "This basket is heavy."

"What? I'm hungry."

"Me too. But you carried it like it's nothing."

"I have years of experience." I didn't flex with my arms but I smiled instead. I already explained my morning workout routine and the many ways I've learned to carry my children on my back supported by a wrapped sash. I didn't even get into the pregnancy pains.

With the basket in both hands, he tilted his head to indicate I should follow. We went through the curtain that separated the shop from his workplace. We moved around piles of materials and boxes through another doorway. This led to a stairway to the second floor instead of the joining kitchen area.

I looked around in awe. I hadn't been here yet. I hadn't asked, to be fair. This almost felt too intimate in the way that his dresser, bed, and a dining table were all within view.

A blush whispered over my cheeks at an errant thought and I focused on the simple decor and layout as Kavi unearthed the basket's contents.

"It's not much but it gets the job done," he said as though he could anticipate my thoughts.

"Your shop seems more vibrant—more like you," I pondered.

"Well, I spend more of my time running the shop. It's nice to have something beautiful to look at." Kavi winked at me then emphasized, "You're beautiful."

"I came with a basket of food. Of course I'm beautiful," I laughed. I lowered the scarf wrapped around my hair and draped it on a chair. I then sat cross-legged at the low table on the offered cushion.

"I was entranced by you long before I knew you brought food."

We held each other's gaze for a heartbeat or two.

"You're beautiful," I practically whispered. Even though I wanted to shout it on the roof of his home.

He blinked as his smile widened. I ached to run a hand through his hair. I hoped he didn't see my eyes flicker to other intimate corners of the room.

As we looked at each other it felt like we were holding a conversation.

What actually came out of Kavi's mouth was, "Well, let's enjoy the spread while it's still warm."

<hr>

After enjoying some pakoras and samosas–having our fill of fried eggplant and savory pastries–I leaned away from the table and supported myself with my hands. I packed some feni, a bottled alcoholic beverage, but we didn't open it yet. I wondered which one of us would uncork it first.

This was the first time we would drink together and I wondered what would unfold.

"You'll have to tell the chef that this was incredible," Kavi said. "Don't tell my *dadi* but this might be the one rival to her recipe."

"I wouldn't dare. I don't insult anyone who knows how to prepare a good dish."

Moments like this brought me pause. We were from vastly different worlds. And if we took more steps toward each other, what would happen? Would I live here—would he live in the palace with me? Would we go somewhere else to make a new place for ourselves?

I hadn't thought this far ahead and I felt somewhat anxious. Turning my attention elsewhere, I tucked these thoughts away. This wasn't the time to dwell on the future.

"So, your birthday is coming up."

"Yeah, I'm looking forward to it." Gods, guide me.

"And if I remember correctly, you're turning 27, right?"

I nodded.

"Sorry. You being the princess and all…"

"Well, you can make it up to me by telling me about your birthday."

Kavi grabbed the wine bottle and used the accompanying tool to twist away the cork. I held up my glass as permission to pour me some. He then poured himself a small amount.

"Well, my birthday isn't for another few months but we were actually born in the same year. It makes it easier to remember birthdays like yours."

"Oh wonderful!" I beamed. "We'll have to celebrate together. Maybe something grander than a meal like this."

"This is perfect—are you kidding? These moments…I wouldn't trade them for anything."

My mind whirred as he took my hands in his. What could happen in a couple of months? I half-imagined what it would feel like to transform my attraction to deep, real love. In my mind, I could see him lifting Sanjana into the air and him showing Devraj how to paint.

"Where is your mind going, princess?" My vision focused and Kavi was smiling at me.

"Don't mind me. What were you saying?"

"I wasn't saying anything. But I don't mind you staring."

"Well, don't let me distract you. You brought up my birthday."

"Right," Kavi took a sip. "This is your first birthday back in Ushallav. I know you're having a party at the palace but I thought…maybe you could spend part of your day here."

My answer clogged my throat.

Rushed, he clarified, "Well, I don't know if you know this but this neighborhood holds a small festival during your birthday week. And I thought you might like to join in on a celebration to honor you. I think my aunties would faint."

I did know about these festivals. They happened every year across the kingdom. I've secretly always wanted to go but I've always celebrated with my huge family. One year, I even meant to sneak out and finally experience these local festivities but a much younger Damir made the trip to see me. I think we managed to sneak off to steal some kisses before joining the fray.

"I could see if I could make it work but I'm not sure," came the confession. Orchestrating these dates was getting more and more difficult as others started catching on to my schedule. I couldn't think of bringing my kids here just yet. And celebrating my birthday without them…

"I've been meaning to tell you," I beamed. "Yes, we're having a big celebration for my birthday. But it would mean a lot if you would come."

Kavi practically guffawed at my invitation. Several emotions twitched in his expression but he settled on a smile. "That's…really wonderful. I'd love to come. I don't have the fanciest garb but I'd come in my work clothes if it means being there."

"We can have the tailors make something for you." It was hardly an expense for me. Besides, half the gift of his presence would be seeing him dressed in something shiny and silky—befitting the place he held in my warming heart.

"I have also invited some guests from the north. You see, I reached out with an invitation before I met you. I think it'll be a nice opportunity to catch up and revive old alliances."

I tried to suppress the gnawing in my gut. There wasn't really any other way around it and yet I still cringed at the revelation. Mostly because I wasn't fully transparent about the kinds of alliances I was hoping to revive or forge. He already looked a few degrees deflated.

"Well, I'm still invited, so I'm taking that as a win," Kavi shrugged. "You're not inviting any Makaarians to the party, are you? Will your ex-husband get an obligatory invitation?"

I cringed and frowned at that. It was something I tossed around in my mind. Part of me almost invited them out of politeness but ultimately, I decided against it. It was all too fresh. Maybe things would feel different in the years to come.

"No," I shook my head a bit wearily. "The guest list is already full."

Kavi wiped his forehead as if he was sweating bullets. "Kavi—"

"I don't want you to worry about me. It's your birthday. I'm honestly so happy you've invited me. And you've given me an opportunity to show you how much better of a dancer I can be compared to your prince friends."

"I hardly know them," I rolled my eyes with a smirk. "I just want you to be prepared. Part of being in the royal family means that everyone will be watching me very closely. Everyone knows I'm looking to remarry and they'll over-analyze who I do and don't talk to. I'm sure by the time you return home, all your neighbors will already know the answer to 'so how was the party?'"

That earned a chuckle from Kavi.

"Are you inviting me as a friend or as someone more, Anjali?"

He gave my hands a squeeze.

"I'm stuck in my thoughts again." I clenched my jaw in frustration and willed the questions away. "What I want you to know is that this is all new to me, and it's hard to know how I feel. It's hard to describe. All I know is that I really enjoy being around you and I want to keep exploring where this will go.

"Sometimes, it's difficult to know if I'm doing something for me, or my children, or my parents, or my country. I reached out to the princes because I thought it might make my parents happy that I was making a smart, political match. But they could all be ugly, uneducated, or humorless dolts. I don't know."

"You married King Damir for our country. To ensure future peace," Kavi said. He emphasized "peace" with his hands holding mine. "You get to ensure your own happiness now. I'm a bit biased, but I think you deserve that. I hope you'll find happiness with me but you'll know when it's time."

I blinked away tears and he used the pad of his thumb to dry my cheek without smudging my makeup.

"Just know that they'll have to work really hard to secure a dance with you," Kavi grinned. He planted a soft kiss on my forehead and I wrapped my arms around his waist.

"Next time you come to the palace, we'll get your measurements."

That earned me a thrilling smile.

CHAPTER
SEVENTEEN

Kavi and I hardly saw each other during the next two weeks. As the days became longer, we filled the sunny hours with planning. Kavi was right—this was the first time celebrating my birthday since I married Damir and moved to Makaar. This was a big deal, and word spread like mad about my guest list.

"Come in," came my answer to a knock at the door. "Go see who it is, sweetie."

Devraj scrambled to his feet from his coloring station on the floor and opened the door. My handmaidens were on the other side.

"Hello, mighty little prince," Ziya greeted.

"I'm Devraj!"

"We know, princey-boy," Dipa teased. Devraj guffawed but let the women in and they took their seats.

Wordlessly, Sanjana relocated into Dipa's lap and played with her braid.

"Sanjana, you need to ask first."

She shyly looked up at my handmaiden.

"Your hair is so very pretty," my daughter said. The braid in question pooled in Dipa's lap like a length of rope.

She quietly asked for permission and Dipa nodded—clearly not wanting to get in the way of this parenting moment.

"All right. Let's see," I began, looking at some parchment with my own notes. "What else do we need to prioritize before party time?"

"We've planned and confirmed all the details three times over," Janitra answered. "The food, decorations, outfits, and music are all accounted for. All you have to do is get dressed up, arrive on time, and enjoy the event."

"We really ought to talk about our role," Pari added. "You keep telling us that we ought to enjoy ourselves and let the palace guards focus on security."

Based on the pointed look she and the others gave me, I understood that they disagreed with this idea.

"This is a party but there are a lot of political moving pieces," Janitra insisted. "This is your birthday party and your opportunity to…interact with your guests. We all are united in the idea that we will be on alert so you and your children are safe."

I sighed. They already knew I could handle myself, and I'd sacrifice a shiny crown or a beaded, embroidered gown if it meant defending myself or those I loved. I just wanted to give them the night off. Their gift to me would be having a good time with their guests.

"We're not making any comments about your strength and abilities. You are royalty—one who lets Abhijita shine through your features," Janitra continued rather earnestly. "But it's our job to use our goddess-given strength to help you."

"Gurpreet put you up to this, didn't they?" I tried to joke. They glanced at each other before turning to me.

"They're double- and triple-checking our security guard team to weed out any ill will." Dipa pressed forward like she didn't quite want to address my comment.

"I think we all recognize that this party will be equally joyous and diplomatic." Ziya glanced over notes of her own. "We know you more than you realize. There will be enough eyes and ears so when the party is over, we can give you all the information you need about your suitors."

I took a heartbeat or two to look the women in the eyes. This was silly. Of course, this is what they're here for—this is what they trained for. I probably sounded much more defensive than I truly felt.

"What's a suitor?" asked Devraj. "Do they wear suits like Papa?"

"Well, suitors don't have to wear suits, Dev," I laughed. "Suitors are people who are very kind and maybe want to be in love."

"Sweetie, your father was a suitor for his wife, Einora. There are people who want to fall in love with your mother," Dipa clarified.

Ziya snorted and Janitra gave her a look. We smiled as Dipa's answer seemed to satisfy my son. I held up my hands in peace and surrendered.

"Of course I need you," I conceded. "I wish you could have a moment of fun after all the work you've put into this occasion but I'll appreciate having you there with me. For the ups and downs. I don't think I can embarrass myself in front of another man ever again."

That earned the easy peals of laughter I fished for earlier.

"That does remind me. Devraj, Sanjana. Listen to Mama for a moment." My children looked up when the attention was fully on them.

"Remember that list of people I showed you before? Some of those people will be at my birthday party. You don't have to meet anyone if you don't want to but they might want to say hello."

"Okay!"

"Are they kids like us?" Devraj asked innocently. I laughed.

"No, they're adults like Mama," I answered. "You'll get to meet lots of kids at the party, though. They'll be traveling from very far away. You'll have to show them all your dance moves."

"And point out the good sweets," Dipa added, wrapping her arms around Sanjana still on her lap, earning a delighted squeal.

"The list of people are grown-ups who might be suitors. And I might marry one of them."

"Marry somebody?"

"Yes, Devraj."

He squirmed uncomfortably. Normally, I'd gesture for him to come closer for snuggles but he returned to his coloring and pointedly turned a fraction away from me.

Janitra looked at me and I could see concern and empathy. My handmaidens were well aware that Devraj was missing his father terribly but didn't want to leave his mother and sister. He was stuck between two parents; his little heart was full of so many feelings. Sometimes we addressed his reactions directly and sometimes we let him be.

"No one's getting married right away," I clarified. "I just want to talk to some of these people and see if they're the right fit for us."

A flicker of annoyance and frustration passed through my mind: why was I still picking up the pieces of this divorce? We absolutely wouldn't be in this position had Damir remained a widower until I returned home. Why was I still the bad guy?

"Your artwork is looking great, Devraj," Janitra said, looking over his work. "Is that supposed to be me?" She pointed at the depiction and then flexed her arms as though posing for a painter.

"No," he giggled. "It's Mama!"

"Oh, well the drawing is very beautiful so I had to ask," Janitra joked.

I nodded at Janitra in gratitude and cleared my mind. Devraj was a child and going through his own difficult, messy, frustrating time. He could be angry with me, Damir, Einora, or anyone necessary. We'd still be here and hold him closer—even if he was facing a fraction away and scribbling ferociously.

"If you and I don't like anyone on the list, we'll crumple it up and start over," I reaffirmed. Devraj tucked his chin closer to his chest; his moment of warmth with Janitra frosted over. He didn't want to admit he could hear me.

"Yeah, we'll beat 'em up if they're bad." Pari planted her fist into an open palm. Devraj covered his face with his hands so we wouldn't see a smile crawling across his angry visage.

"Well, let's hope this feels more like a party than an interrogation session," I sighed. I knew Pari was joking to crack a smile and break the tension. I was getting tired of everyone enunciating how their jobs were to protect me. Couldn't I just celebrate my birthday, kiss Kavi in public, and maybe flirt with the princes if they were cute? Heavy would the crown forever be.

"What about…your new friend?" Dipa asked, almost in a whisper. "Is he okay with the current arrangement?"

"Oh, yes! He's already been fitted for his clothing. He seemed excited about the invitation."

"And the rest of the guest list?"

"Well, he saw it more like a challenge."

Janitra nodded and pursed her lips. I looked at her for a beat until she met my gaze.

"You look concerned. Or as though you'd like to say something."

"Gurpreet and I have looked into the festival he was talking about," Pari spoke up. "His family seems to really like you. In a he-knows-more-about-you-than-we-know-about-him kind of way."

"I'm used to Ushallavi citizens caring for me and the rest of the royal family. Some are a bit enthusiastic but he's not a fanatic."

"We all have the honor of serving you because enough *fanatics* thought they knew what was best for you." Dipa's words were barely audible—touching on moments that altered my life and my children's lives indefinitely.

Were they…wary of Kavi? And did they really think I was too blind or stupid for wanting to date a commoner? A kind and considerate and creative man? Someone I chose for myself?

I felt embroidered fabric in my hands and realized I was gripping my skirts too tightly. I loosened my fist and tried to fold my hands in my lap.

In my mind, I was seeking ways to extend grace to Devraj even though I could sense that the only person he wanted me to marry was his father. That was not going to happen. But if everyone else was going to stand in the way of my genuine efforts to connect with other options…

I didn't realize the room was completely silent until all I could hear was my own breathing. My long, deep inhalations and exhalations were much louder than I intended.

"Gurpreet is already doing their job to ensure we're all happy and safe. You can focus on just the 'happy' part," I said with measured enunciation. "I'm not going to sneak off, I'm not going to isolate myself, and I'm not going to compromise my dignity."

"Anjali—"

"Please leave."

Sanjana approached me once the other women took their leave.

"Mama, is it nap time?"

"Yes, sweetheart." I sighed and let her hold my face in her tiny hands. She pressed my cheeks toward my lips and laughed at the silly expression she molded.

"Don't be sad, Mama. I love you," she chirped pleasantly.

"Thank you. I love you, too. Do you want to take a nap too or play?" It was very dignified the way I spoke through forced pursed lips.

Devraj practically materialized to my left and buried his face in my shoulder.

"I take it you want to nap, Dev?" I asked as Sanjana let me go.

He whined in the affirmative.

"Okay, let's rest, little grumps."

"You're a big grump!" Sanjana insisted.

"Yes I am," I countered. "And hungry. Let's grab some snacks."

***

The air grew increasingly tense and quiet as my hand-maidens realized I had entered the training room. I could tell based on their sweaty countenances, they'd just ran a training session together and finished.

Much like my training facility back in Makaar, sorcerers were able to create moving images and locations that flickered across the walls. With captured light and sound, I and my fellow Abhijita followers could chase after thieves or save hostages as practice. It was often much more fun than pushups.

Their panting grew still as I neared them. I noticed

Janitra's eyes flickering from Pari to me like she was un-sure of what to do next.

I spoke before anyone could.

"I want to have a good time at the party. So I wanted to apologize for what I said earlier." I swallowed before continuing. "You're just trying to do your job so I can do mine. Please feel free to continue your set plans, as I trust you will help me find the balance between being wise and having fun."

My arms hung stiff and tense at my sides. I could feel my hands grip tighter and I couldn't will them to relax. For a moment, no one moved or spoke; just Dipa, Pari, Janitra, and Ziya schooling their breathing to a calmed state.

"It's going to be an incredible time," Ziya smiled. Her hands were on her hips and then she lightly tapped my bicep. "I think we're all a little nervous and excited—you especially. And you should be. It's a big night for you. You deserve it."

"We just finished a training session and we're going to stretch a bit. Will you join us?" Dipa asked.

I nodded. And with that, we silently strode to the corner of the training facility where rolled up carpets waited for us.

"My queen." Janitra drew close into a whisper. "Is it normal for royalty to…apologize?"

"Sure. Just because I can use direct language doesn't mean I should let it sting—especially the people I love most."

Janitra whistled, impressed.

"If it makes you feel any better, I plan on trying all the drinks. I plan on having a good time."

"I better see you on the dance floor, then." My smile grew.

"If things go your way, you'll be too focused on Kavi with the hair to notice my moves."

We unfurled the rugs and began various breathing and stretching practices. By the time we finished, the tension all but disappeared in my muscles and my frantic thoughts.

CHAPTER

EIGHTEEN

The day before my birthday became a flurry of preparation, alluring smells, chatter, and anticipation. Of course, things felt much lighter after I talked to my handmaidens and cleared the air.

Janitra poked her head in while a makeup artist worked on my face. "Your brother has officially received and greeted our third prince, Ekwueme. That just leaves the Elpídio prince and they're all here and accounted for."

"Have Harshad and Pavti made it yet?" I asked. My younger brother, Harshad, was apparently traveling with Pavti and promised to be back in time for the party.

"The kids are just finishing up lunch and they'll join you for final fittings," Pari announced. "Ziya will bring them and the head seamstress."

"Don't forget to keep sipping water. I've also brought you some tea that will clear your head and help you avoid headaches." Dipa held out both drinks and I sipped the tea while the artist paused his work.

I anticipated this hustle and bustle, which is why I chose to spend this day preparing for the party, dancing and celebrating until dawn, and then spend my actual birthday sleeping and conversing with our out-of-town guests.

I'm practically a genius, I thought to myself with a satisfied grin. My eyes fluttered shut as the makeup artist begins applying sparkling powders to my eyelids. I started to daydream of faceless-yet-somehow-attractive princes flirting with me, admiring my children, and wondering if they could extend their stays to get to know me better.

I dwelled on my near-intimate moments with Kavi and wondered if tonight would be the night that things felt so right—right enough that we'd do more than just kiss and embrace.

Somehow, almost as if I planned it so, I anticipated that this birthday celebration would be quite the memorable one.

Janitra broke the spell by saying close to my ear, "I wanted to let you know that Damir and Einora send you a birthday gift. I've put it in your room. They sent some other things for the children. I hope that's acceptable."

Curiosity filled my veins. "Thank you for doing that. I'm curious what it is."

"I'm sure whatever it is, it's lovely," Janitra answered. "I secretly hope it's some good Makaarian chocolate.

And if it *is* chocolate, I not-so-secretly hope you're up for sharing."

This part of my birthday celebration was purely diplomatic. Sure, I love a good entrance but my parents truly insisted on something a bit more formal and traditional. But considering the circumstances and the attendees, they made the right call.

In the hallways, I could hear Gurpreet's tenor voice raised above enthusiastic drums.

"Join me in welcoming the woman of the hour, Ushallav's precious gem, and Abhijita's devoted disciple! Queen Anjali—accompanied by her heirs and handmaidens!"

The percussion set the rhythm of our arrival. Already sweaty, my children swayed and bounced to the driving beats. My handmaidens and I, dressed in matching iridescent opal fabrics, swished, swayed, and clapped as our procession traveled through the hallway and into the large gardens and gazebo overlooking the glittery seas. Torches and large stone pots of flowers lined the round outdoor pavilion.

As our feet touched the open space, the rest of the musicians joined in and played for a good ten minutes. It was an opportunity to dance as an entourage, show off our glittering visages, and pull guests into the space to dance with us until the musicians freed us from their spell.

I steadied myself to look around and soak in the festive atmosphere. The flowers surrounding us were the right shades of white, lilac, and sky blue; against the sunset, it felt like we were lifted into the clouds and far away from responsibilities, hard truths, and reality. Here, anything could happen—including a future full of love.

Just like my party to celebrate Janitra joining the ranks, curved tables laden with food formed a second ring around us—perfect for snacking and conversing.

The procession ended and we stood in the middle as we caught our breaths and laughed joyously. My eyes couldn't quite focus on anything more than the flowers, the tables, and the sea of people. Somewhere stood six men who I wanted to socialize and dance with. Where was Kavi?

"A perfect entrance." It was almost as though my thoughts summoned the very man I sought. He took my hand graciously in his and I let him kiss it.

"Kavi," I breathed. Truly because I was out of breath and smitten all at once.

"Let's take a look at you. Only you could gracefully dance in all this finery," he continued.

My whole outfit was a mix of deep turquoise, light turquoise, and that iridescent opal. I wore a sleeveless top that showed a hint of my stomach and matching sleeves that covered my biceps down to my wrists.

Over that, I wore a billowing light-teal gown with a high slit so as to cover one leg and show off the other. The sleeves opened from my shoulders to elbows with small pearls gathering the material just under my elbows. The light turquoise sleeveless tunic crossed over my chest and held in place with a corseted sash and ended in a high-neck look. And then of course, I wore heavy and ornate earrings and necklaces—all pieces I commissioned from Kavi, my master jeweler.

My long hair was intricately braided behind me and I stuck with a small circlet visible on my brow for the evening. I wore matching slippers that I imagined I would ditch by the end of the night—along with at least one of my ornate layers of clothing.

Kavi matched me—something we fully intended. Except his long-sleeved tunic was such a deep blue it almost matched a night sky. His turban and dhoti were of a similar light teal color. His hands and earlobes were decorated with his own jewelry designs. His perfect smile pulled the whole look together.

We embraced.

"I've got to formally meet the princes. I'll come find you for the first dance," I promised. He kissed my hand before melding into the crowd.

I looked around—dumbfounded that my kids weren't nearby. Within seconds, I saw that Pari and my parents were making eye contact with me near one of the tables with food and I nodded in thanks. My children were more interested in playing with their cousins than watching their mother flirt with jewelers and princes.

I nodded to Janitra and she helped clear a path. We practiced the art of greeting and talking politely to guests and well-wishers while keeping a steady pace in the right direction.

We finally reached a face that I imagined a skilled painter could do justice.

Expertly holding a goblet of wine stood Yeong-Gi, prince of Haneul. His entire outfit was onyx black—including the sweeping embroidery on his robe that danced in the firelight. He wore a high collar tunic and matching trousers. His robes billowed in the evening air but only graced the right side of his body—attached at the waist with a stiff obi. His black-brown hair was shaped into a high ponytail with two tufts of hair framing his face. Gold earrings lined his pointed ears and gold glitter streaked his upper eyelids.

He was conversing with Newen, prince of Calfuray. Where Yeong-Gi's outfit swirled in luxurious dark shades, Newen chose a bright, patterned appearance that complimented his brown skin. Considering the warmth of the season and climate, I was impressed that he wore a dazzling embroidered makuñ, or poncho, with lines of every color creating a V pattern toward the middle. The neckline was widened enough to expose one of his broad, tattooed shoulders. His braided hair grazed over that exposed shoulder and down his chest. His headband and beaded earrings twinkled in the light. His white trousers allowed the mostly-reds of his makuñ shimmer.

Lounging on a low couch, princes Ekwueme and Bernadino of Fumanya and Elpídio already seemed deep in conversation. Ekwueme's beaded and bejeweled locs were drawn away from his deeply brown face to reveal a jovial smile. For the party, he chose to wear a white long sleeved, tailored tunic over wide trousers that resembled a pair of dhoti. The reds and oranges of the shimmering material reminded me of a dramatic sunset. He wore matching beaded necklaces that hung to his stomach and a folded cloth over his shoulder that looked similar to a dupatta.

Bernardino ran a tanned hand through his wavy dark hair as he laughed. His white billowing shirt was dangerously unbuttoned, already exposing much of his hairy chest, and rolled up at his hairy forearms. His deep emerald pants billowed and gathered at his knees to show off a pair of gleaming shin-high boots. His red embroidered sash brought everything together. Next to him lay a wide-brimmed hat—probably the widest hat I'd ever seen.

I had a moment to take them in before reaching them—Janitra standing just behind my right shoulder.

"Welcome, welcome! It's so good to see you."

I spoke Ushallavi but my fingers moved to translate my words into signs. With all our various languages, our families established a sign language to allow us to learn a common language for diplomatic use.

To my right, I could hear a soft gasp from Janitra. Was she impressed? Probably because the four stunning men turned to look at me and answered in kind.

"Nice entrance, Princess Anjali," signed Ekwueme.

Yeong-Gi smiled warmly. "Judging by the fanfare, I thought you were getting married—and I missed my chance."

"It's been ages!" Bernadino signed before pulling me into an embrace. Then said in broken, charming Ushallavi. "Thank you for the invitation."

"I think the last time we saw each other was when my older sister got married," Ekwueme signed.

"I think you're right," I agreed politely. I didn't remember making the trek to see the wedding. It was fully possible that happened while I was in hiding. He was probably misremembering; dutiful Ray wouldn't miss something like that.

Soon, it was a cross of five different languages but the signing to unite us. I didn't forget Janitra.

"This is my newest handmaiden, Janitra," I explained. Then I addressed her, "Sorry, I should've warned you about the signing."

"Don't worry," Janitra smiled. "Your translating is helpful. Tell them they all look particularly handsome tonight."

I smiled as Ekwueme made eye contact with me.

"We know *some* useful Ushallavi words, Janitra." His grin broadened. "But yes, we wanted to look our best for our dear friend Anjali tonight."

Janitra laughed like she knew she'd been caught trying to be clever. But after a moment of conversing, Janitra excused herself to grab us both some refreshments.

"Come join us on the couch!" Bernadino encouraged. "We've been catching up on how we've been faring since one of our last playdates. What have you been up to, Anjali dear?"

I could feel stares near and far on the back of my neck but it didn't matter; let people think what they want to think. Everyone could only guess what we were saying unless they understood the different languages spoken out loud.

When I eventually felt just a bit too overly perceived, I stopped speaking for a moment and just used my hands.

"Where do I begin? I have two great kids and recently divorced King Damir. You read my letter, didn't you?"

"Honestly, I'm just here for the party. Dutiful Yeong-Gi probably memorized the whole missive."

"Bernadino, Anjali already has two children. She isn't looking to adopt a third," Newen added with an arched, amused brow.

Yeong-Gi did offer a bow in my direction. "You survived in the forests. That's pretty admirable. Glad to see you in good health."

"Thank you," I bowed back. Everything about him was elegant and sharp like a cut gem. "You all had quite the journey. How are things up north?"

Newen smiled. "It's not much of a story. And in a good way. Let's party now and catch up tomorrow. I'm loving this song."

With eagerness and a jovial wink, Bernadino took Ekwueme's hand. He took Newen's hand, who took Yeong-Gi, who reached out for mine. Like cousins, we laughed and pulled each other into the fray of dancers.

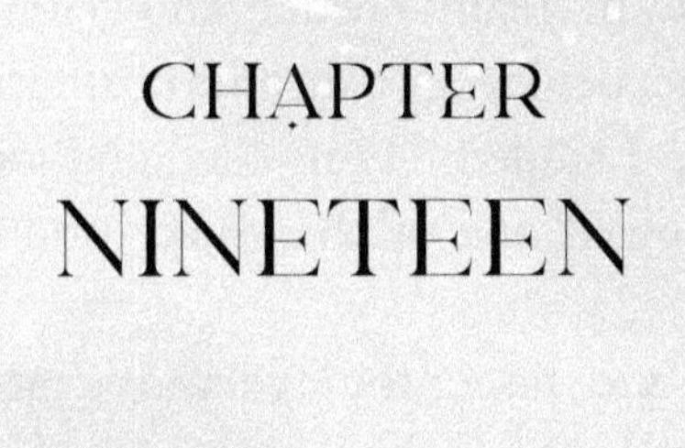

CHAPTER

NINETEEN

The rest of the night was filled with moments I'd never forget. My favorite food, my favorite people, in my favorite place. I was proud of myself and the ultimate dance I performed: making my rounds around the dance floor and devoting my due attention to my children, my suitors, Kavi, my handmaidens, my family, and myself.

When the handmaidens (mine and my mother's) escorted all the children back to their beds, they then gathered all my aunties, uncles, siblings, and parents. I knew the partying was just about over when guests were slowly leaving the outdoor party scene and going inside to rest and recover.

"You really know how to celebrate a birthday, Anjali," Bernadino complimented. He walked arm-in-arm with

Ekwueme toward the guest quarters. As I waved good-night, Newen approached me. His skin was still glistening with sweat from all the dancing.

"Thank you for inviting us—myself included," he murmured.

We shared a brief glance that didn't need translation. I added him to my list because he divorced several years ago. Not as amicably. Out of everyone here tonight, we understood each other's pain quite deeply and simply. He looked like he really needed an evening to leave his somber feelings behind in a distant northern kingdom.

"Rest well," I smiled. He nodded and joined his company and followed one of the palace attendants toward their rooms.

Yeong-Gi and his entourage waved at us from afar as I knew they'd retired for the evening. Everyone in his traveling party, including his elders, looked so fresh and young. I doubted getting a full night's rest was the only way they retained their elven youthful features.

That left Kavi smoothly making his way to his cart.

"Kavi," I called out. I waved to catch his attention. He smiled over his shoulder and waited for me to join him.

"We have a room for you here so you don't have to travel home so late."

"No, it's fine. I'd rather not leave my shop unattended for too long."

I took a step back, slightly surprised and caught off guard. Was he cross with me? His words had a rough slice and his smile didn't crease his eyes like it usually does.

My mind went back to the way that we danced and danced and danced. If I wasn't dancing with my children,

I saved all my dancing for him. I really only danced with the princes if it was a large group dance that required changing partners.

I always came back to Kavi. So why did he seem so far away?

"What's wrong, Anjali?"

"Something's wrong."

"Are you okay?"

"I was just fine until just now. You seem guarded."

Kavi sighed and shook his head with a smile. "I think we're both tired. I'll see you tomorrow."

I knew if my questions went unanswered, I wouldn't rest well. If I did something, I wanted to know now.

"Did you have fun?" I tried. I held out my hand for his and he acquiesced. He placed a kiss on my hand.

"You're quite the dancer," he answered. "It was a nice time."

"I saw two of the princes get a little too reacquainted," I smiled conspiratorially. "I'm hearing wedding bells and they aren't tolling for me."

"And that's supposed to be funny? Make me feel better?"

My smile dropped.

"Kavi—"

"Maybe you didn't notice but while you were doing that hand language thing, people were talking. And I could hear them just fine. They knew you personally invited me tonight. And yet you were all smiles and all charm with them."

"I danced with you. With *you*," I returned. I couldn't hear the voices or movement of anyone around us. I thought Kavi and I were truly alone. I clenched and unclenched my fist. "You're clearly upset and I want to resolve this."

I just had the time of my life and felt so proud of my party-planning abilities. And the one person who brought some light into my life was dimming right before my eyes.

"Look, I don't understand politics," he began, waving his hands in the air with frustration, "but I don't understand how you debase yourself to make these foreigners feel better about themselves."

"What's not to understand? They are my childhood friends and allies. We have an understanding and a respect for one another. We live in a time where everything is neutral or good. We have peace—may Zayant sleep undisturbed and Tamul remain wide awake. I'm fine and I'm not debasing myself, so don't be upset on my behalf."

Kavi dropped my hand. He didn't seem to understand that I wanted to do anything to avoid another generation of war and disaster and hopelessness—we didn't need to allow pride in one's country to threaten peace.

"Maybe if you spent more time with your people, you'd see things in a different, more clear way." His eyes bore through mine, lost of all mirth.

"What are you saying?" I whispered slowly. It was like a live coal was in my throat. His tone had me on edge and grateful my children were far, far away.

"We brought you home, my queen. We brought you home and nursed you back to health. It wasn't safe for you in Makaar—"

"My own handmaiden betrayed me, Kavi. Don't believe the gossip. The Makaarians have their own ways but they never threatened my life."

"But you're safe here—where you belong," Kavi insisted. "So why go seeking the northern princes for love when you already have it right here?" He gestured with two fingers toward his chest.

"Speak freely, dear," I said through terse lips. His eyes glinted as he quickly looked to our left and right. "Eyes on me."

His eyes slid over me like someone else inhabited his form.

"I've been working here on commissions for weeks, months. I know my way around, so to speak. These other princes—your former husband—don't know you or cherish you the way I do. The way your people do. We know how much you've suffered and we're stepping in to help you."

"Who's this 'we'?" A shiver coiled up and down my spine.

"Anjali, do yourself a favor and send your princes away. They will play you just like Damir did—"

"That's enough—"

"No one else loves you or our gods or our ways. And as much as we know you can handle yourself, we—I—don't want to see you get hurt again." Kavi at this point was yelling and pleading with me. "If you choose unwisely, things could go very badly for you."

Choose unwisely? Letting this man breathe the same air as me, my children, and my parents was starting to sound like an unwise choice.

I flexed my arm muscles as I breathed in and out. I was prepared to high kick him in his windpipe if he dared accuse me of choosing unwisely again.

"You're safe, my liege," Kavi murmured, clearly seeing my building rage. "I saw to that. I'll see you soon." He dared to plant a kiss on my cheek before completing his journey to his cart.

Standing rooted in my solid, defensive stance, I didn't ease until he was truly out of sight.

Several images and memories flooded back. Mysterious figures cloaked in all black. Matching black arrows. Dead handmaidens. Myself nearly joining them in death. A tortured Einora. A treacherous Leela.

My past was not fully dead—just waiting.

I could hear a swish of skirts and a familiar, comforting hand rested on my arm.

"Just say the word," breathed Janitra. She felt warm to the touch like a furnace.

In Makaarian, I answered, "The walls have more than just Eyes. I must bring this to Ray at once. You and the others must go after him."

"Pari and Dipa suspected as much. They're hiding in the cart as we speak."

A smirk played on my lips. I clearly didn't need Kavi's protection the way he hoped I would.

"And just when I thought things were going well," I sighed.

For once, Janitra didn't try to say anything witty. She just kept a reassuring hand on my arm.

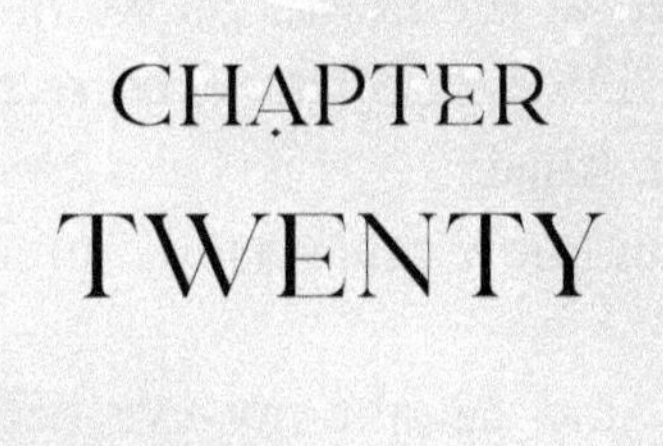

CHAPTER

TWENTY

After a fuzzy moment of time, someone gently approached me. I released my forehead and received a cup of chai. I took a sip and tried to calm my breathing. I hoped the combination would stop the rapid pounding in my left temple.

Was the headache from all the alcohol or Kavi? All I knew is that I wanted to be anywhere but here–Ray's office.

"I can feel you staring, Mother."

"Beta, that's your second cup," *maan* answered, as if it were answer or justification enough.

She held her evening robe closed over her sleep clothes with her left hand and held my father's hand with her right. They didn't appear angry, afraid, or upset—just stunned by what we had just shared with them.

We sat together in Ray's office. I sighed, hating the silence. Just like always—I just broke something and my big brother was off cleaning it up.

As I stared at the dregs of my cup, a knock sounded at the door. I flinched and quickly found a secure spot for my teacup as Ray entered his office and took his chair.

"Your maidens apprehended Kavi before he got too far from the palace. They reported that he didn't put up much of a fight and went quietly."

Father sighed at the news. "So we question him and go from there. Do I understand correctly that he was threatening you, Anjali?"

"And did you know this was his intention?" Mother added.

Ray sighed and caught my eye before turning to our parents. His gaze said, *You better tell them something before I do.*

"I just thought he was an honest craftsman and artist. I know that our people really care about our personal affairs but this feels excessive. I wouldn't have known had he not let down his guard."

"Or maybe he felt comfortable showing his hand," Ray suggested.

"It's possible that he felt threatened by our international guests," Mother pointed out. When we glanced at each other, she added, "I watched him the whole night—he was our beta's special guest and I was interested in what he was doing. I noticed he didn't seem comfortable. He didn't socialize with anyone. Thank the gods he didn't approach the children."

She shuddered at the thought.

I didn't meet anyone's gaze as I talked through the clues.

"He seemed, well, very charming. We spent a few dinners together—nothing serious. I wanted to have a slow courtship and he seemed fine with that. But he seemed very adamant that I marry him or someone like him in the future. And a couple of times he used the word 'we,' meaning him and someone else. That sounds familiar, doesn't it?"

I looked to Ray.

He replied, "It sounds a lot like Leela. She wanted you to divorce Damir and return to Ushallav—and when you wouldn't do that on your own, she stepped in. She hoped to reawaken the animosity Makaarians and Ushallavi people are healing from by manufacturing a martyr. Perhaps they're not two fringe Ushallavi zealots but part of a larger group of people."

My stomach twisted.

"What exactly have you learned about Leela since we last spoke about it?"

My parents looked between us with unease.

Ray, almost looking guilty, answered, "We have a problem, and it's called the Black Wings."

***

Arrows spun from everywhere and out of nowhere, thudding into Swaran. Another tore through Gamani and more pierced through Maliha and Neha. I crawled and crawled and crawled.

If what Ray said was true, then Kavi was a part of the Black Wings—the group who murdered my previous handmaidens to stir up hate and rip open old wounds. They did not share the dream I had—I wanted to co-rule with Damir, to show the world that we were stronger together. We didn't need to fight over ideologies anymore. The possibilities were endless. But Devraj had barely turned four years old before those dreams were ripped to shreds with matte black arrows.

And now, we were faced with another attack but of a different caliber. Instead of killing me, why not court me, manipulate me? I fought back angry tears and self-deprecating thoughts. Why not change my mind and heart from within or push me into a corner I cannot flee, right? What would happen if someone like Kavi did get the chance to marry me—how much more would he slowly kill any of my other dreams or aspirations?

I gripped the fabric around my thighs and knees—I was still dressed in my festival clothing but added a blanket around my shoulders for comfort. My hair spilled down my back and over my chest.

Defeated. Embarrassed. Furious. I felt like such a fool, and I felt even more enraged that everyone chose to sympathize with me instead. No one yelled at me or blamed me for my stupidity when I felt as though I deserved much worse.

"Do we know what they want? Do we know why they're doing all of this? Again?" the words hissed between my teeth like steam. "And are you confirming that Kavi is part of this group?"

"The short answer to these questions is yes, Ray answered gruffly, "But it's already past dawn. Everyone needs some solid rest. My guards and I will get detailed answers soon enough. Just know that he's not going to hurt you or the children. Someone is also watching his residence and sifting through for more clues. If anyone makes a move, we'll be the first to know."

I drooped in fatigue.

"Why are you all so quiet?"

Silence greeted me for a heartbeat.

"Beta, are you all right? What you've gone through is terrible but we're relieved that you're safe."

Father touched my arm and I grimaced at his gentleness.

"Things could have been worse," I countered. "Kavi tricked me. And I was so…so desperate for someone to love me that I let him. I should've seen right through this or vetted him more thoroughly—"

"And what would your keen eyes see?" Ray argued. "You didn't know he was an agent for Black Wings. Until this evening, we all saw him as a regular citizen. You have every right to be angry but don't be so angry with yourself. Be angry with me, at least. I was starting to collect information on this group and should've stopped this before I knew for sure he was good for you."

"But I would've hated you for that," came my bitter reply. "If you told me that you forbade me from seeing him, I would've resisted."

"You are a strong and noble spirit, Anji," *maan* interrupted me. "Kavi chose to exploit that. It doesn't diminish who you are or who you want to be."

I sat back in my chair and scowled.

"If I were younger, you would be scolding me," I countered. "You would've punished me for being so careless with my safety."

Some part of me wanted to carry the full blame for the panic rising in my chest and throat but I also wanted my parents to bear the burden, too. My time as a betrothed princess was fairly rigid. What should've been a happy time was also stressful.

If I was engaged to any prince right now, this would be a much more tense conversation. But right now, it felt like I was getting away with being so ignorant and blinded by…love? A connection? A desire to be desired for once?

"You've already put yourself in a dungeon of your own making, Anji," Father said in a somewhat warning tone. "There's nothing more we could do that you haven't already done or said to yourself."

"And we don't want to punish you, love. That's not what I want to spend my time doing while you're here and back home," Mother added. "This is a problem but we already have solutions and actions in place. We will seek the truth about this group and learn what there is to be done with them. They nearly took you, our daughter, from us. So allow a parent to be defensive of their children—especially when there was nothing you could do to deserve such danger and violence in your life."

"Come here, beta." Father took me in his arms and I let him embrace me. Mother stretched her arms over the both of us.

Now I was the stunned one. There was some deep dark thing in me that kept telling me that I was a creature that my parents loathed or resented. I failed their dream—according to this hateful creature in me. I don't think I ever had a frank conversation with them about how they felt about the divorce or my attempts to find a new husband.

Maybe I should've stuck with Mother's initial advice and followed my gut instead of whatever was feeding off of my shame and despair. It wasn't gone, but it shrunk ever so slightly.

My parents let me go from the embrace and I looked over to Ray who merely witnessed what happened.

"Anjali, we can talk at a later date about vetting future suitors," he began, "but for now, we're implementing very serious security measures."

I wasn't a fan of the sudden seriousness in his tone.

"Go to your children and get some sleep. Tomorrow, everyone in the royal family will be divided and sent to secret locations just like we trained as kids—"

"You must be joking," I practically yelled. Based on the looks everyone gave me, I was the last to learn of this decision.

"This is what handmaidens do. You trained them for this and they've already agreed. I can't tell you where the children are going but they'll be safe with your handmaidens—you may choose who will accompany them."

At one moment, I wanted to feel the brunt of the blame, and now I felt very defensive. My parents, my brother, and my handmaidens knew about this plan and agreed to it. This fact felt much more enraging than it probably should have. I didn't think I could handle another emotional pendulum swing.

"Why do all of this? Do you not trust me?"

"I don't trust Kavi," Ray firmly interjected. "I don't trust his people. You told me that he suggested that he and potentially more people are aware of the layout of the palace. They could move to free Kavi or harm our family or the staff. I cannot allow either to happen. So who will accompany you?"

I sputtered, "Janitra can join me. Will you tell me where Sanjana and Devraj are going? Ray, they're going to panic if you separate us. Devraj cannot go through this again—!"

"They are the heirs to the Makaarian throne, Anjali. If the Black Wings will resort to murder to interrupt your marriage, I will not entertain any alternative plans and endanger my niece and nephew. You can hate me now but you'll thank me later, sister."

I remembered learning about this emergency plan as a preteen. I could see the logic—the locations were never spoken aloud so there would be no visual or oral record should anyone misuse the Eyes to attack the palace.

As a child, I thought this would safeguard us against Makaarians who wanted war—not against my own people. I suddenly felt like the walls inched closer and closer. Could I trust myself or my own people?

"This feels like we're playing right into their hands. We're afraid—which is exactly what they want. Kavi only showed his hand to scare me and force me—us—to reason with them as if they have power over us."

"You're not changing my mind, Anjali. You'll say goodbye to your children and you'll say hello before you know it," Ray countered, folding his arms. "Once we know more of who or what we're up against, we'll reconvene and take the next steps together."

Defeated, I mirrored his actions and folded my arms defiantly.

"I was foolish," I conceded.

"Whether you intended to or not, you found answers that I could not. So there's that." Ray gave a small, tired, sympathetic smile.

When the meeting grew cold, I embraced my parents and spoke to them a little while longer before guards escorted me to my rooms.

I tucked myself in between a sleeping Sanjana and Devraj. I had mere hours before a new day would begin and we would have another tough goodbye.

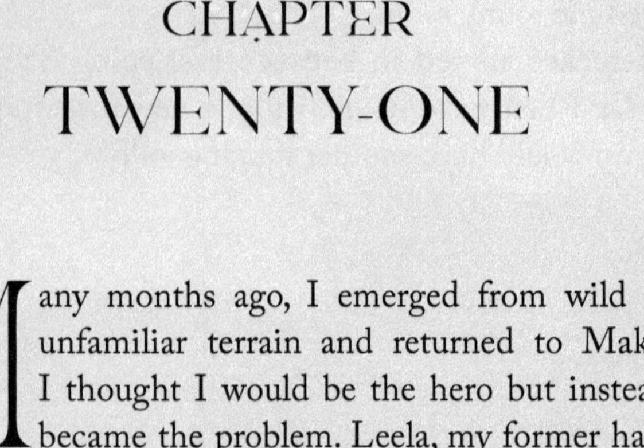

CHAPTER
TWENTY-ONE

Many months ago, I emerged from wild and unfamiliar terrain and returned to Makaar. I thought I would be the hero but instead I became the problem. Leela, my former handmaiden and enemy, also returned from obscurity. She didn't like that I was working with Damir's new wife, Einora, to find my assassins—Leela's associates as it turned out. And once she nearly drove me to madness, Damir thought it was best to hide us away in his castle while his guards faced Leela—a beautifully trained warrior.

Had I not resisted, Leela would've earned another victory. But this time, after much convincing, I agreed that I would not buck against Ray's secret decree. I would follow orders and then waste no time reuniting with my children.

I still wanted to roll up my sleeves and beat the answers out of Kavi myself. He would certainly get an idea of how frightening I could be when someone toyed with my affections.

"Where are you going, Mama?" Devraj sleepily asked. He woke up to the sight of me packing some of my things.

I argued with myself over how much to share—I didn't know any details by design. That unknown was probably going to scare him more than the alternative.

"I have a surprise for you, Devraj and Sanjana. Well, it's a surprise for me, too, so I don't have a lot of information. But you're very brave and bright so I'll tell you what I know, sweetheart."

Confused, Devraj inched closer.

I would show no fear—hopefully they would not be afraid.

"Your Uncle Ray has told us that we're spending a short time apart. The whole family—yes, your cousins too—will all be spending some time in different secret spots. I know this is a lot to hear before breakfast but you'll be spending time with Pari and Ziya."

"Where are you going?"

"It's a surprise. Uncle says it'll be very nice. But this is just a short trip and it's to ensure the palace is safe."

"Are there bad guys here?"

"Of course not. If there are ever any bad guys, they go in the dungeons and they can't come out. Uncle and I will check to see if there are any more and then we can come back."

"Will they take my toys?" Sanjana asked. I smiled at her choice in priorities.

"No. Ziya will beat them up if they even try."

Sanjana gave a sort of wicked, mischievous smile at the thought.

I could see the wheels turning in Devraj's head.

"Are we going to see Papa?"

"Probably not, sweetheart. Not for this trip. You'll still see him in a few months as promised."

I put a hand on his chin.

"But hey, if that's your surprise trip, you'll tell me all about Papa, Einora, and Gregori for me, okay?"

He nodded dutifully, wistfully.

"Now, let's pack your favorite toys and we'll grab breakfast. Your Uncle Ray is eager for us to be off."

"Why are you not coming with us, Mama?"

Devraj wouldn't let me off the hook so easily. I pursed my lips before replying,

"Remember when the bad guys attacked us in Papa's castle?" I didn't have the heart to say Leela's name but Devraj knew what I meant.

"Just in case there are any bad guys, the handmaidens will fight them first—to protect you. And protect me. You are my whole world, and sometimes the bad guys want to harm innocent people to harm someone like me or your Uncle Ray."

Sanjana wrapped her little arms around me, and it was like we were enduring another day in the forest together. She must've had lingering memories of exploring without going too far from me. This was the first time we were separating and my heart splintered with guilt.

"Uncle Ray promised it would be a short, fun trip.

I can't wait to hear about your adventures and see your drawings. Will you be good for Ziya and Dipa?"

"Okay."

"Yeah."

Such half-awake and deflated responses.

"I had to do something like this when I was your age."

"Really, Mama? What happened?"

"Well, it was practice—in case we needed to do this for real. This is for real this time. But I got to spend a few days at the lake with my siblings. It was kind of fun."

Devraj looked like he half-believed me.

"You'll be back and I'll be back very soon. I promise." I kissed their heads and they snuggled close.

"I love you so much," I murmured in their messy manes. "I hope you know that. You are the most important people in my life. I love you forever, and nothing can change that."

I looked up from our family hug to see all four handmaidens: dressed for travel and armed for unforeseen conflict.

"All right, let's get moving."

And move we did. I saw my children off in a carriage—giving Ziya and Pari my bravest look. While Janitra helped me load my carriage, one of Mother's handmaidens applied my disguise. It usually involved makeup to change my facial features but this one even involved a wig.

I didn't even know what I looked like until Janitra, Dipa, and I arrived at our new location and I could pull my disguise away.

"You're smudging your makeup," Janitra winked, and I smiled despite such a draining day.

"Let's see where my dear brother has sent us," I merely answered. To be honest, I still wasn't comfortable in enclosed carriages, especially since I entered not knowing where I was going or who would be waiting on the other side.

I pulled a scraggly brown wig off my head and folded some false glasses before reapplying the low-hanging hood over my forehead. I left the carriage and costume pieces behind me and stepped out and down from the carriage.

When I looked around, I felt embraced by trees. Not the kinds that I traversed before. Years ago, I traveled with Claudiu and the Gavril people through all kinds of landscapes and climates as we followed the Traveler's Path and I recovered from a near-death experience and birthing Sanjana.

Something felt different. This felt like a moment of peace instead of one of survival.

It helped that Gurpreet was right there with a similar cloak and a calm expression.

"Let's get you settled in, friend." They pulled me in for a quick hug and took one of my trunks. We were just partying the day before and now we were…following orders.

Once my eyes focused after the uneasy sleeping in the carriage, I could see a columned entrance to a round building. I gasped softly. I'd been here before. I came here with my mother when I was younger—a moment with my newly-minted handmaidens and my mother before my wedding day and moving many miles away.

Another sanctuary for Abhijita—a place of discovery, learning, and healing. Nothing much had changed since I visited this place nearly a decade ago.

We entered the round tiled entryway and admired a similar ring of Abhijita statues in triumphant, strong, sensual, alluring, and divine poses. Our sanctuary placed much closer to the palace was more like a well-decorated training ring. This was the softer sister with some areas to train but mostly through stretching and dancing.

"Are the hot springs still hot this time of year?" I asked softly. After the wild night of dancing, eating, drinking, and more dancing, my body ached for a long soak.

"I had the same idea," Gurpreet grinned. "I know that you miss your kids and your boyfriend is locked up but hey, why not hide away in style?"

I winced. "It was a bit too good to be true, huh?"

"It makes sense that there wasn't much information I could get about him," Gurpreet answered. If I didn't know better, they sounded a bit disappointed. "Dating is going to be difficult from here on out but I don't think this is the end."

I thought about how I professed some budding feelings to Claudiu before facing rejection and then immediately opening myself up to Kavi. And then if it weren't bad enough, I stopped in my tracks and put my head into my hands.

"What's wrong?" Dipa asked, alarmed.

"All the other princes are still at the palace," I moaned into my palms. "I didn't even think about saying anything to them."

"That's your brother's job," Gurpreet shrugged. "I'm sure at least one of them will understand the situation you're in and not let it discourage them or turn them away."

"Well, that leaves Yeong-Gi and Newen. I saw Ekwueme and Bernadino pair off at least twice during the party."

"Oh yeah," Janitra piped up. "They were definitely stealing kisses by the end of it."

Gurpreet's eyebrows shot up in surprise and intrigue. "I need to hear *all* the details."

The anxiety in my stomach would not dissolve. I fiddled with my two braids as we sailed toward a spiraling staircase taking us to the floor below. Sconces lit the way to a long hallway of doors.

"This is my room," Gurpreet pointed out. "The three rooms across the way are yours."

The rooms were cool and somewhat more modest than what I was used to but I was grateful. This wouldn't be forever and I hoped the secluded space would serve as an extra protection against…everything I didn't want to think about.

Janitra extended an arm toward the doorways and I just picked a room. I knew they were all fairly uniform. The bed waiting inside was soft and welcoming.

I dropped my trunk and Gurpreet set down the other.

"I'll show you around the rest of the place once you rest for a bit. You've had a long day, and you look like it."

I pointed to my painted expression. "I don't think my disguise was meant to make me look approachable."

Gurpreet snorted and closed the door behind them. Janitra and Dipa waved from the doorway.

I went to the wash basin and washed my face. After I changed into more suitable clothes and combed my hair, I climbed into bed and felt my tense muscles melt and ebb away in the cool, dark space.

CHAPTER
TWENTY-TWO

It wasn't a guarantee but Ray promised that we would get a message in a week's time—we'd get an update and the carriage would arrive if it was time to return to the palace. The longer I sat in my room, the more I missed my kids and gave into paranoia. What if there was someone here that would betray me—give away my location?

Gurpreet must know everyone here, I reminded myself. And they wouldn't hesitate to ensure my safety. Gurpreet was my closest friend and was here for me now.

I rubbed my face in exhaustion and looked at myself in the mirror. What was I going to do while I waited for Ray's message?

As if in answer, I heard a knock at the door. I opened it to find Gurpreet.

"I came to see if you were available for supper," they said in the doorway.

"Supper?"

"Yeah, you've been in here all day. Assumed you needed some time to rest after everything that happened. Want to talk about it?"

"Haven't you heard all the details?" I asked wryly.

"Sure but I'd much rather hear about it from you."

"I don't know if I'm up for your gloating right now," I half-joked. But that didn't earn me a laugh or even a sly grin.

"I'm not gloating. You were in danger and I want to know if you're okay," Gurpreet said. Without waiting for much more, they closed the door behind them and lit some sconces and candles in my room. I blinked at the sudden added light to the space and plopped back onto my bed and Gurpreet took a nearby chair.

"Sure, I know that Kavi isn't who he says he is, but I'm more worried about you. You know I've had some crazy exes but not *that* flavor of crazy."

My thoughts jumbled and tumbled in the recesses of my mind. How *did* I feel? I was so focused on ensuring my kids weren't scared or upset with me. Whatever energy I had left was spent ensuring that my parents and king weren't mad or disappointed in me. I didn't think—didn't dare think—about my own feelings.

My voice felt pretty hollow when I answered, "It's…a lot."

In a rare moment, Gurpreet threw their arms around me. "You handled yourself well. Although if Ray allowed it, Kavi wouldn't be alive long enough to question. But I'm still glad you're here. I can ensure you're safe and you don't make any rash moves."

"What, like date someone from a secret group that is conspiring to control or end my life?" I asked sardonically.

"No, like spiral when you're defeated," Gurpreet practically tsked. "You've always set the standard so high for yourself."

"Gurpreet—"

"No, Anjali. Hear me out. It's serendipitous that you're here. This is a sanctuary for weary souls. Not necessarily of the body but of the spirit. Abhijita practically led you here so you could finally have a moment to yourself. Every inch of this place is meant to help with the healing process and get you back on your feet."

I sighed, exasperated. "Gurpreet, I know that dating a terrorist is pretty low of me but I don't think Abhijita needs to heal me of this. Sure, it's a blow to the ego but I didn't get that far with Kavi anyway."

Gurpreet bit their lip for a moment before speaking.

"I'm talking about what happened to you years ago—when you were separated from your family, your hand-maidens, and your home. That's a lot and not an easy thing to forget or put behind you."

"But we caught Leela. Einora helped me find the truth and we brought her to justice."

"But her people are still here. We don't even know how many more Kavis are out there."

"I won," I spat. "I lived and won the combat. I protected my children and I won."

"Is that true?" Gurpreet challenged, crossing their arms over their chest. "You've crushed one ant but not the anthill, Anjali. And even though Leela's not alive, she's still in your mind, isn't she? All this second-guessing will affect your fighting, your parenting, and everything else you want to do."

"I'm not broken," I practically whispered, quaking.

"I didn't say that."

"You're saying that I'm in need of healing."

Gurpreet stood up and smoothed their clothes.

"I can tell that you want to do what you want to do. So are you coming to dinner or staying here?"

"Have Dipa bring me something. I'll stay down here."

"Works for me," Gurpreet sighed and took one last look at me as they stood in the open doorway.

"Oh, Anjali, you're still here," Janitra said from outside. "You coming with us?"

She poked her head in behind Gurpreet and waved. I could tell she had already changed into the comfortable cotton clothing that sanctuaries like this provide visitors and patrons.

"I'm not feeling up to it. I'll be eating here," I answered through a tight frown.

"We could join you if you wished."

"That's not necessary, Janitra. Go enjoy the rest of the evening." I was talking to her but still staring Gurpreet down.

"You and Dipa can bring her a plate," Gurpreet said to my handmaiden. "Anjali is still exhausted and could use some time."

I seethed as the trio closed the door and left me alone.

The past was where I left it—in the past. Why would I dig it up now—to further remind myself of my lowest moments? If Gurpreet was scared of a little spiral, then why push me into one? My children are alive because I survived and protected them. And Kavi, or my past, weren't going to deter me from a happy future.

CHAPTER

TWENTY-THREE

I munched on my dinner and mulled over what Gurpreet said earlier. They had always pushed me. I'd let them. Out of everyone's genuine thoughts and forwardness, there was always something refreshing about how Gurpreet worked. It was one of many reasons why I went to them even when it stung. Especially when it stung.

Maybe my bite of food had some extra spice in it but it stuck in my throat. I had to actively swallow my food and felt it go down dreadfully. I could feel my jaw clench and even quake.

Like a candle flame rising to life, I knew why it felt like Gurpreet pushed me too far. Because they knew I hadn't ventured this far yet. I hadn't opened the lid off this chest of emotions.

As much as I hated to admit it, they were right. My past *was* still eating me alive. I thought that by leaving Makaar and that forest behind, I showed them both that they couldn't hurt me. But I felt a sudden surge of anger toward the Makaarians who let me down and turned from me.

I arrived fully trained and fully equipped to lead us all to a prosperous, glorious future. I knew what to expect and I met their coldness with my fire—my love for Damir and my love for my dreams.

And yet that training wasn't enough—not when my patience was whittled down every day with each cold shoulder, each averted gaze, each moment I swore I could hear them using words meant to insult my heritage.

I'm a good person. I gladly gave my life to my children. I willingly co-parented with my ex-husband and his perfect second wife. I marched myself—all beauty and power and grace and smiles—to a foreign land that threw me away.

I was thrown away. Discarded. Disregarded. Treated like Damir's second when I was the first queen he married.

And I bet they love her. I bet they breathed a sigh of relief when I graciously and rather maturely let them be in love. I could've stepped in, grabbed the crown off Einora's head, and wiped the smirks off the lords' faces. I imagined myself in dark velvets and dark, curled hair and making my decrees. I could demand their love. I could demand Damir's loyalty. I could actually fight for what was rightfully mine.

Why did I cave? Why did I do "the right," kind thing?

For so long, I wanted to give everyone grace. How could they know I was strong enough to outlive Leela and her wicked plans? But they just had to move on so quickly about it. I didn't care if Damir apologized or felt guilty about it. I don't know if it was his idea or he was pressured by the old grumps in his court—he still played his part. He still gave my crown to another woman.

And where did that leave me? I should feel so lucky that I get to raise my son and daughter. I should be *so* grateful for my life—as if I didn't fight tooth and nail to preserve it.

I give. I serve. For all my bluntness, I hold my tongue. I wear my crown well. And yet.

And yet I was back home and I had no idea what my future would look like, and I didn't know who to punish for that. I'd punished myself long enough, and it was still to no avail. It was time for someone else to step in and take my lashes.

My vision blurred. It wasn't until my eyes failed to adjust that I knew to wipe them.

Tears. I was crying. Sobbing. I couldn't remember the last time I cried that hard, so hard that my eyeballs throbbed and my forehead coiled so tightly.

My ears registered my screams and sobs. I had been fully unraveling in my mind that I didn't realize the destruction outside of my body.

In my raging thoughts, I realized I threw my pillows. The modest décor on the wall leaned skewed and crooked. The candles sputtered like they quaked at my outrage. My leftover food squelched under my foot.

I gazed into a crooked mirror. My tears carved twin paths down my makeup. My hands shook. It felt like I both knew and couldn't recognize that rage. It was always there—seething and rippling under my skin. As if the rage felt perceived, I felt goosebumps rise and my hairs stood up in attention. I felt white-hot energy in my arms, my fingertips, my chest, and in the back of my neck. It was like freezing water filled me and I never felt more awake.

I was alone. My sleeping children were safely hidden away. I didn't have to watch the space I took up or the sounds my throat made.

My hand rested on my beating chest. I didn't have to be quiet. I didn't have to use nice words. I didn't have to translate my fury into some kind of palatable emotion or demeanor. I didn't have to be benevolent.

Those hands went to the jeweled circlet woven into my hair and shakily freed it from my tresses. It wasn't until it delicately rested in its velveted box that I fully unleashed myself to myself.

I would tell myself exactly how and what I felt. And I would hold myself and dry my tears and swear to myself that I would never ever abandon myself again.

***

"She's fine. I've got this. Thank you."

I strained my ears, holding my breath.

"She didn't hurt herself. I'll clean this up."

I heard a swish of fabric and bare feet calmly traveling away.

When I woke up, I realized I was sprawled in my bed. I wasn't sure if I put myself here or if Gurpreet carried me. That's who I saw wiping the wine stains from the cool tiles. I tried to sit upright but immediately slumped back. I had no energy in my limbs.

"There she is," Gurpreet murmured to no one in particular. "I know you were upset after our conversation but this is new."

I found a fresh cup of water at the side of my bed—a gift from Gurpreet. I drank and cleared my throat.

"You don't need to do that. I'll do it."

"You're a queen. When was the last time you cleaned your room?"

"I'm not a queen," I bit out.

"Hey. Your Majesty. Yes, you are. Cut the bullshit."

"Shut up, Gurpreet."

They signed and briefly looked at the mangled food on the floor.

"I'm sorry," I whispered.

I curled in a ball and stared at the wall. I heard Gurpreet rise to their feet in the way their clothes rustled and their knees popped. I half-expected them to exit through the doorway but I soon felt their weight on the bed behind me.

"Looks like you finally let yourself be angry," Gurpreet sighed. "Finally."

When I didn't retort or reply, they continued.

"It happens a lot when people come here. This is a safe place to feel every feeling—every feeling the gods and our ancestors put inside us. I don't know who told you otherwise, but you're allowed to be angry. It's painful and you won't exactly feel rosy afterward but I'm glad you finally let yourself feel."

"What do I do?" I asked. I held my arms out like they knew the answers but wouldn't fess up. "I'm not married to Damir—and I really don't think I want to be married to him even if I had the opportunity. I'm not a queen anymore. It was all I ever wanted to do and all I was trained to do. What am I without…everything?"

My back was turned to the circlet intentionally. I didn't want to look at the perfect, sparkling thing.

"I'm not your friend because your family runs the kingdom. I'm not your friend because of your marriage and connections. I'm your friend because of you. I love who you are without everything. And because I know you so well, I know that you'll figure out what or who or where makes you happy and you'll go for it.

"Not everyone has a second chance to chase after their destiny. You knew the moment you opened your eyes that you were royalty, and you knew you would marry Damir before your first menstruation. It's not your fault that you're here. You didn't make a mistake that landed you here. But I know you have the capacity to find your new happiness."

"Have you dated men recently?" I groaned.

Gurpreet laughed and I felt it.

"You know I avoid it when I can. Your family's money is going to attract a lot of riff raff but your kids will probably help you cut through the duds. But what does it matter? You don't need to be remarried right away to stop feeling like this."

I groaned some more.

"Also, I don't know if you're technically not a queen because you're not married to a king, but you're not a nobody. We'll figure it out. We'll help you figure it out. I can't think of anyone stupid enough to tell you to hand over the family jewels."

"Whoever wants them can have them," I sighed. "They've been nothing but trouble."

"I know you well enough to know that you don't mean that. I know you weren't meant to live a normal life and I know you'd regret it if you turned your back on all of it."

"I can't even do that if I wanted to. I'm co-parenting with Damir, which means I'm helping raise the heirs to his kingdom."

"Sounds like queen's work to me." Gurpreet shrugged.

My friend let me breathe slowly for a moment before asking, "Do you feel better?"

"I guess? I don't know."

"The grounds are gorgeous this time of year. Maybe we can go for a walk or dip in the springs tomorrow. I don't think you want to resign to solitary confinement in this room."

I looked around at the chaos I left.

"We can move you to another room."

"That's not necessary," I interrupted. After a pause, I conceded. "Actually, yes please." The thought of sleeping here and reliving my burst of rage brought fresh tears in the tight corners of my eyes.

And as we picked up my things and picked up the garbage, I told Gurpreet everything that happened between me and Kavi. They listened thoughtfully.

"I just felt hopeful for once. Things were going slowly but surely in the right direction. At least, I thought they were. I still feel foolish."

Gurpreet, ever the loyal friend, reminded me, "While you are capable of doing foolish things, they don't make you a fool. Kavi is the fool here. Even if he was playing the part of the suitor, he couldn't keep it cool long enough to string you along."

"Maybe acting isn't his strong suit. Imagine being so bad at acting that you give up a secret organization. Should've stuck with the jeweler gig," I murmured.

Gurpreet snorted and laughed. "There you are."

Their words lingered long after I settled into another, cleaner bed.

"Maybe when this is all over, I can spend time with you and it won't be out of an emergency."

"Don't think for a second that we think any less of you because things have been difficult and dangerous. I wish you could see how far you've come. I'm serious! And anyone is lucky to have you in their lives. Hopefully you'll see that someday—sooner rather than later."

CHAPTER
TWENTY-FOUR

Later that night, I find myself in a carriage again. I pat myself down and look around. I'm wearing my nightgown as my hair swishes unbraided around the small of my back.

When did I get here? Am I going back home to my children?

I look out the window.

"Stop this carriage!" I cry, not caring who hears. But I don't even hear my voice; it's like it came from many paces away. I look out the window and take in the sights—the forest. That forest that holds too much pain and too much of my past.

"You can't make me go back there," I want to say but the words aren't audible. Logically, I know those woods would take days to reach from the sanctuary—according to my fuzzy knowledge about the sanctuary's location. Someone would have to knock me out for nearly a week for me to be here now.

Is this another dream? I withdraw inside my carriage and grasp at my chest and clothing—seeking anything solid to ground me.

I conclude this is a dream and try to wake myself up.

And I sat up after a struggle to pull away from the images. I didn't want to see them again, and my body had listened. I opened my eyes to see complete darkness. I remembered I was back at the sanctuary with its cool, sunless interior.

"Why that damn forest?" I moaned to myself—like I was a teenager throwing a half-awake, half-asleep fit.

After realizing I was still at the sanctuary, I calmed my breathing and fell asleep again.

I'm back in the carriage again—this time, it's clear that the colors are far more vibrant than what my eyes see in reality. It feels like I can see too much, like I wasn't in a world I'm familiar with.

And now, someone is sitting in the carriage with me. "Nani?"

It feels real; my mother's mother is sitting diagonally from me. She did not survive the wars we fought with Makaar. She sits in a beautiful sari like the ones she wore when she was still alive. She looked old but still in her prime—just the way I remembered her looking when I was a young teenager. Her long braid has strands of bold, beautiful silver.

"Anjali, you're missing out on this view." She smiles and points out the window to my left. But I don't want to look out there—that's where the forest was. That's where part of me died and the rest had been forced to learn to survive.

And my grandmother is right *there*—why would I care about a pretty view?

"Nani, you're here!" I scramble to her side and she embraces me.

It's at this moment that I start to feel as though I'm dreaming again but I don't want it to end. I want to be here with my nani for as long as possible.

"Anji, don't let this pass you by," she nearly scolds me but chuckles. I look out the window across from her and I don't see the forest anymore.

I'm back in Makaar, and sharing a moment with Damir and Devraj, before I left them to visit my Ushallavi family and give birth to my princess. That feels like a few lifetimes ago at this point. Grandma never got to see this part of my life.

From my vantage point, I'm sometimes watching myself and other times occupying my own point of view. It's jarring but I smile softly at the little, unbroken family.

"This is what Devraj wants," I find myself saying. "He wants his parents to be together."

"He has his parents," my grandmother smiles. "He has everything he needs to be a good king one day."

My eyes well with tears. This dream is too bittersweet. She never met Devraj—am I imagining what I wished she would say, or was this really her, sharing a message from wherever she was resting?

I decide that it doesn't matter, because it feels like my grandma is bestowing a blessing on my Devraj and my mind can rest, for now. He does have his parents, and not even the Black Wings can alter that.

I sit back in my seat after crouching for what feels like hours at Nani's side, and stick my head out the carriage. When I look back at my grandmother, she isn't there.

I look up and I feel tears rolling down my cheeks. I gasp. I see someone I've known my whole life and feel drastically under-dressed for meeting for the first time.

Abhijita is sitting across from me.

The goddess could have been dressed in anything but sits with me in the simple cotton tunic and trousers pro-vided at the sanctuary—her sanctuary!

"Goddess," I sputter. How could I bow in the cramped carriage? I fall to the floor and fold into the best full bow I can manage; my head presses against the floor as I feel the carriage carrying us away—somewhere.

"Anjali." The voice is just as colorful as the too-vibrant shades I see in this dream. Is this still a dream or is this now a vision? I feel the anxiety rising up in me—what if I wake up and this moment is gone? What if I forget?

I scramble to my feet and sit across from the goddess I've worshiped my entire life. Her outfit is the only plain thing about her. Her skin is a shade or two darker than mine but gold, sparkly freckles across her cheeks, nose, arms, and shoulders. Her wild curly hair tumbles into a pile on the seat next to her. She's so tall and wide that the carriage in my dream is stretching to give her ample height and leg room.

"Abhijita," I sputter, clearly gawking and staring. She smiles and the colors shimmer and deepen more than I thought possible.

"Thank you for being here," Abhijita continues.

"Your sanctuary," I guess out loud.

"Yes. It's where I can reach you best. How are you enjoying your stay thus far?"

My mind takes me back to an earlier moment when I was yelling, screaming, and crying in a candlelit room. I tuck my chin in embarrassment.

"That's not the worst I've seen, daughter. You're grieving."

"I am." There's no point in lying or pretending. I'm in her sanctuary and she sees more than just what I reveal on the outside.

"I know you're in a place of pain," she says, looking around at the carriage which is steadily driving on. "My children look their pain in the eye and outgrow it. I know that will happen for you, too."

"What if I don't feel like I have a choice? It feels like no one knows what to do with me. I'm trying to not let my past hurt me but nothing seems to help. Everyone looks at me with pity rather than answers."

"I sent you your mother's mother to comfort you. If she were alive and with you, she would've told you of the people she struck down for the future of Ushallav. She died full of many regrets. But we've worked together to mend them.

"There might not be legends or folklore about your situation but you're not alone in these struggles. I know many of my children do and will look to you for the answers that you're fighting so hard to find."

Tears pool in my eyes and trickle down my cheeks.

"I don't want to be the blueprint. I just want to be free."

To my astonishment, Abhijita extends one of her long, beautiful arms and wipes the tears away with her fingers. And she doesn't stop as the tears continue to unfurl.

"I know. You're not meant to suffer so you can be a lifeline for others. But I promise you that I'm always right here, and I will help you find your footing. Your past will not cage you forever."

"Thank you, goddess." Is this what it means to speak? I can't believe my goddess is consoling me.

"Anjali." She cups my face. "I love you."

I feel each letter, each syllable, and each intonation in my bones. I cry and cry, finding myself in Abhijita's impossibly large arms. The colors swirl in my vision and it feels like the sky itself is embracing me.

"You're going to see things in your dreams," she says, her voice all around me. "There are so many choices and futures that await you. None of them are right or wrong—just yours. When you're ready, you'll leave the carriage."

With that, she lets go of me and rises to an impossible height—too large to fit a carriage in my waking world.

"You're going?"

An impossibly perfect laugh escapes her lips. "I don't want to influence you with my bias. It's better to see for yourself and choose for yourself. I'll be waiting outside when you're ready."

The carriage still lurches forward but the door opens for her and she steps out. She waves farewell and disappears from view.

It's just me in my carriage and we pick up speed. I'm swaying from side to side, still reeling from Abhijita's presence. I wipe what feels like a gallon of tears from my face.

The colors swirl and I'm back in the palace—my home. I stick my head out the window again, eager to see what my goddess needs me to see.

I'm back at my party—still dressed in my night clothes. There I see all kinds of people. Their facial features aren't that clear but I instinctively know who I see.

Damir. Einora. Benedikt. Janitra. Dipa. Pari. Ziya. Gurpreet. Claudiu. Yeong-Gi. Newen. Ekueme. Bernadino. Even Kavi. There are some people here I don't think I've even met before.

And it's almost like in an instant, I know why Abhijita removed herself from the carriage—even in my dream, I feel all my favorite places tense and tighten. I crave sensual touch and connection—I thank the gods that Abhijita was not here to witness the blush creeping across my cheeks and neck.

Who will I approach first? They all look to me with kindness in their eyes—as though any one of them would be a safe new home for me, should I wish it. Abhijita said she would wait outside the carriage when I was ready.

Who is the key to that? Do I decide that now before I wake up?

I hear her voice but I don't know where she is.

"Yes, you are grieving and you will get through it largely on your own. But I bless you with the knowledge that you don't have to do it in solitude."

I lock eyes with someone in the stunning crowd and I wake up.

CHAPTER
TWENTY-FIVE

I gasped, realizing the dream was over. I'd never felt such a longing to throw the covers over my head and pick up a dream right where I left off. But instead, I got myself out of bed and lit a few candles. I wrote everything down as clearly as possible.

I'd received answers in dreams before—like unlocking the details about the black arrows to help me seek justice for the slaughtering of my handmaidens. This dream felt even more tangible and straightforward—like Abhijita herself wanted to ensure I remembered and took advantage of her wisdom.

"Thank you," I breathed to the goddess who might be listening. I scribbled out pages and pages of notes—even a simple sketch of the Abhijita who visited me. I never wanted to forget that—my goddess came to help me.

I looked at myself in the mirror. Dried streaks of tears were visible on my face but I could see horizontal streaks where someone wiped them away.

When I looked down at myself, I saw something else. My nipples were peaked and I knew it wasn't because of the cold. I took advantage of my solitude, lay myself back down, and used my fingers to release the longing stored in my body.

"Okay, so you're horny," Gurpreet shrugged. "I didn't think you needed a goddess to spell that out for you."

"Hey," I interjected, blushing. I looked around the small garden path we trod and wondered if others could hear Gurpreet's raised voice. "I was going to keep the dreams to myself until Abhijita showed up. And you're one of the top experts on everything about her."

"That's correct—I just didn't think I needed to spell it out to you that it's been a while since you've slept with anyone, and you clearly miss that sort of intimate connection. Unless you and Kavi—?"

"We only hugged and kissed. Thank the gods it never went further than that."

Gurpreet held up their hands in a mock surrender like they merely asked a question and didn't want anything more.

"Gurpreet? Is Abhijita trying to play matchmaker with me?"

My friend gave me a sidelong glance and said, "Our goddess is many things but I think she just wants you to be happy. Maybe the key isn't marriage but maybe it's the safety of a deep, meaningful relationship with someone. And I know that you pay enough people to help run the palace and keep the country on course, so I'm talking about someone who doesn't just view you as their queen."

I let the words sink in. The goddess definitely had a special interest in my life—unless she visited everyone here at the sanctuary all the time and I was no one special. Either way, I wasn't going to flippantly discard the insight I gleaned from my dreams.

"You know that our pantheon of gods were once noble mortals before ascending to something higher," Gurpreet added. "Abhijita was a woman who had a very difficult life. She lived many of the horrors inflicted on women and femmes that are considered archaic today. Her subjects train their bodies and spirits to be strong. But there are so many shades of what it means to be strong and beautiful. And that's why we worship her. She allows us to be the kind of strong, beautiful people we long to be."

Gurpreet wasn't looking at me as they waxed poetic about our goddess. I know they wouldn't say it out loud but it was not easy—nor made easy—for them to be accepted in this sanctuary. Abhijita was largely worshipped for her femininity; Gurpreet was an answered prayer for those who didn't conform to any set of gender expectations.

Gurpreet's triumphs could fill volumes. I was so proud of them for their well-earned connection and position. They showed me that it was possible to be so spiritual and yet so…free. They didn't care if people looked curiously at their revealing clothes or balked at their candor.

Abhijita gave them permission to be their own kind of strong and beautiful, and Gurpreet didn't reject such a priceless gift.

"Interesting that you saw men, women, and nonbinary people in the last part of your dream," Gurpreet mused. "I wondered about that but thought you were so into Damir that it didn't matter. But it matters now. It seems like Abhijita is trying to tell you to stop limiting your possibilities. Maybe you're into all kinds of people, and now you have the perfect opportunity to explore. If that's what you want."

I suddenly felt like a young teenager admitting she had a crush on someone. As a princess, I didn't really dwell too much on who I fancied because I was already and always betrothed to Damir. Sure, I dreamed about beautiful princes like Yeong-Gi. But would things have been different if I knew I could choose?

"Who are you daydreaming about? Is it me?" Gurpreet teased.

"I shouldn't have told you that part." I rolled my eyes. "Am I still speaking with a spiritual guide and dream interpreter or not?"

"Okay, okay, Your Majesty. This is fun for me but I know you've gone through a lot." Gurpreet smiled but with empathy. "The professional side of me would tell you that traumatic events of every kind can separate our minds from our bodies, and we can feel unsafe. But it's okay to reconnect with your body now."

"But the friend side of you would say—?"

"Girl, you are either in love or want to be in love so much! And that's something worth pursuing. But based on what you've told me, it sounds like you're waiting for everyone to vote for your next partner. And it's not their decision."

"Okay, I understand that. I'm not saying you're wrong, but it's just not that simple. The royalty in me doesn't make this part any easier. Claudiu outright turned me down, Damir fell in love with someone else, and I almost threw myself into the arms of a terrorist…"

"Abhijita didn't punish you in your dream, and neither will I," Gurpreet replied. "But knowing that you might actually be attracted to all kinds of people has me thinking of way more people to introduce you to. If you want me to, of course."

Gurpreet was giving voice to the thing I felt like was true deep down but difficult to make real by saying it out loud.

I…liked men. Now I thought I also liked women. It felt right to admit to myself. I didn't know if that truth had any beginning or end but it was still the truth. I still looked back fondly at my times with Damir. And Kavi was also very attractive. Maybe if he was a completely normal person who actually liked me, we could've gone further.

For now, I wanted to explore this blooming feeling of excitement and hope within me. I didn't feel ashamed to admit this in my heart; it just felt new and fresh. Like learning the steps to a dance and not immediately mastering the moves. I would fumble, but eventually I'd find the rhythm.

CHAPTER

TWENTY-SIX

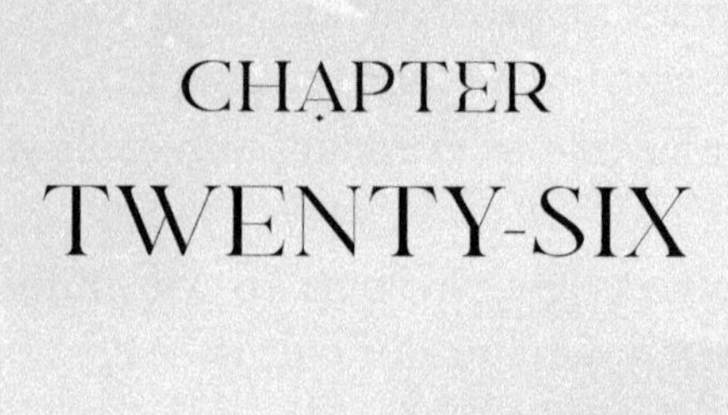

After the powerful highs and lows in my quarters, I decided to make the most of the open-air and above-ground amenities. I at least had something pretty to look at while I pondered Abhijita's message and what I was going to do with it before returning to reality back at the palace.

And what a scene unfolded as I ventured into the outdoor gardens. The design reminded me of organized chaos; bushes and trees were trimmed just enough to create some pathways but were still allowed to sink in deep and have their space and provide natural shade. The trees stood so tall and thick that it felt like we were in another world entirely.

Blossoms in trees shed their petals in the gentle breeze. Everything was so soft that there wasn't a need for shoes.

Someone tuned a flute in the background before playing soft scales.

I smiled as a troop of dogs–mostly dark shades of gray, brown, and black chased each other. One of the fluffier dogs looked up at me. Her black fur mixed with white and silver reminded me of a starry sky.

"I'm sorry, I don't have any treats," I shrugged. The dog stopped her panting and her floppy ears dropped a touch. She gave me what looked like a quizzical expression before licking my exposed shin and running off.

"Akela," someone else called with an exasperated laugh. "Stop licking everyone." The woman gave me an apologetic look as she corralled the dogs. I wondered if she owned those dogs or they were just here. I hoped I would see more friendly animals during my stay.

Maybe I should let the kids adopt an animal. Would that improve things when they were in Ushallav? I thought to myself. I shook my head. *One big thing at a time, Anjali.*

As I explored the grounds to take in the familiar and new sights, a new level of observation flooded my senses. And blood flooded to my cheeks at the realization.

Due to the safe, secluded nature of the sanctuary, patrons typically viewed clothing as optional. And this wasn't news to me; during training, warrior women would change their clothes all the time without a raise of the eyebrow. My handmaidens regularly saw all sides of me—when training, dressing for the day, giving birth, and beyond.

And if the patrons weren't in various states of dress or undress, many of the statues decorating the grounds—depicting women and femme people of all types—complemented that atmosphere. I was standing under a statue of someone proudly displaying top surgery scars while gazing into a long oval mirror.

Of course, I've seen hundreds of tasteful, artistic portraits and statues of Abhijita nude—so why did I suddenly feel so shy? At least my mother wasn't here right now.

I silently prayed that my sudden bashfulness and prudishness didn't show clearly on my face. I felt like a newly-born soul and didn't want anyone else to see me on such shaky footing. I was safe and I was under Abhijita's care, I reminded myself.

To prove that there was nothing shameful about my surroundings, I visited one of the outdoor hot springs. I found them past the edge of what looked like a constructed patio. There before me was a set of stone steps that led down directly into the springs. I smiled, noticing an orange, striped cat taking a nap on one of the steps; not caring that others wanted to pass by. He looked like he wanted to be close but not too close to the steam.

I relished the feeling of lowering myself in the steamy water. I sighed contentedly as I gathered my hair in a bun atop my head and rested my neck against a towel. The wind blew gently, scattering blossom petals across the ground and the surface of the water.

Idyllic.

I half wondered if I could fall asleep here and experience another stunning dream-vision like I had the night before. I could admit that since my dream of Abhijita, I had had a disappointing string of normal nights and nonsense dreams—nothing with any particular meaning or noteworthy characters.

Maybe more information would come now if I was in such a meditative state. I closed my eyes and enjoyed the solitude for an unchecked amount of time. Even if I didn't reach a deep sleep state, I couldn't remember the last time I was alone—no chaperones, no siblings, no handmaidens, no children…

A twinge of guilt furrowed my brows. I hoped the kids were well. I hoped Ziya and Pari were handling things well—they were more than capable, of course.

"I thought you were supposed to be relaxing."

My eyes fluttered open as I heard the water slosh to make room for more visitors. Janitra and Dipa sat across from me, settling in the warm water.

"Everything all right?" Dipa asked.

I sighed. "Just when I was enjoying my soak, I started thinking about Sanjana and Devraj."

Concern bloomed across their faces. Dipa reaches out an arm. "I'm sure they're all right. I think we can be assured that if we receive no word from the king, it's a good sign."

I nodded. "I still worry. And I still feel guilty."

Once I spoke, I realized that I'd only really spoken to Gurpreet about what happened since I arrived here. If I remembered correctly, my handmaidens got their orders to go get Kavi, then immediately got their orders, packed their bags, got their rest, and traveled with me or my children.

After the days of rest and restlessness, this was the first moment they took to approach me. There was so much to tell them—even if it felt painful or embarrassing to dredge up again.

What was there left to say? Where would I begin?

"There's your famous pondering face," Janitra teased softly. "You could just enjoy the hot springs and not dwell on the painful things."

"If it makes you feel any better, Gurpreet has ensured the other patrons here keep your stay a secret. Most don't even know why you're here. They assume it's a holiday, if anything," Dipa added. "You did just have a birthday, so it makes sense."

I sighed, smiling. "I keep forgetting. My birthday party was a couple of nights ago. I hope everyone had fun. It was fun in the moment."

"That was a legendary party," Janitra smiled. "It's been a while since I've danced that much, and I thought we partied hard during my handmaiden ceremony celebration."

My handmaiden drew swirls in the water, causing the flower petals to stir. Some clung gently to her skin. She didn't seem to notice my distracted stare.

"Thank you," I smiled slightly at Janitra and Dipa, "for apprehending Kavi and not teasing me about it. I take this mistake very seriously. I never ever want to make such a careless choice again."

I stiffened my posture as though I was awaiting judgment—verbal or nonverbal.

"We've been with you as much as possible from the moment you met him," Dipa answered. "You didn't make any careless choices—he did. He chose to endanger you and your children. He had the opportunity of a lifetime to court you and this is how he chose to play his cards."

"We don't judge you, Anjali," Janitra murmured—just above a whisper. "We're with you—always."

Emotions roiled in me. A series of mantras flooded my thoughts. *My body is safe. My mind is safe. My heart is safe…my children are safe.*

"I'm up for a snack," Dipa sighed. She gave Janitra a quick look. "I'm going to grab something to eat. Please try to relax, Anjali."

I nodded as she stood and stepped out of the pool and wrapped herself in a towel. I suddenly had to pretend like it was no big deal that a beautiful, muscular, naked woman stepped out of the water. In no time at all, she and her belongings were gone and it was just me and Janitra.

After a moment passed, Janitra stopped drawing spirals in the water. In Makaarian, she said, "Gurpreet told us you had an important dream. They didn't say much more but I helped clean up the mess in your room after you moved into your new one. Please, Anjali. Please lean on us."

An appreciative smile crept across my face. Perhaps I could be honest in Makaarian—assuming the other women around only spoke or understood Ushallavi.

The wind wove through the tree branches and scattered more flower petals on us. Now petals were sprinkled over my shoulders and hair. I rubbed my wet hands over my face.

In steady Makaarian, I walked Janitra through my dream. I tried to just share what I saw rather than what I felt—those emotions were for me. Maybe Janitra could see something between the margins that I could not. And maybe she could tell the other handmaidens so I wouldn't have to explain over and over again.

"Wow, that's quite the dream, or vision, I suppose," Janitra said after I concluded my recount of the dream. "I can see why you needed a moment of solitude."

"I feel like I have to tell you something," I stammered. Janitra stared back, curious.

"Remember the last part of my dream? Just before I woke up, I saw someone in that crowd of people, and one person in particular stood out."

"Yes? Do you remember who it was? Do you think it's significant?"

"You tell me." I exhaled before adding, "That person was you."

The silence was a bit awkward and long for my liking but I sat with it instead of dipping under the water and holding my breath.

Janitra looked for a moment at the petals lilting in the water before looking up at me.

"That's…interesting. Did Gurpreet have an interpretation for that?"

"I didn't tell them that detail. Just you. I'm sorry if it makes you uncomfortable."

"No, no. It's an honor to be in the same dream as… Abhijita."

She seemed stunned by all the details I shared but lingered on the newest revelation.

"Maybe Abhijita wanted you to know that you can trust me," Janitra smiled politely. "You chose me to be your new handmaiden and I'm sure that was a difficult decision to make. But I'm always here if you need me.

You don't need to be embarrassed about seeing an ally in your vision."

"It's still a lot to process," I admitted. My heart thumped in my chest. I couldn't tell if it was bashfulness from earlier or the mischievous glint in Gurpreet's eye when we last spoke but I found myself wishing, gods I wished, Janitra had a different response to my dream—her part in the dream.

Just like how my dreams introduced me to colors that I didn't think existed in this world, I saw Janitra in a new light. Of course, she was always strong, beautiful, and jovial. Why did it feel like I was the last one to really recognize it fully?

"I've had some time to think about what I really want—for me and for the children," I dared to say, "and I've sort of discovered something about myself. The dreams really made this clear to me. Maybe it's silly, considering my age. But I think I'd very much like to court women as well as men."

Janitra nodded, curious. "That's perfectly fine. And it doesn't matter how long it takes to know that side of ourselves."

"Ho-how long did it take for you? You said that you don't fancy men. I'm assuming you've dated women?"

Janitra actually let out a chuckle and I felt a blush engulf me. "Yes, Anjali, I've dated women. I never really had an attraction or romantic feelings for the boys around me. I thought that it might just be due to the fact that I was around a lot of Makaarian boys. But I found that when I shared a kiss with my first girlfriend, well...I knew."

She smiled with nostalgia, not really looking me in the eye.

"Well, if I choose to court women in the future, I just want to ensure it's a real feeling inside of me. Maybe you can help me not mess it up."

Clearly, you're messing this up, I couldn't help but think to myself. I wanted to tell her what I had started to…feel about her. I wanted to figure out what this all meant. Was I feeling lonely and desiring company and turning to the first person at hand? Or was the dream trying to tell me something that was real that I was ignoring?

Mother told me to trust myself. I desperately needed to trust myself.

"I think you'll know what's real," she replied, finally looking at me. Gods, I wished more than anything that what I felt right now was real.

CHAPTER
TWENTY-SEVEN

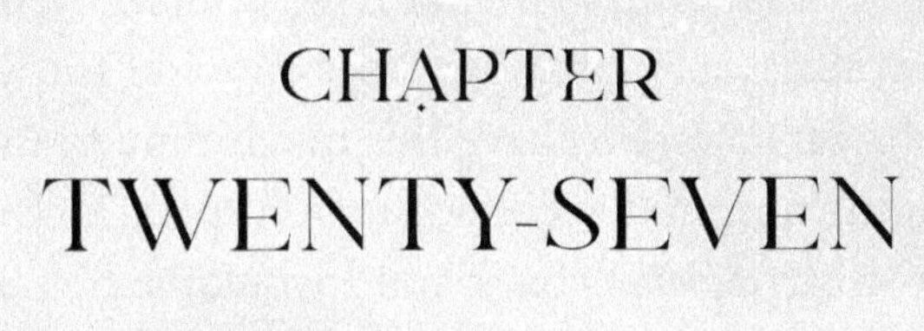

I threw my head back, panting. I felt my heartbeat as I reveled in my self-induced ecstasy. As I lay in my bed, I looked up at the ceiling and the shadows flickering and dancing. I wondered if this moment to myself would be enough to get me out of my stupor.

Surely, this was all I needed. Now, I could focus on my children, the political ramifications of my recent dating choices, the princes that might still be at the palace, and whatever else was temporarily off my plate.

And yet, all I could think about was the flowers decorating Janitra's skin and the water rushing off her body as she left the hot spring. In my mind, I reimagine this over and over again.

As I had touched myself, I'd thought of how I would much rather touch her. I remained stuck in my thoughts when all I wanted to know was what she was thinking about—what she thought about me.

I jolted awake moments later. I realized that I had dozed off after my private moment and I was still in my state of undress. Shivering slightly, I found my clothes that I had tossed onto the floor earlier.

"What am I doing?" I asked the ceiling.

I felt so unlike myself—like I was bumping into too many emotions, and time just kept slipping through my fingers. It was so rare to have this much time to myself— time I didn't want to have. I wanted Gurpreet to come tell us that the carriage was back and I would be home by the time my children woke up for breakfast.

I didn't want to be alone with my feelings, my needs, myself. This was next to torture.

"Abhijita, goddess of my strength, what am I doing?" I plead again. "Please show me. I feel like I'm too…"

I couldn't bear to say it. I always believed that Abhijita was a real figure, a goddess. But after my dream, it felt like she really heard me. She had told me that she loved me. I shuddered and grimaced to think of her expression if she heard me finish that sentence with anything negative.

Placing my palms together and pressing my thumbs to my forehead, I prayed.

"I'm so close. Please help me. It's so hard to take this leap into the dark. Who should I marry? Should I marry anyone? Should I go back to Makaar and reclaim my throne? Am I really attracted to women? Is that selfish or will that help my family?

"What am I? Am I still a queen—am I something else? What would best serve you—serve Ushallav? I just—these questions are all too heavy for me. And I can't do this alone. I'm tired."

I stood with my hands still positioned over my forehead. My skin started to sweat as I kept my posture. I waited for a prolonged moment—wondering if anything would happen. I looked across the room and saw myself in the reflection. I lowered my arms and finished dressing myself.

I wasn't sure what time it was but I hoped that there was still some available food. This troubled queen was hungry.

My stomach felt better once it was calm and sated. Moonlight and a handful of dying sconces lit my way. I made some tea for myself to bring to my room.

As I padded down the hall toward the stairs, I thought I could hear someone shifting in the night. It could've been my canine friend doing some night hunting. But when I looked out the main doors, I realized someone was leaving with their things.

At this sanctuary, people came and went whenever they needed to. I stood as a prime example.

In my thoughts, I wished the woman well on her journey as I headed back to my room. If anything, I had a strong desire to pack my things and go back to the palace in the dead of night, too. But unless my children were already there, that wouldn't solve my problems or calm my anxieties.

Instead, I went back to sleep and began to dream before my tea could even go cold.

I'm back in my carriage, and I'm strangely relieved. I'm not sure how I got here but I'm delighted that my passionate pleas are being heard. At least, that's what I hoped.

For some time, I sit alone and the carriage rolls merrily along. Greens and blues blur and move past me. I'm not sure I want to look through the window even though I hoped this dream was an opportunity to parse through an answer from Abhijita.

I'm just sitting there and wondering what I should do next. If anything, I'm enjoying the ride. It's calm, peaceful. Possibly the first time I've been in this situation and not felt a sense of dread. Maybe that was an answer in and of itself: things that made me feel unsafe are no longer that frightening. I could do this.

Just when I'm settling into my seat and thinking about looking out the window, the carriage stops. The door opens and four women pile into the remaining three seats. The water works begin.

Swaran, Gamani, Maliha, and Neha. Gamani and Swaran are smiling and gripping each other's hands, Neha sits to my left, and Maliha is directly across from me.

My original handmaidens. Their faces are so clear and jovial. They wear beautiful gowns and dupattas like they are just arriving to a party.

"Are you really here?" I burst out with surprise.

I hold out my arms and start crying. I don't know if I can literally feel them but it doesn't fully matter. Their presence is such a gift. I never got to say goodbye to them—never got to lay them to rest in reality and in my heart.

"Oh, Anjali, it's so good to see you. It's so good to see you, friend," Neha says in my ear.

"Oh, you're crying," says Maliha. She giggles a bit. Am I crying? It's a dream but still she dries my tears with her finger.

"How are you here?" I ask incredulously. "I've been having visions lately but I can't believe this is happening."

"Oh, Abhijita said it was okay," Swaran answers.

"We heard you were at the sanctuary. Is Sanjana with you? She's getting so big!" Gamani adds.

"Wait, this is all so much. Are you…you're dead, right?"

"Yes but we're doing well."

"You don't have to worry. That's why we're here. You worry so much. We're happy, we live happily—"

"And you speak with Abhijita or know each other?" I ask incredulously. "She came to me in a dream earlier this week. Did she send you?"

"She did!" Maliha answers. "I think she has a soft spot for you. It helps that you're at the sanctuary but you've been through a lot and we've really wanted you to know that we're always here. We're always here to protect you."

I notice that Leela is not among them—and I'm glad for it. If she shows up, I won't hold back. She'd be gone for good.

"Interesting that we're meeting you here," Gamani says, looking around the carriage. "So many good and bad memories here."

And I realize that she's right. I was in this same carriage when everything had unraveled and rotted. I remember talking with my handmaidens and looking forward to our time in Ushallav—time they never got to enjoy. Leela took away their lives and tried to take away my future.

"I think I'm stuck," I answer somewhat shyly. I don't remember ever lying to them but I don't think I had ever expressed such a hopeless feeling to them before.

There is silence and we hear the wheels moving onward.

"It makes sense that you'd return to this place—when things weren't so painful. But there's a whole world out there waiting for you," Gamani continues. "And we'll be here until you're ready."

"That's silly. You've already passed on. You're with your ancestors and with Abhijita. You don't need to be stuck with me."

Maliha smiles softly. "You're right. You don't need to worry about us. But we can, of our own will, give you courage when you need a little extra."

I smile. "You probably have to leave soon, don't you? I don't want to wake up—now or for a long time."

"It's not quite morning for you," Neha answers. "We'll be here with you as long as you'd like."

"I don't know what to make of all this. But I want to listen to how you're doing. Gamani and Swaran, you're positively glowing. Tell me you finally got married?"

And for no time and all the time in the world, I listen to my handmaidens talk with vibrancy and laughter. They are clearly happy and at peace. Could I ever be at peace like them in the waking world? I promise myself, hoping I would remember when I awoke, that I won't deny myself happiness—for myself and my children and for my handmaidens.

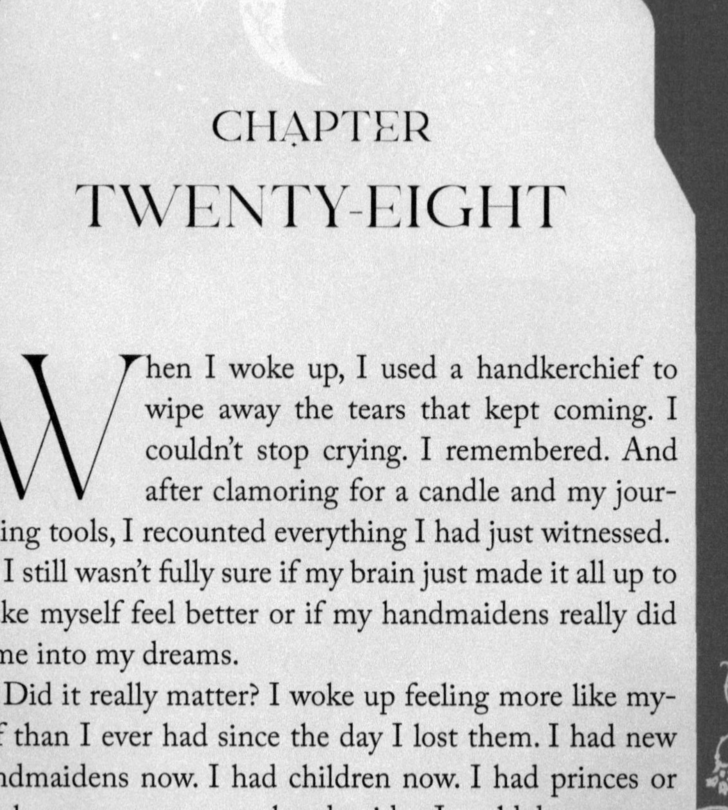

CHAPTER
TWENTY-EIGHT

When I woke up, I used a handkerchief to wipe away the tears that kept coming. I couldn't stop crying. I remembered. And after clamoring for a candle and my journaling tools, I recounted everything I had just witnessed.

I still wasn't fully sure if my brain just made it all up to make myself feel better or if my handmaidens really did come into my dreams.

Did it really matter? I woke up feeling more like myself than I ever had since the day I lost them. I had new handmaidens now. I had children now. I had princes or maybe even a very pretty handmaiden I could date as soon as this evacuation was up.

There was so much to live for and I hoped it wasn't too late to start. So after I finally dried up the last of my tears,

I washed my face in a bowl of water and dressed myself. I knew there was a large room for bathing and beautifying, and I was long due for a clean, painted face.

When I opened the door, I saw Gurpreet and waved. Almost surprised to see me, they approached.

"Are you all right?" my friend asked. "You've been sleeping a lot since you've been here. Not a bad thing but I thought I'd ask anyway."

"I've wanted more dreams and Abhijita provides," I grinned. "But I haven't had a proper wash in a while and I'm heading over there now."

I left it wide open for a joke or a jab but Gurpreet instead nodded solemnly.

"I'm here if you want to talk," was all they said.

"Where is Janitra and Dipa?"

Gurpreet looked around as though trying to remember. "I'm not sure but I can send them your way if needed."

"Oh, that's fine. I'll probably run into them during the day. I just wondered if they were okay. I haven't really been myself since being here."

Gurpreet took my arm and gently pulled me closer. "I think time's almost up. Soak in whatever you need from the sanctuary before it's time to go home."

"Is everything okay?" I asked, wondering if I was reading their expressions correctly. They seemed uneasy.

"I think so," Gurpreet responded distractedly. "I've got some things to attend to, so I'll feel better once I take care of them. I'll let you know when I get official word from the palace."

"Thanks, Gurpreet. I'll hopefully see you around."

They smiled before taking their leave in a different direction.

I took my towel and headed to the baths. I smiled contentedly when I entered the large glass structure that allowed sun through the foggy panes. Much like the natural springs, there were pools of hot water decorated with statues, soaps, perfumes, and brushes. I must've been a late sleeper because hardly anyone was here. Most women, including Dipa, were already clothed and leaving.

"Dipa, good to see you," I greeted.

"Anjali! I can stay with you if you'd like. Do you need help washing your hair?"

"You can stay but don't worry about me. I can take care of it. Are you enjoying our weird little holiday?"

"I guess so," Dipa shrugged. "I miss the others. And I know it's hard on you, so I worry about you."

"I've had some, uh, interesting dreams. But I feel like I've learned some helpful things to better face what's to come at the palace."

"Face what things specifically? If I may ask."

"Well, beyond figuring out Kavi's real intentions, I need to really, truly move forward." I don't want to hold myself or my handmaidens back.

Dipa brightened, relieved. "I was worried about how much time you've spent alone over the past few days but it seems like it's only been to your benefit. Well, I promised to meet up with some of the others for lunch, so I'll leave if that's okay."

"Of course! I'll see you later, Dipa."

She smiled before leaving and I began removing my clothes and lowering myself in the water. It felt so good to scrub my skin and massage the oils and soaps in my hair. I didn't realize how much I smelled or how sluggish I felt over the past few days.

I let myself sit in the still-warm water and enjoy the sensation of cleanliness.

"I didn't think I'd find you here," I heard.

I opened my eyes to see Janitra stepping into my pool of water and situating herself across from me.

"Janitra! Good morning—or maybe good day. Time doesn't feel normal here," I babbled as she settled into the water.

"I ran into Gurpreet and she said I'd find you here."

"I'm glad you found me." I blushed noticeably but I didn't quite care. I wanted her here—especially since I looked and felt much better than the last time.

Janitra grabbed some of the partially used soaps and a new brush and started rubbing circles on her arms, upper chest, and the back of her neck.

"I've been meaning to talk with you," I started. "I—are you upset?"

Janitra looked everywhere other than my eyes and she had a frown on her face. She had come to this particular spot, so why did she act like she had to be here? I wondered if things would change in my favor if I sat up straighter, maybe revealed more of my chest. My wet hair tumbled over my shoulders and in the water like seaweed.

Anjali, control yourself.

"I didn't sleep well," she answered. "Forgive me."

The edge on her voice gave me the impression that she didn't really need my forgiveness.

"I just wanted to be straightforward and I hope you can be honest with me. I wanted to say…ah, I want to say it but I'm so nervous," I began. "I would really really very much like to court you. I think you're strong, talented, and smart. You could say no and we could go on like nothing happened. You could say yes and we'd figure it out. If you wanted to date, we would be as equals—just two Ushallavi women."

"You're not just an Ushallavi woman," Janitra responded. Her facial features softened almost instantly, leaving behind the sullen expression. "You're the queen. You're incredibly strong, you're the bravest person I've ever met, and you're the most beautiful woman here and anywhere. You'd really court me?"

My heart leaped and my cheeks warmed. "Yes, I absolutely would like to. I'm also so so sorry that I had you come with me to meet with Kavi. I try not to think about it, to be honest."

"There's nothing wrong with liking both men and women—or figuring that out later. What matters is that you can date anyone you want."

She looked up at me while she spoke, then leaned over to touch my hair where it framed my face before lingering her touch on my right cheek.

"I trained for untold hours so that I could be worthy of being of service as a handmaiden," she smiled. "I don't ever want to leave your side. And if I get to be by your side and date you, I would really love that."

"But what if things don't work out? I wouldn't expect you to resume your handmaiden duties if we were to grow apart."

"You just proposed we date, and then you're thinking about breaking up? I don't want to think like that, Anjali," Janitra grinned. "I just want to be in this moment. I promise I'm not as intense as Kavi or his people…but I am feeling rather starstruck."

"That is wonderful to hear. But seriously, are you okay? I know you said you didn't sleep well but that seems like only a part of it." I knew the mood had immediately brightened but I desperately wanted to know who or what made Janitra look so sad or angry.

Janitra retreated to her thoughts, and I wondered if this was what it was like watching me getting lost in my thoughts.

I did my best to be patient. Whatever it was, I wanted to fix it.

"I was thinking about your dream—the one that included me. It's not every day that a queen reveals these feelings about someone like me. I wasn't sure how to react or respond. I'm the handmaiden."

She let that last statement hang in the air like it required no further explanation. "Are you willing to do all this…for me?"

"I admit, I'm new to this. My relationship with Damir was a political one. Yes, I loved him, but we didn't have to make this choice or even ask each other to court. It was done. But this is all me—my choice for once. So if I'm doing something wrong or making you uncomfortable, tell me immediately."

I took her hand in both of mine. "You've been in my life for a short time but I already know that you're a caring, funny, and clever woman. All I ever want to do is know what you're thinking and I want to know more about your life and who you are when you're not a handmaiden."

"My queen, I'm blushing," she laughed. The steamy water was adding a rosy sheen to our shoulders and faces.

"Janitra, please call me Anjali."

"Okay," she whispers. "Anjali, I'm blushing."

"I'd really really love to kiss you," I breathed.

I barely began another breath before Janitra gently guided my face toward hers. Her right hand cupped my left cheek and kissed me. And kissed me. And kissed me. I closed my eyes and heard the water rush around us as Janitra positioned her legs around my lap in a straddle as she deepened her kiss. My toes curled as the space between my legs went very warm very quickly.

***

"Are you sure? Does this feel a bit too soon?"

"Maybe?"

"Anjali." Janitra breathed my name and all I could do was melt in response.

Earlier, I'd sheepishly asked if we could spend more time alone and in privacy and we all but flew to her quarters. Her room was nearly identical to mine but covered with so many more candles. The light flickers across our wet hair and oiled bodies.

I watched as she took her robe off and it felt like I was seeing her anew. I wasn't looking at a handmaiden; I was looking at a woman who's a really good kisser.

She laid down in the bed—likely going to be barely

wide enough for two. I stood over her before crawling next to her. We were so close that I eagerly stole another kiss before reaching out a tentative hand to her chest.

I felt her smile against my lips as we began what felt like chapter two of our kiss. Everything felt so good, and the thrill heightened as we positioned ourselves so close to each other.

"I want this so bad," I breathed. "But maybe it is too soon."

Disappointment iced up my spine. My mind thought of all the things I wanted to experience with her. But I just finally acknowledged my attraction to women, Janitra specifically, not even a day ago.

As if continuing my thoughts, Janitra added. "Of course. I want you to be comfortable. I'm not going anywhere, so we don't need to hurry. Besides, you must be thinking of your kids."

She was correct; there was so much waiting for me—us—back home in the palace. Indulging in sexual fantasies didn't feel right.

"Thank you for understanding. For now, being here like this feels really good." She nestled her face into my neck.

Janitra's hair splayed around her like rays of the sun. Mine pooled over my chest while locks slid forward and over Janitra's chest like a waterfall.

"There's time to learn and try out all sorts of things," Janitra whispered.

"All sorts of things?" I raised an eyebrow as if accepting a challenge.

"Anjali, not everything you do is dire. You can relax. It's all new—enjoy it." She gestured to her body as though indicating the thing that was new and something to enjoy.

"Janitra," I began—but fell short. I was at a loss for words. All I could think to do was tighten my arms around her. She relaxed in my embrace, and it became my new favorite feeling in the world.

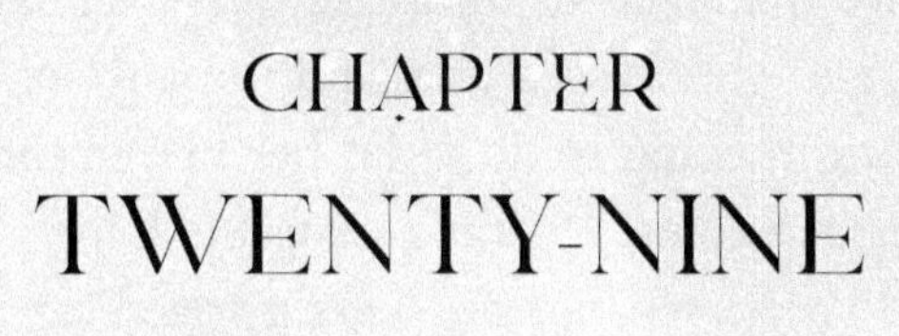

CHAPTER
TWENTY-NINE

Janitra and I spent an afternoon and evening together, and it felt like a dream. The kind of dream that only lasted for an hour but felt like eons. It felt good to talk to her and interact with her beyond the connection we had as queen and handmaiden. With her "yes" to my desire for courtship, there was so much to learn and discover.

We went back and forth and decided to sleep in separate rooms–only because the provided beds would not fit the both of us. So early the following morning, Janitra ensured she was the first thing I saw when I awoke. She kissed my cheek and thus began the day.

"You don't have to do that," I insisted. Almost as if out of habit, Janitra positioned herself behind me with a brush in her hand. In response, she handed me the brush.

I continued the work and looked in her mirror for reference. Janitra just smiled and watched.

"Does Dipa know?" she asked.

I nodded. "She looked like she suspected as much. Am I really that easy to read?"

Janitra kissed my right cheek and locked eyes with me as we both saw ourselves in the mirror reflection.

"Maybe your handmaidens just notice these things," she answered.

After we managed to untangle ourselves last night, I did manage to get dressed and find Dipa to let her know. It was the right thing to do to let her know: she was now the only handmaiden accompanying me here.

I noted the raised but not-so-surprised expression on her face as I briefly caught her up on my experiences at the sanctuary. She didn't know every single detail but it seemed like she didn't need to for her to register the full picture. The small smile on her lips turned in a way that seemed more than just polite but approving.

"So you trained in Makaar, then traveled here to audition for the handmaiden position. What would you have done if someone else got picked—or if I…?"

I blushed and trailed off. What I really wanted to ask was how would our paths continue on if I hadn't examined my attraction to men and women. What if I hadn't declared my budding crush? Would she just be at my side but never close enough? I broke my own heart thinking about it.

"Anjali, it must be the mind of a queen to always be thinking of the past or future but never the present. What matters to me is that we're here together and we can see what today brings." Janitra shrugged as she applied some lotion to her arms and spoke.

She added, "But I suspect that this was inevitable. If not here, we would find each other in another place and time. Aren't we so lucky that we get to be like this now instead of waiting?"

My brush faltered in my hands as I pondered. Ruminating the past and plotting the future was how I survived. I had unearthed Leela's intentions and found closure by digging up my past. I was seeking the best life partner possible by thinking of how my choices will result in the happiness of my children.

Didn't everyone over-analyze their options before grasping at them?

Janitra lightly tapped the crown of my head. "Anjali, dear, you need to learn how to think aloud."

I blinked and chuckled. "I just…all I want to do is make good choices. I hope that whatever I do is a blessing to my children, to you, the Ushallavi people—but enough of that for now. I would really like to hear more about you. Do you always stay in the present or do you sometimes think about the future?"

"Hm, I'm presently thinking about getting some food."

I gave her a wry smile. We linked arms as we stood up and left her chambers. It felt good to walk around the sanctuary grounds as a unit rather than a queen being doted on by her handmaiden.

We grabbed some late breakfast and sat outside basking in the not-too-hot, not-too-cold weather. Together, we spread a stretch of cloth. I sat with my legs stretched out and Janitra made herself comfortable on her stomach.

"You asked me about my future, or whether I think about it," Janitra began, chewing thoughtfully on some fruit. "I don't think I've ever put a ton of thought or detail into it. All I knew was that I wanted to get out of Makaar. My parents had always resisted the idea of returning, and I don't know if they'll ever explain why. But I wanted to join my people, and training seemed like a way to remember who I was and where we came from. It led me to you, didn't it? Who cares whether you might have chosen another handmaiden—because you chose me then and I choose you now."

I wiped my mouth to cover the moment my heart skipped a beat. Being romanced had never felt so thrilling and fun. "I wish I could think like you. It sounds like there's a lot less noise in your head."

Janitra took another bite, and I watched her. Gods, she looked good doing just about anything.

She murmured, "Sometimes, I wonder if I don't expect a lot to protect myself—like how you over-think to protect yourself. But I can't deny that whenever I trust in Abhijita, things just…work out. I don't feel afraid."

Janitra, if memory served me, was only a year younger than me but it felt like we'd live two different lives. Janitra spent her days preparing for what was to come, and no amount of preparing made my divorce sting any less.

There was something sweet, hopeful, and inspiring about Janitra. She seemed to know my story, my tendencies, and the little corners of my life and still agreed to court me, kiss me, be closer to me. I needed this right now, and I hoped I was exactly what she needed, too.

"I guess we'll have to prepare somewhat for whatever happens when we return to the palace," Janitra spoke, bringing my thoughts back to her and my breakfast. "Do you think…your family will accept me? I hope your kids will like me."

"My my. We've only been together for a day or so and we're already thinking about that?" I joked. "I don't even know if my own son likes me right now. He's not happy about being away from his father. He doesn't understand the situation and I feel like the villain for not wanting to just…be a shadow in the Makaarian courts."

I looked down at my plate. This trip to the sanctuary felt like one long hangover. What would happen once my head cleared and my life resumed? I expected to spend time untraumatizing my children, meeting with my brother to hear what he learned from interrogating Kavi, apologizing to several confused princes, and otherwise cleaning up the mess I left after my birthday celebration.

So much to do, and my stomach soured at the thought.

I felt Janitra grip my hand reassuringly.

"Ask me what I think about my future," she challenged with a grin, looking up at me. I kissed the hand that gripped mine.

"What do you think about your future, dear Janitra?"

"I'm hopeful that it'll have something to do with courting the beautiful and brave Queen Anjali, getting to know her children, and kicking any ass that needs kicking."

We smiled at each other and I felt a blush and wave of emotion swirl up my neck and ears.

"Whatever's to come, we've got this," Janitra said, taking a bite of mango.

"Anjali."

I looked up and saw Gurpreet.

"Want to join us?" I asked, gesturing to the remaining food. They squatted and took a bite out of some rice.

They murmured, "We're leaving first thing tomorrow. We just got word from the palace—it's safe for everyone to return."

"Really?" I sputtered. I scrambled to my feet even though no one else was standing.

This time tomorrow, my children would be back in my arms. Like a lit candle, my brain suddenly sparked with thoughts about them—were they scared? Angry with me? Was I a bad mother for thinking about kissing and touching Janitra when I should've never stopped thinking about them? Janitra was right—would they like her? What was I doing picnicking when I could be packing?

Gurpreet stood and held both my wrists—calmly and yet firmly.

"The children and handmaidens are safe and healthy. You have plenty of time to pack and spend your time however necessary to prepare."

Janitra was at my side. "Everything's fine," she reassured.

"I just feel…everything," I answered. "Like I regret the hours I could've spent writing letters or preparing to face the princes—"

"Maybe some sparring will help with this anxious energy, Anjali," Gurpreet suggested. "Janitra, you better come with us if you're able."

"Of course."

"Janitra doesn't have to if she doesn't want to," I insisted. "She's no longer—"

"I know," Gurpreet said, finally flashing their signature wry smile. "I was merely inviting her. I figured your heart wouldn't be fully in your punches unless she was nearby and able to watch you show off."

"If you think that this teasing is going to distract me from the mother's guilt, well, you may be right." I gathered my plate of food and gave Janitra a kiss on the cheek.

"What? None for me?" Gurpreet joked. I gave them a kiss on the forehead and looked forward to wrapping my hands and doing something beyond stretching and meditating.

***

"You loved Damir, right? You had some good moments."

To my knowledge, this was the first time anyone—let alone my handmaidens—broached the subject. Janitra sat across from me and Dipa. Our bodies swayed with the movement of the carriage—a real one this time.

We were already halfway home, and I wondered if this was Janitra's way of getting me to talk instead of brood.

"Yes. From the moment we met, I loved him. I thought we were fated to be together and bring about all these big, grand changes. And even though we were betrothed, I loved spending time with him," I mused. "Despite it all, we had a very deep connection. I didn't want to divorce him, and sometimes I regret it. It feels like I failed, although there was nothing more I could do."

"He loves Einora," Dipa said simply and sadly. It was true. Fate and betrothed marriages don't stop anyone from falling in love. "I don't think that means you failed anything."

"Yes," my voice cracked. "You'll see why Einora suits him when you meet her. It's difficult to hate her. She makes a good replacement."

Janitra gave me a pointed look as though she strongly disagreed.

Dipa looked between the two of us, intrigued. I'm sure she had a lot to report to the other two handmaidens. I felt sure that they would see the changes with their own eyes.

Before boarding the carriage, I gave Janitra some jewelry and clothes so she did not have to wear her handmaiden clothes. If she was to be my equal, I wanted her to look the part. And she looked gorgeous while doing it.

"My queen," Dipa murmured, "Sanjana and Devraj already love Janitra. She helps them practice Makaarian. Sanjana is obsessed with Janitra's hair and Devraj insists he dangle off her arm whenever she lets him. They like all of us but I think they already love Janitra."

Dipa and Janitra exchanged glances and I noticed Janitra's eyes glitter and glisten.

"A very helpful observation," I answered. I gripped her arm with affection and gratitude and she smiled.

"This arrangement is going to be a lot more enjoyable than your other prospects," Dipa shrugged. "May the gods give a moment to breathe before whatever comes next."

I took a long, controlled breath as I looked out the carriage window. The details of the trees and gravelly path rushed by but not with the same vividness as the dreams I experienced at the sanctuary. But the parallels felt familiar. My goddess told me that when I was ready to get out of the proverbial carriage, everyone I knew and loved would be there to receive me.

And for the first time during this long week away from my children, I was dying to throw open the doors and face what would greet me.

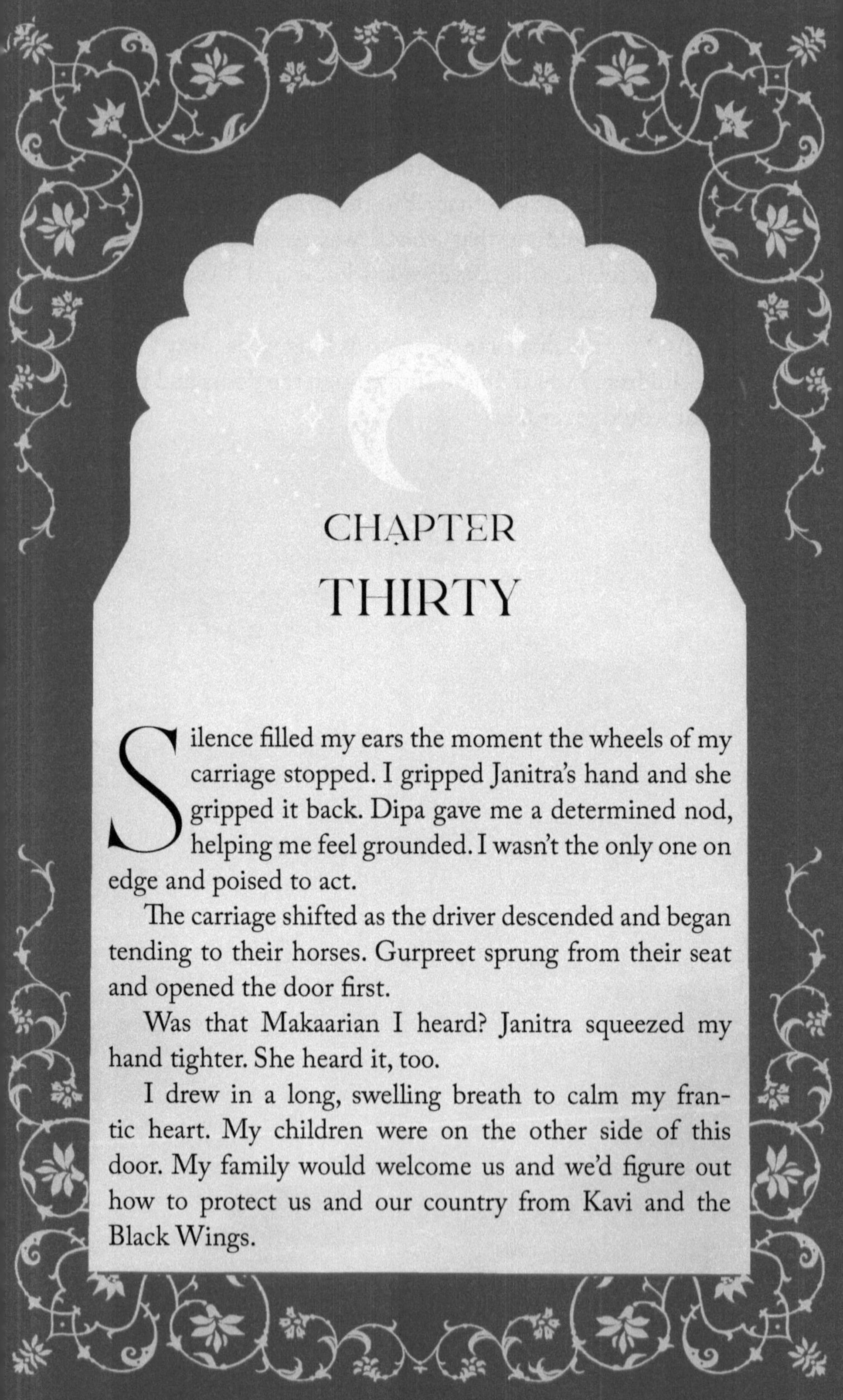

CHAPTER

THIRTY

Silence filled my ears the moment the wheels of my carriage stopped. I gripped Janitra's hand and she gripped it back. Dipa gave me a determined nod, helping me feel grounded. I wasn't the only one on edge and poised to act.

The carriage shifted as the driver descended and began tending to their horses. Gurpreet sprung from their seat and opened the door first.

Was that Makaarian I heard? Janitra squeezed my hand tighter. She heard it, too.

I drew in a long, swelling breath to calm my frantic heart. My children were on the other side of this door. My family would welcome us and we'd figure out how to protect us and our country from Kavi and the Black Wings.

Nothing could prepare me for the stern expression to greet me. More for Janitra's protection, I released her hand as I descended the carriage steps.

Damir. Flanked with Makaarian guards, diplomats, and his frowning advisor Benedikt, my ex-husband stood rigid and formally. He gripped our children's hands like they were the one thing holding him back from expressing more emotion than the storm swirling in his eyes and down-turned mouth.

The sight of Devraj and Sanjana at his sides turned my stomach. Hostility. More hostility—just like when I returned to Makaar after years of hiding. The parallels were not lost on me.

"Mama," Devraj called. His excited and warbly voice broke my stare into Damir's expression. I knelt down and held my hands out. I half-worried that Damir wouldn't let go, but the kids were free to tumble into my arms.

I kissed their foreheads, cheeks, temples—anywhere I could. I wanted to forget Damir and his stupid entourage and his stupid, angry face.

What was he doing here, and how dare he look supremely pissed at me?

"I'm home," I told my children. "I missed you so much. Are you okay?"

Sanjana and Devraj talked over each other—sharing their experiences, good and bad.

"Papa is here to visit us," Devraj informed me. He ran back to his father and smiled up at him. "Is he staying with us?"

"I don't know, sweetheart," I said to my son but looked at his father. I was so shocked that he was here—I wasn't sure if I should be relieved, concerned, or both. Someone, likely my brother, was going to get an earful for not informing me that my ex-husband was here.

Looking at Damir, I finally addressed him. "Good to see you're in good health. We have much to discuss."

As if biting his tongue, he nodded gravely, and motioned for us to cross the shaded palace entrance together. I gave Janitra and Gurpreet a quick, wary glance before picking Sanjana up and joining the throng inside.

I felt icy, cold emotion coursing up my back and settling in my shoulders. It took active breathing and eye contact with Dipa, Gurpreet, and Janitra to keep my nerves calm. It felt like I was about to get scolded by Damir. And for what?

I followed protocol. I let my handmaidens do their job. Everyone was safe. I had returned at a secret time and at an early hour to ensure security. And yet, my body was frantically trying to prepare me for a physical fight when this fight would be with words and emotions. I only felt angrier.

This room was full of too many people—the heat contrasted sharply with the icy stress keeping me on edge and damn-near volatile.

One of Ray's advisers gestured for us to enter the king's office. Ray needed to up that man's salary or I needed to add him to my staff. I was impressed with how I couldn't read his face as an angry divorced couple was about to come to blows.

My handmaidens were hot on my heels, giving me comfortable space. It was like wearing a long cape that fluttered heroically behind me.

Damir and the children went inside first. I turned around to face the mixed entourage. I held my hands up and everyone froze in place.

"Please give me and my family a few moments of privacy before joining us," I said as calmly and queenly as possible. "The children haven't seen their father in quite some time and I want to hear his message privately. Thank you for your understanding."

Makaarian and Ushallavi faces alike broke into shocked, confused expressions. My parents, both dressed in early morning yet formal clothing, were approaching with haste.

"Gurpreet, please fill them in. I'll talk to them soon. Everyone's okay."

My friend nodded and signaled to my handmaidens. They would smooth down any ruffled feathers. I gave a narrow-eyed look to Benedikt's aloof frown before entering the room and shutting the door.

I sighed before finding my seat.

Out of the three adults in the room, Ray was the most formal and prepared. He even wore his turban and crown. I was wearing a traveling tunic and garments and Damir was dressed in his usual Makaarian suit whenever he's opened to the public forum for complaints.

I looked around for things for the children to do. Was there a way to keep them within sight but not hear all of this? I felt stretched, tired, and defensive.

"Everyone else can come in and we can talk things out with them momentarily," I began, "but you better explain why you're here and what you think you're going to accomplish here."

Shock flickered over Damir's expression. I'd never seen him this angry. He's never struck me unless we consented to sparring but he looked like he wanted to slap someone.

"How dare you speak to me like that?" Damir sputtered. "I had to hear from your king that you've been courting, I don't know, a terrorist?"

He growled like fire-breathing dragons of Makaarian lore. I kept my lips tight and arched an eyebrow. I wanted to give him room to speak before snapping back at him.

"Anjali, you can court and marry whoever suits you. I only want your happiness. But don't you think you could've informed me that this man is a danger to you, to me, and our children? I had to hear from Ray that you ran away and spent time at a spa and left our children here?"

Ray held up a finger milliseconds before I could speak.

"As I told you earlier, I sent her there for her safety," Ray interrupted coolly. "Our forebears set the standard and we followed protocol, which meant she went to a location that I determined and she only discovered upon arrival. You can interrogate your ex-wife and children but you'll only find that everyone is safe and healthy.

"As for putting the Makaarian heirs in danger, Anjali sought out Kavi per my request. She was able to get Kavi out of hiding and expose his entire operation. You should be thanking her for getting to the heart of the reason why she was attacked three or so years ago. They radicalized Leela and could radicalize more. I have made a copy of the report for you to analyze but do not raise your voice at my beloved sister until you have digested the full story."

I didn't look at my brother and tried to not look as shocked as I felt. It felt like he was a teenager again and I was ten years old as I watched him fully cover for me. Ray and I knew I went into this out of attraction—not to gather intel.

Damir looked at the two of us and at the children. They were playing in low whispers behind Ray's desk and they were uncharacteristically quiet. Listening.

I used a low voice in case the others outside could hear. "The Black Wings have been gathering in the name of keeping the Ushallavi bloodline 'pure.' Our previous marriage and our children go against everything they hold dear. We are in the middle of apprehending them and bringing them to justice. You and your people can either aid us or leave us to our work. But know that everything I do is for the happiness, health, and long future of our children."

Janitra was waiting just beyond the door. I wished she was here and was equally glad she wasn't. This was my reality—her potential future. Did she want to deal with me and my ex-husband?

"Why are the children here then?" Damir questioned with edge. "They shouldn't be here while you're weeding out these people."

My breath sharpened and the hairs stood on the back of my neck. I looked down and realized Sanjana was in my lap. Whether she was there for her comfort or mine, it didn't matter. I held her tiny hand and felt my eyes tighten with emotion.

"Damir, at no point have the children been in danger. If they're not under my direct care, they are surrounded by handmaidens, palace guards, and my side of the family. They hadn't formally met Kavi," I explained, my anger slowly deflating. "They live in a world much safer than what we grew up with but our work still isn't done. You can't protect them without me—and I can't protect them without you."

Damir licked his lips and clenched his jaw. He looked at Sanjana like he wanted to hold her and never let her go. Devraj stood next to me and held my upper arm.

"Papa," my son called.

"Go on, Dev," I encouraged softly. He tumbled in his father's lap and let himself cry.

"I don't like yelling, Papa," he wailed. Sanjana whimpered sympathetically and I patted her back.

"No one is yelling, Devraj," I said. "And it's okay to be angry. Papa loves you and wants you to be safe. So do I and your Uncle Ray. Sometimes grown-ups get angry when they are really sad and want to cry."

I didn't look at Damir but I rocked my daughter and let him speak for himself.

What I wanted to say was *I trust you, Damir. Do you trust me? Have you ever trusted me with…all of this? Your dreams and visions of the future?*

"We have an opportunity to continue this somewhat private conversation before letting everyone else into the room," I said—not quite a threat but more like a warning. "Now is the time to process whatever you need to process. So do me a kindness and talk with me like I'm your equal."

Anger still prickled my words but the fury wasn't so strong. I was still upset that he thought so little of me and was about to scold me for courting someone else.

I didn't have a say in his second marriage because he thought I was murdered. Like hell would he have any sense of superiority and opinion of who I wanted to replace *him* with. I only felt calmer because Ray was absolutely on my side and wouldn't let these Makaarians outside his office scold me like a child.

Damir let out a long exhale and looked me in the eye. "I arrived with anger and thought I would have to have to bring the kids back with me for their safety. I feel a bit better now that I could hear about this directly from you. And the kids look well."

I suspected that this was the closest thing to an apology Ray and I would get. An empathetic part of me knew that if the roles were reversed, I would fly to Makaar fueled by my fury. I would incapacitate everyone in my path first and ask questions later. He was a concerned parent; I'd be worried if he were any less alarmed.

My eyes flickered over to Ray. I blinked a few times and gave a fraction of a grateful smile.

Thank you, brother. And I'm sorry.

"King Damir, I can give you this report and you can look it over with your advisers. How would you prefer to move forward?" My brother spoke like he was trying to de-fang a poised snake.

My brother was trying to discern whether we could reason with Damir. I could tell that he wouldn't let him strongarm and take the kids away at the first sign of political danger.

After a long sigh, Damir nodded. "Let's grab some breakfast and get to work. Does your staff still have that flavor of chai I miss?"

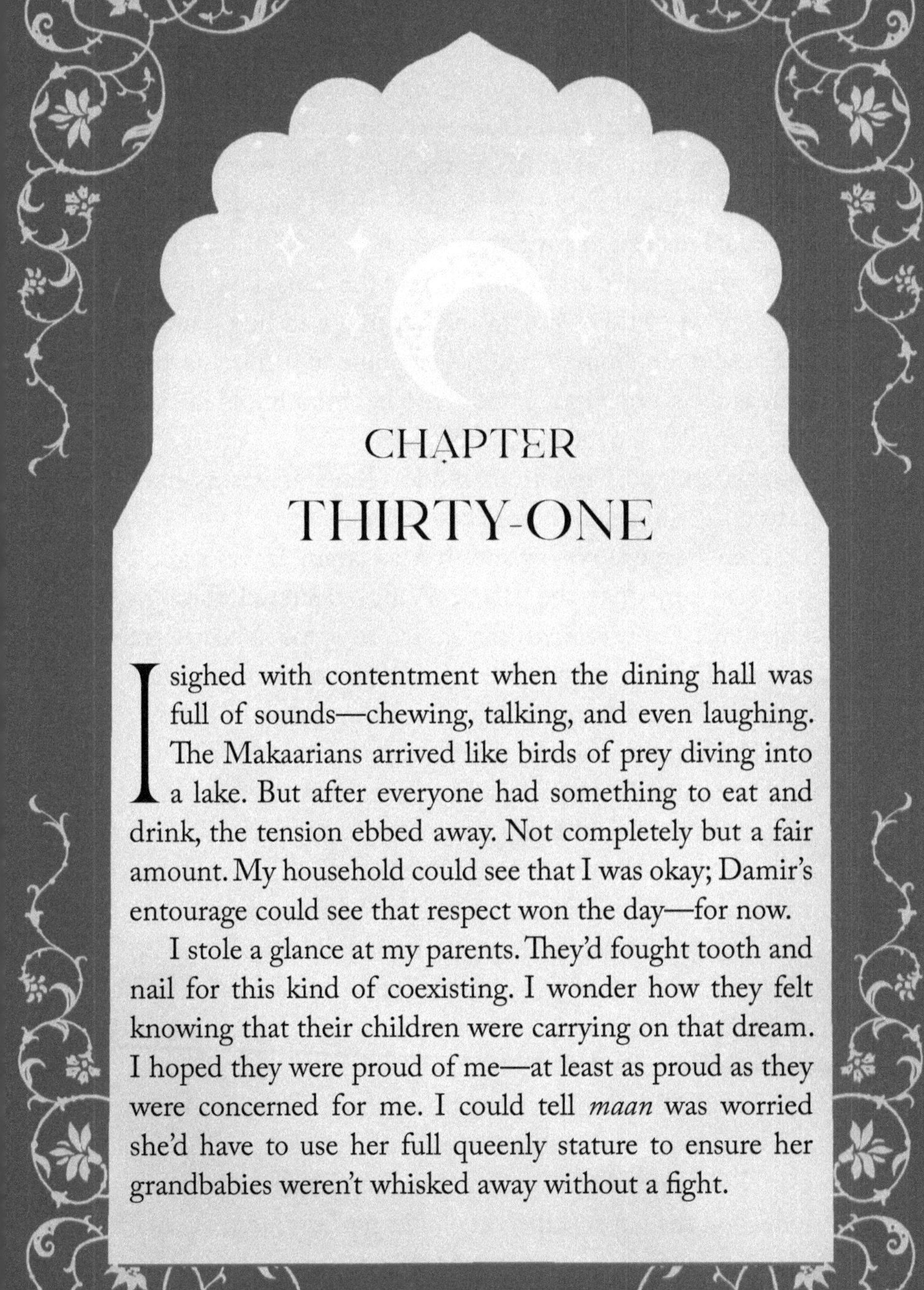

CHAPTER
THIRTY-ONE

I sighed with contentment when the dining hall was full of sounds—chewing, talking, and even laughing. The Makaarians arrived like birds of prey diving into a lake. But after everyone had something to eat and drink, the tension ebbed away. Not completely but a fair amount. My household could see that I was okay; Damir's entourage could see that respect won the day—for now.

I stole a glance at my parents. They'd fought tooth and nail for this kind of coexisting. I wonder how they felt knowing that their children were carrying on that dream. I hoped they were proud of me—at least as proud as they were concerned for me. I could tell *maan* was worried she'd have to use her full queenly stature to ensure her grandbabies weren't whisked away without a fight.

Sitting with my handmaidens proved…new and interesting. This was absolutely the worst time to tell anyone of my experiences at the sanctuary, and I hoped that the discussion would remain off the table. But eventually, I would tell my family—the world—that I saw Janitra as my equal instead of my handmaiden.

I stole a glance and a wink across the table. I had to get through all of this—just to see her in a wedding gown if she'd take me. Something in her polite and mischievous grin as she scooped some food into her mouth told me she had a similar thought in mind.

Pari entered her serious mode. "Ray's assistants have vetted the full palace before our arrival."

Her voice was so low and in Makaarian. It was a good guess as any that the Black Wings operated through Ushallavi. I appreciated her choice to speak Makaarian; in case Damir's people were listening in, they wouldn't assume we were keeping anything from them.

"What do you think?" I replied.

Pari shifted uncomfortably. "I'm trusting the king's judgment but it's still very tense here in the palace."

"We must always walk the line between trust and distrust," I returned in Makaarian. "You know as well as I do that I nor any royal figure will ever be fully safe. So we do what we can and we trust in the Eyes to guide us."

"I've been meaning to give this to you," Janitra added in Makaarian. I startled a bit at the sound of her voice and the feel of something pressed to my thigh. She slid a piece of parchment and didn't let go until it crumpled in my grip. I did my best to avoid a blooming blush. I discretely looked at the paper, expecting an important message.

In careful script, she wrote,

The reason why my family left Ushallav was to escape the Black Wings. I only learned the details once I became an adult. Someone my mother and father knew from the war days strongly convinced them to join, and they left soon after for their safety. I'm sure guaranteed protection from you and Damir could convince them to help you identify key figures.

This covert stuff was sort of exciting.

I smirked at the note. We rarely used our written secret code for handmaidens but Janitra was a quick study. I folded the note and tucked it in my trousers. The information was still really valuable and helpful.

I didn't know that the Black Wings had such a long history. I hoped I could meet Janitra's parents and not only thank them for raising their daughter but also for being so brave in the face of so much danger.

I felt a meaningful stare a few seats away. Damir met my gaze as I looked up and acknowledged the staring. It was possible that he saw Janitra pass the note.

The children ran back and forth between us, eating at his side and mine, so we both had small plates with half-eaten breakfast. At this point, they were both sitting pleasantly near their father. If they were scared or upset, they didn't show it. Damir was equally unreadable.

His expression banished my good-natured smile. I had never completely forgotten that the Black Wings struck my family way too close to home and whatever he might think, I took it seriously. I merely connected with my handmaidens as we found a moment to have some joy. They had been begging me to lighten up and heal; he was demanding I retain seriousness to avoid consequences.

"How are Einora and Gregori doing?" I spoke up. If he was going to stare at me, he might as well humor me with an update.

"Baby GeeGee!" Sanjana squealed. "Is baby GeeGee here?"

"No, baby," Damir smiled—the way parents want to smile when they actually feel weary. The smile didn't stretch as far as I knew it could. "But he misses you and can't wait to see you."

He looked my way and addressed me. "Einora is Einora. She's worried about how you're doing but knows you'll find your own way. She lives for your letters."

I smiled a bit. I'm sure my sad smile didn't fool anyone else. Einora captured his heart the way I couldn't. She was the woman he'd married for love when he thought I was truly gone.

I couldn't wait to tell everyone at this table—even stupid Benedikt—about the woman I wanted to be with. The thought made me giddy; I had found someone I could even imagine being with or even marrying.

Janitra touched my knee under the table with a whisper of a touch.

I'm here, it said. She didn't know that much about Einora, so maybe she thought this was a much more painful question than it sounded.

The pleasant conversations died down without prompting. There was an energy in the air—like it was time to get serious and earnest once more. Before sitting down for breakfast, we made a quick plan.

The group of Ushallavi and Makaarian adults would split into three directions. One group, led by my parents, would be with the children in a safe location of the palace. Another group would follow me, Ray, and Damir back into his office. The third group, including half of my handmaidens, would patrol the grounds and alert us of anything out of the ordinary.

So when the eating stopped and the awkward silence grew, I set down my napkin and adjusted my dupatta.

I thought about Janitra's note. What I had gleaned from Kavi's words and deeds was that he represented a people who wanted Ushallav to remain "strong and pure." They disagreed so much with my marriage and joint dream with Damir that they would do just about everything to keep me "pure"—including nearly killing me and an unborn Sanjana.

So how were we going to handle this? How would we address the growing hostility from unsatisfied subjects without letting them control my life? Would they come after the kids—the physical manifestation of everything they hate? Would they convince their neighbors to wake the god of war, Zayant, and put Tamul, the god of peace, back to rest?

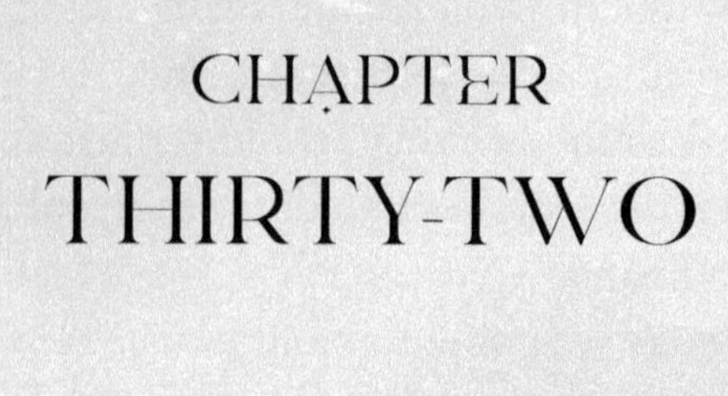

CHAPTER
THIRTY-TWO

After several hours of discussion, I felt we were close to a solution. After a pause for resting and cooling down (things weren't entirely peaceful in that seemingly-cramped room), we returned for more deliberating.

"I need to share my information with them, right?" Janitra asked in a low, nearly conspiratorial tone.

I sighed, unsure. Her note was interesting but I wished we could share it privately with Ray first. What if Damir and his entourage took it the wrong way? She was putting herself and her family in danger.

"It's your childhood. It's your parents," I reminded. "I just…I trust you. If talking to them means that we get your parents any kind of justice for what happened, then let's do it. But I can share it as anonymous intel."

"Sure, just like I heard that you dated Kavi to get information out of him," Janitra winked.

I rolled my eyes and guffawed. "Let's just say I owe Ray for weaving a forgiving tale."

"I think it's important to share," Janitra said, returning to seriousness. "Sure, there are some extreme ideas in Ushallav but there are people who don't listen or agree. Kavi doesn't represent all of us. Maybe with time and protection, Damir can learn more from my parents."

I scrunched my face, unsure. I trusted Janitra to do the right thing by her family but I hoped the Makaarians wouldn't eat her words alive. Not on my watch, certainly.

We could afford to speak a bit freely—we were resting in my personal chambers. Although with all the talking back and forth, I wasn't particularly in the mood to raise my voice.

Janitra cupped my face in her hands and kissed me solemnly between my eyes, on my nose, and on my lips.

"I know you're not too keen on introducing your ex-husband to my parents but they'll be fine. I'll be fine," she smiled into the kiss.

"Maybe you should be the one protecting me from the Makaarians."

Janitra folded her arms to make her already-muscular arms look even more imposing.

"Don't talk to my queen like that," Janitra said in a low voice—practically a growl. Terrifying and alluring at the same time.

"Well, let's go see what we accomplish this afternoon." I sighed wearily. "This is my present and your future. You don't have to endure all this if you don't want to."

She took my hand.

"Something tells me that you won't believe me unless I tell you every day of your beautiful life. But I came all this way for the chance to be handmaiden. And you chose me for something greater. You can't get rid of me so easily."

And why would I want to? I didn't realize how dull the pigment of my life was until I had my children—but Janitra filled my life with colors that didn't have names yet. I'd endure what was to come to ensure I never had to return to a monochromatic outlook on life.

We all settled back in our chairs after our brief break. We all naturally turned to Ray to facilitate the conversation again. Even though everyone was talking about the task at hand, I felt burdened by all the implications–all the seemingly-innocent dinners that led us to this point.

Here, I'd been trying to decide how to go on with my life as a divorced queen that wouldn't upset anyone. And for a while, I was blissfully unaware of the nation's problems. But there were people who thought I should've fought for my throne and secured our position of power within Makaar. While others had killed my handmaidens and nearly took my life in their attempt to keep us apart.

All I wanted to do was raise my kids and have the love and respect I deserved from a partner. Beyond that, I wasn't sure what I would do with my time and talents. But I would hope I would be of service to someone if given a chance to breathe.

I grimaced. Kavi wanted to get close to me to control my future. Even just associating with him would fulfill his dreams and kill mine. And if we had gone so far as to get married, I couldn't bear to think of what would have happened to my children or our connections with Makaar or other countries. We'd kiss all our plans to grow in respect and prosperity goodbye. How could Kavi be blind to that?

I should've never looked his way. For now, I had to forgive myself for coming earnestly to the relationship; he didn't.

As Ray began with some mild pleasantries, one of his staff members passed around drinks. I rolled my eyes after Benedikt only drank his glass of water after watching Ray take some meaningful sips. He had been here all day—using our rooms, eating our food, and drinking our water. Did he think he was special enough to be served poison?

There was sweet peace in knowing that Damir kept the man in the divorce.

Benedikt frowned in my direction. Maybe I was too easy to read. I blinked and shifted my view and looked elsewhere. He was certainly less full of himself when he was here in my domain than in his. He was such a disagreeable man when he thought he knew more about ruling than me.

As he leaned over to whisper something in Damir's ear, I had a wicked thought. The way they leaned in to speak reminded me of Janitra leaning in to say something witty or compliment my hair. I looked at the two men with different eyes. Maybe Benedikt was more devoted to his king than he cared to admit.

Not my problem. Not my problem. Not my problem…

To pull me out of a spell, Janitra put her hand on my arm. What did she say?

"With Queen Anjali's permission, I would like to share some personal information that might help us come together."

I gave her a nod of acceptance and encouragement. She stood from her chair and began addressing the room of mostly men with the most beautiful, strong posture I could imagine.

"Good afternoon," she began in Makaarian. "You may not recognize me. I'm new to Queen Anjali's group of fierce handmaidens. But I did not spend my youth in Ushallav. My parents moved me and my three siblings to Makaar as children for our safety. You see, I was too young to really know why, but my parents entrusted me with their story. They were approached by people like Kavi with tales of injustice. It wasn't sudden or outright.

"My parents both served and fought in the war, as I'm sure many of you and your kin fought against us. And while most of my neighbors were glad to be done with the fighting and the dying, some weren't finished. They wanted to pick up the blade and ensure that the world knew just how strong Ushallav could be.

"Leela and Kavi are radicalized people. I urge you, gentlemen, to help us to better understand the people and show a united front. The dream that our late kings and queens had to stop the war and begin the peace live on in Damir, Einora, Ray, and Anjali. There must be a way to show that war will not make anyone stronger or better.

"My parents moved to Makaar to get away from what the Black Wings threatened to do if they gave up their numbers and names." Janitra paused her speech and looked at my ex-husband directly. "If King Damir and Queen Einora can ensure their safety, they could help expose this group of people before their rhetoric spreads further."

"This is a lot of work to clean up someone else's mess," Benedikt spoke up. *Oh good,* I thought, *the water whetted his whistle.*

Ray tilted his head but didn't interject. He appeared like he had an inkling of what Benedikt meant by "someone."

"Oh, there's many a Makaarian who has their own opinions about the choices the royal family makes." Janitra paced the room, making eye contact with the others who sat around Damir and Benedikt. "Just because the Black Wings are of Ushallavi descent doesn't mean that every Ushallavi person agrees. If I've learned anything in the service of Queen Anjali, it's the delicate dance of pleasing one's subjects and making the decisions everyone would prefer to delegate away."

"Leela and the others willingly killed Queen Anjali's previous handmaidens and nearly took the queen and princess with them," murmured Pari. "We wouldn't be here unless Leela had acted on her radical brainwashing."

"Janitra?" Damir spoke.

"Yes, my name is Janitra, Your Highness."

"Janitra, that must've been painful to leave your homeland to preserve your life. Did your parents ever tell you if the Black Wings were a global entity?"

My lover's lips curled a fraction, impressed. She bowed her head grimly. "In honesty, they didn't go into the details in order to protect me. But with the intel that Anjali acquired through Kavi, they're starting to get bolder, more confident. In a turn of irony, they seem to be open to outside help to gain more control in Ushallav. You may think this is a little spill from our country but without a united front, you may have spills and messes of your own."

Damir's jaw tightened at the thought and Benedikt gripped his thighs.

"The handmaiden speaks boldly, plainly, and truthfully," Ray interjected smoothly. Janitra took her seat next to me. I could feel her warmth and energy pulsing. "Our parents promised to lay down our weapons and see reason. Yes, we will spy and capture dangerous, radical individuals before they destroy us from the inside. But with a clear alliance, it won't matter whether our choices are popular; we'll ensure the Black Wings have no safe place to roost here or anywhere."

"Is that what you told the princes from the north?" Benedikt asked.

"Are you referring to my birthday party?" I quipped. "Hardly the place to talk politics. You can tell us how you really feel once we truly address the Black Wings situation."

Ray tsked a bit too loudly and I knew that was a warning for me.

Damir didn't look flustered about the reference to the princes or my birthday party. I could tell something was cooking in that mind of his.

"Janitra, thank you for sharing your story with us. We have to accept the fact that this could be a regional problem if we let it fester. And at the heart of this, the children remain in far too much danger." Damir straightened. "This actually changes everything. I have an idea."

And with that, things actually got interesting and we put our heads together to change our course.

CHAPTER
THIRTY-THREE

Per Ray's insistence, I stayed put for most of the day. That was perfectly acceptable because I didn't want to leave my kids in any sense of the word. After all the stress of the morning, we found ourselves in the playroom, relaxing from the travel and politics.

At some point, Gurpreet slipped in the room and handed me a short note detailing where the kids stayed during the week. It turned out that all the kids stayed together for the week, so they enjoyed their time with their cousins. My handmaidens reported that nothing was amiss beyond Sanjana missing me more than they imagined.

Considering the way she pressed her small body into the crook of my neck or in my lap, I could tell she was fine but not ready to separate too quickly. I stroked her hair as I read her some books and played games with Devraj.

My son was clingy for a moment but quickly became talkative. I missed him so much that I could hear him talk about anything and everything, and not stop him.

"Is Papa coming to play? I saw him during breakfast. He's here at the palace!" Devraj spoke hurriedly and repeated himself.

"I'm sure he's coming to play soon," I answered, not sure he could hear me.

I looked at the door—Janitra had already offered to get Damir and show him the way to the playroom. They would arrive any minute.

I'd given her a concerned glance as she went to find Damir. She insisted on playing the part of a hand-maiden even though I didn't want her to. She promised we'd take things one step at a time; this was a temporary measure.

There was no sense in dealing with a previous partner all while announcing I had a new one.

I tried to appear calm and focused on Devraj's recounting of a joke his cousin taught him as Damir and Janitra entered and joined us.

"Papa!" Devraj shrieked with glee. Damir smiled wearily and took our son in his arms.

"Hello, little prince," he replied, pulling his son close and picking him up.

I locked eyes with Janitra.

A blush bloomed across my face as she gave a quick sign in the language I shared with the northern princes that said, "You're safe. Watching over you."

She gave me a whisper of a wink and a smile as she left the room once she saw we were properly united.

After a moment of watching my children clamor for their father's attention and his listening ear, Damir looked to me and murmured almost sheepishly,

"Happy belated birthday."

I let out a somewhat delirious chuckle. "Thank you, Damir. It's been quite the week—I nearly forgot it happened. Everything happened so fast. Thank you for the presents."

"Do I get presents?" Sanjana asked sweetly.

Her little voice sounded sweet as she spoke Makaarian after quite a long break.

"Of course, of course," Damir smiled.

"We already got them but haven't opened them yet, sweetie," I said, cupping her little face with my hand. "We better send some gifts with Papa for baby Gregori and Einora."

"I have a present for Gregori!" Devraj declared, producing his prized drawing. His depiction of our family included all six of us. I silently wondered if he'd ever add a seventh person—someone like Janitra.

"Gregori will love this." Damir smiled down at the drawing. "You're going to become the family artist at this rate."

Before my stay at the sanctuary, I might've been cold, far away, and inaccessible to my ex-husband. I would've wanted him to feel all the shame, anger, and grief that I carried and unleashed that fateful night in my solitude.

But as we interacted as the four of us, I genuinely listened as Damir recounted Einora's continuing recovery from giving birth several months ago. Her encounter with Leela had set her back, to put it mildly, so she'd been on bed rest since we last saw each other. Gregori luckily hasn't missed out on attention and care, as Einora's female family members had finally stepped in. I smiled in satisfaction that she took my advice to reach out for assistance.

I wasn't necessarily empty of my rage or grief at what happened to me—and the things Damir let happen to me. However, I did feel like my fierce grip on my emotions loosened just a touch.

I had love and support from my family and handmaidens. I had hope in Janitra that I was capable of being in love and being loved. And I had myself—I already promised I wouldn't betray myself ever again.

"Are you ready for…what's to come?"

I nodded. "With more and more information, we're more prepared for whatever they're going to throw at us. So far, my track record is promising."

I tried to give him a winning, confident grin but he didn't look as jovial.

"I know you're prepared but I'm still worried."

"What are you worried about, Damir?"

"This plan puts you in direct danger—again and again. Can't a handmaiden or guard serve as your decoy?"

I lingered on the question. Sanjana was splayed on the rug gripping her blanket in a gentle nap while Devraj sat cradled in his father's lap. He had a horse figurine galloping up and down any surface within his reach.

"The people still call me a queen, even though that's not what I do anymore. You know as well as I do that there are some things that ought to come directly from us. Whether anyone else agrees, I want to face these people head on and show them that they can't control me or my family. I have all the support I need, so I am confident I'll succeed in doing what needs to be done."

Damir pursed his lips in thought, not looking at me.

"That handmaiden—Janitra was her name? She cares for you."

It wasn't a question. It was an observation.

In a half-serious, half-joking manner, I replied, "I'd certainly hope so. It's part of the job description."

"As someone who still cares for you and your wellbeing, I can tell when you're in love and someone's in love with you."

"I—"

I didn't have a joke or retort. Was I that obvious? And better yet, was it so obvious that the feelings were mutual?

"I don't know if I ever thanked you for the way you treated Einora when you had every right to tear her down, dismiss her, or hate her. Or really, you had every right to hate me. You still have every right to hate anything about this. But you showed us a great kindness. The least I can do is show that same kindness to you and whomever you spend the rest of your life with."

Still stunned, all I could think to do was smile contentedly at Damir.

I didn't need his blessing or permission to court anyone but it meant something that he would say such kind, supportive things to me in front of our children.

We were a united front then and we were united now. A hope burgeoned within me that with this added armor on my soul, we really did have a fighting chance to face the Black Wings and pluck every last feather away.

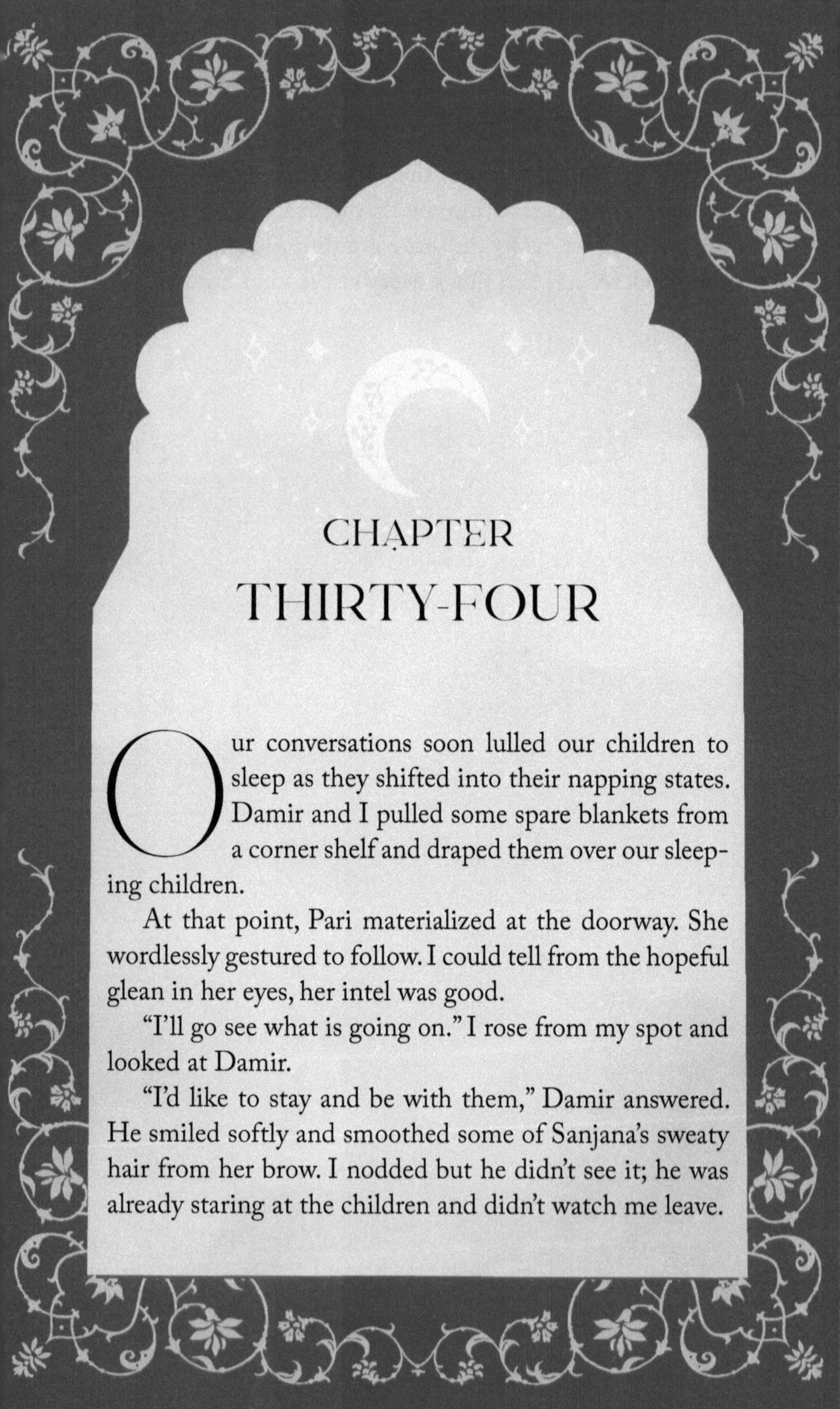

CHAPTER
THIRTY-FOUR

Our conversations soon lulled our children to sleep as they shifted into their napping states. Damir and I pulled some spare blankets from a corner shelf and draped them over our sleeping children.

At that point, Pari materialized at the doorway. She wordlessly gestured to follow. I could tell from the hopeful glean in her eyes, her intel was good.

"I'll go see what is going on." I rose from my spot and looked at Damir.

"I'd like to stay and be with them," Damir answered. He smiled softly and smoothed some of Sanjana's sweaty hair from her brow. I nodded but he didn't see it; he was already staring at the children and didn't watch me leave.

I gathered my wits and followed Pari out the playroom and into the hallway. She lead me through the hallway and to my office. It felt nice to return to some normalcy instead of lingering in my brother's workspace.

Waiting for us stood Gurpreet, Dipa, Ziya, Janitra, and four princes. I gasped in surprise—more at the sight of them wearing highly casual garb and without makeup.

"A pleasure to see you all," I spoke aloud in Ushallavi but signed to the princes. Janitra couldn't help but smile and wink at me. I didn't translate myself for my hand-maidens as I signed, "Are you hoping to blend into the crowd today?"

Bernadino gave me a crooked grin and signed "It doesn't sound like an insult coming from you. Did you fall out of your carriage, dear princess?"

Ekwueme laughed and smiled at the sass but I expected that much. Those two had always acted as though they were my distant, mischievous cousins.

Standing with his hands behind his back, Yeong-Gi broke this pose to sign, "We chose to stay behind with limited staff. Your translators have attempted to explain our options. We're here to provide full support from the north."

"Did you know this?" I turned to Gurpreet but quickly added, "They've chosen to stay and aid us."

"We've cobbled together as much," Gurpreet replied. "But with you here, it won't take all day to figure out what to do with them and for them."

A smile tugged on my lips. "Prince Yeong-Gi, you have the ability to disguise yourself and others, correct?"

The prince nodded. "I understand you need help tricking some would-be assassins. With adequate rest, I can disguise several people if needed."

"That will be helpful. What do you know of the plans thus far?"

I filled in the blanks as necessary. The stoic Newen offered to scout with his bodyguards and use their tracking skills to post in the outskirts of town should any enemies attempt to disappear into the foliage.

Ekwueme and Bernadino would be there for the drama. The overall hope was that enough confusion, rumor, and hostility, the Black Wings might reveal their numbers and presence. It was said that it's easier to kill pests when they're exposed to the sunlight.

"You're too valuable to be the bait," Newen spoke up—well, signed. A slight blush covered his already dark features. "Have you exhausted all your options?"

There was a pause and the handmaidens waited for a response. They looked as though they weren't sure why I stayed silent.

"He's asking why I'm choosing to be bait," I translated.

Gurpreet pursed their lips and nodded in understanding but didn't speak for me.

I locked eyes with Janitra briefly but long enough to give me courage.

"Closure," I told the princes. "These people came for me and my handmaidens years ago in an attempt to kill me and invite strife between us and the rest of the world. I want to send a clear message that I won't let them break me again."

The princes nodded solemnly.

"And besides," I smiled slightly. "With Yeong-Gi's abilities, they might see five of me if they're lucky."

***

"My lady? A moment of your time?"

I looked up as my handmaidens crowded behind me expectantly.

"Pari stepped out momentarily and she's just outside," Ziya explained. "She was able to confirm some vital intel. More importantly, she says the food's ready."

After some palace servants brought us some lunch, Gurpreet directed our attention to a map of Ushallav, specifically the palace and the surrounding city and residential quarters.

Like rays of the sun, the map depicted roads that splayed in every direction; the hub being the palace. The very northern part of the map depicted the Northern Sea. If the map continued on, it would depict our northern allies on the other side. As the roads stretched south, little squares and rectangles depicted a cluttered city that gradually spread out into farmlands, rivers, and the roads that lead to Makaar.

"We were able to confirm that many members of Kavi's neighborhood have been swayed to the Black Wing's side and will likely combine forces to retaliate and rescue him," Ziya began. She pointed at a section of Ushallav that I'd been visiting more often in recent times. "I don't know if the citizens truly gave into the Wings' beliefs but it's safe to say that our approach to this upcoming clash could turn the tides."

"Either the people think that the Black Wings have some solid points or they will retain their faith in us," Dipa added. I could tell that "us" meant more than the royal family; they meant Ushallav as a nation.

"Back to the conversation on bait," Gurpreet continued, looking grimly at the map. "We know that the Black Wings have been meddling with our politics around Queen Anjali. It's very likely that they've been planning more for our lady. Kavi was sent to sway her—maybe use her as a pawn."

As my handmaidens and friends spoke, I signed in translation.

"He's hardly your type, dear," Bernadino signed. He rolled his eyes and smiled. I narrowed my eyes as I felt a blush bloom across my face. Ekwueme swatted at Bernadino's arm and held back a smirk. It was as though he thought the prince was funny but tried to keep things serious.

Gurpreet continued, "As previously stated, we need to be smart. They clearly want Anjali in order to hold power or sway here. Obviously, she can hold her own but this could be a real political disaster if they take her or if there's a slaughter."

There was a break in the conversation as Gurpreet finished speaking and no one had anything to add. The room fell silent as everyone weighed the situation.

Did Kavi and his crew really think that I would just join them after everything that had transpired? It felt like they wanted to emotionally manipulate me—have me fight with a fist tied behind my back.

My jaw tightened. They'd put my children in danger two too many times. They knew that was my real weakness. I would find a way to protect them, protect my people, and not give my freedom away to Kavi's cause.

"Using you as a bait would likely draw the more zealous members here and we could apprehend them. They will likely only risk their identities if you're there," Yeong-Gi spoke, stroking his chin. "My people can help with that. How much time do we have before we launch our plan?"

I looked around the room and landed on my hand-maidens' expectant expressions.

"We could interrogate Kavi again—see if he'll spill," I said aloud and with my fingers. "That could help us better answer that question."

"He won't talk to anyone." Gurpreet folded their arms and gave me a look. "Maybe he's waiting for you specifically."

Janitra looked wary. I wasn't sure if she was worried or angry. I knew she would get the answers out of him by whatever means necessary. I took a guess at her thoughts.

"I can give it a try—my way first," I said. "He may still think I don't know his affiliations with the Black Wings."

Gurpreet and Janitra gave me matching frowns.

"It's worth a shot if it means we have a reliable time-line—or the upper hand," I insisted. "I won't let this ass-hole walk out of here a winner."

"Do you think he is manipulating you so you'll do what he wants?" Newen mused. "Yeong-Gi can send someone down there in your likeness and take care of this."

Dread formed a ball in my gut. I didn't want to explain any intimate details to anyone to help the ruse look and sound believable.

"Just let me do it. Please," I insisted. "You can all wait at the entrance in case I need backup."

I wouldn't dare look my friends in the eyes. So what if this was some trick? Kavi and I were unfortunately intertwined and I would take the steps to break free—Abhijita willing.

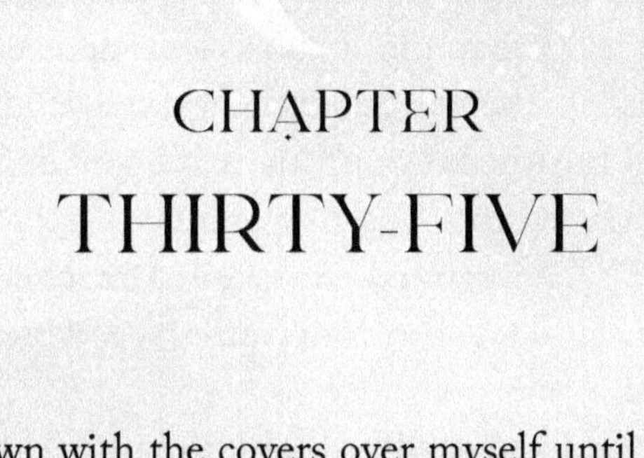

CHAPTER
THIRTY-FIVE

I lay down with the covers over myself until all I could hear was a symphony of calm breathing and snoring. Keeping my own breathing calm, I climbed out of my bed and padded out of the room. The slippers on my feet made my steps hardly perceptible.

Gurpreet silently showed me the way. I followed quiet hallways and stairways down to the dungeons.

"Your Majesty?"

It was more of an incredulous question than anything. A guard stood from their chair and saluted. They expertly positioned their body between me and the occupied cell.

I pulled them close and handed them a note. I didn't want anyone to hear my voice or my intentions. They looked over the note and gave me a look like they weren't sure they believed me but knew that if I wanted to be here, there wasn't much they could do about it.

"It's okay," I assured them. "You'll be here if I need you." We both turned to glance at Gurpreet several paces away—the only visible ally in view.

They palmed a key into my hand and sat in their chair warily but trustingly in response.

Kavi's cell was at the end of a small, stale hallway. The door opened as I turned the key in the lock. In the moonlight, I saw a figure in the shadows shift and stand up.

"Who is it?" The voice sounded gravelly and tired.

"Kavi," I breathed. I don't know if I sounded scared or relieved. I wanted to sound desperate.

"Anjali?" Kavi replied, shocked. I reached out and felt his wrists. I let him touch my face, which he tentatively did.

"I'm so glad you're alive. Thank the gods," I breathed.

"What's going on? Why are you here?"

"My brother, the king, sent me away. I came here to find you as soon as I returned. Are you hurt? Did they do anything to you?"

"They arrested me after your birthday," Kavi replied hurriedly. "I'm fine but they questioned me. Your handmaidens apprehended me. King Ray ordered me to be confined for harming you."

My eyes adjusted to the low light; I could see his eyes shining in the moonlight. It was unclear whether the silver lining his eyes was real or an act.

"Kavi, everything is so, so wrong. I feel like even though you've been in my life for such a short time, you're the only one who understands me and can help me. My handmaidens acted against me—my brother sent me away as punishment…"

"Hush," Kavi cooed. He held me close in a hug–as much as one could. I could hear his shackles stir as he embraced me. I tensed but let out an exhausted sob. "Everything's going to be okay. Anjali, you're shaking."

"No one knows I'm here," I breathed. "Things are going to be very bad if we don't do something to stop it. My ex-husband is here."

That earned me a stunned silence.

"King Damir is here in the palace?" He sounded much too calm about that. That actually chilled me to the bone.

"I think he's here to take my children away. He doesn't trust me. It's not fair! All I've ever done was try to be a good queen, mother, and wife, and some would-be assassins have ruined my life. And my ex-husband is punishing me for all this."

I kept my breathing in check; my confessions of half-truths and half-lies still felt a little too close to home.

"I love my children. What if Damir takes them away and never lets me see them again?"

"That seems a bit extreme for him," Kavi tried.

"But I don't trust his advisers. What if they're making him do all of this? They could use this over Ray's head in the future. I just feel like everyone is acting against me and I don't know what I did to deserve this."

"Your people love you," Kavi said, releasing me so he could cup my face in his hands. "Your people will do anything to protect you and your happiness. Ushallav is with you even if the king isn't."

"What can they do against Ray?"

Kavi's voice dropped even more than I thought imaginable. "If you help me escape, I can get you help. We know that you have the ability to fight but we'd be willing to fight for you. Your hands are already tied but ours aren't."

"Who are you talking about? Who would be helping you?"

"I know some neighbors who have been cheering you on from afar since you arrived. You're a public figure and you've inspired people. You've stuck with your roots and your devotion to the gods through it all. The people will rally behind you against the injustices before you."

"You can't risk your lives for me," I resisted. "This is dangerous stuff."

Kavi let me go and pondered silently.

"The people of Ushallav are ready to stand. They'll stand with you."

He sounded assured and passionate. He kissed my forehead before planting a thoughtful kiss on my lips. It felt nothing like the kiss I shared with Janitra hours before. I couldn't tell if he kissed me because he loved me or if he loved this opportunity I presented him. And to be honest, I was here to toy with this relationship to suit me.

I'd do anything to truly protect my children and my future from Kavi and his ilk. I hoped he would drag out everyone on his list and land them all back here in this dungeon for their crimes against my peace.

"I hired some spies to work around my handmaidens. It's quite possible that Damir will make a move in a few days—maybe sooner—and take my children. I will do what I can to stop him. But I need your help to prevent them from leaving. You need to get ready."

"Wait, what do you have in mind?"

We both could hear Kavi's shackles clatter into the soft hay on the ground. Compared to our whispering, the sound shattered the relative silence.

"The guards won't stop us. I'm getting you out," I explained.

Kavi froze under the moonlight, looking at his hands. It was too dark to tell but I couldn't see any injuries or bruises. Still, he rubbed his wrists in agitation like he was ready to bolt.

"Kavi, I think you're the only person I can trust," I added. I pulled him in for a kiss and he seemed hungry for it. We kissed for what seemed like hours and hours. His lips roamed across my jaw, neck, and chest. I let him but steeled myself. A month ago, I would've melted in his arms. Now, I was fighting for his trust.

"If this works out in our favor," I began tentatively, "I'll fight for you. We'll be unstoppable together. I know you'll get Ushallav on my side but I'll always be by yours."

"Gods," Kavi breathed. It sounded like he was drowning in my skin and words and was coming up for air. I needed him to be drunk on my promises.

"Would you marry me—after all this?"

Kavi smiled in the moonlight. My mind screamed—did he look so sincere because he was truly delighted at the prospect of being my future husband or the prospect that he won me over for the Black Wings. I wanted to vomit but I was so close. My risk would hopefully turn into a reward.

"If you'll have me," he grinned crookedly. I had to admit, he looked handsome in his response.

"I better get back to my chambers before anyone realizes I'm gone," I whispered. "I'll get you out of here."

I took Kavi's hand gently and led him out of the cell. We padded away and passed the guard who gave a convincing show of sleeping on the job. The very first light of morning winked in the sky as I guided Kavi to the stables. He gave me one last hungry kiss before climbing onto the waiting horse, cracking the reins and tearing off the palace premises and out into the world.

Moments later, I shed my simple clothes and donned a nightgown. Janitra stirred on the other side of the bed and I pretended to adjust myself in my sleep.

"Darling," Janitra muttered half-asleep. "Are you all right?"

I sighed into the arm she wrapped around me. Her body heat and blankets warmed me quickly; my encounter with Kavi chilled me to the bone.

"I did my part," I replied simply. As if sensing my heaviness, she pulled me closer and stroked my arm softly until I felt my eyes droop.

I prayed to the gods that I hadn't just royally messed everything up.

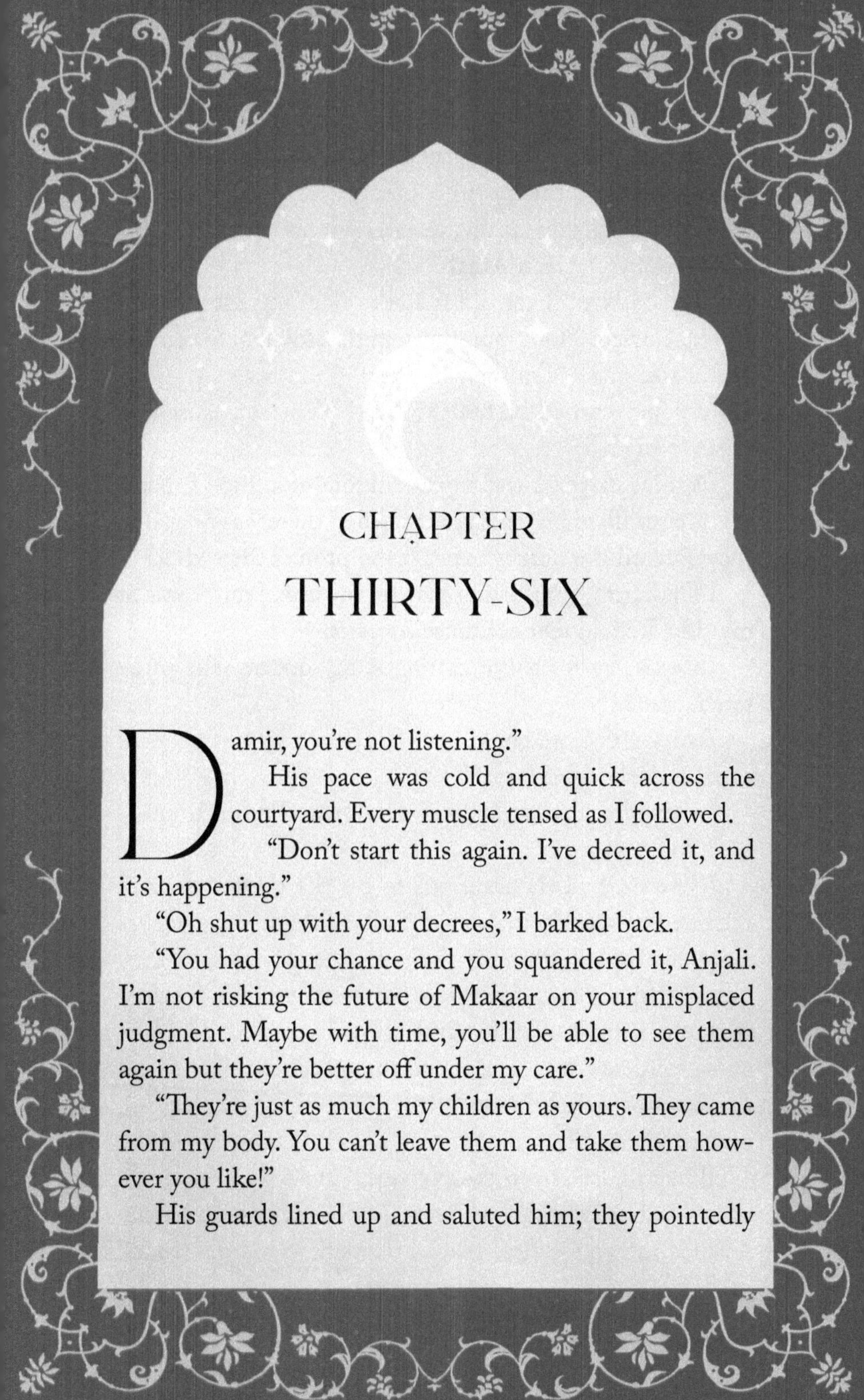

CHAPTER

THIRTY-SIX

Damir, you're not listening."

His pace was cold and quick across the courtyard. Every muscle tensed as I followed.

"Don't start this again. I've decreed it, and it's happening."

"Oh shut up with your decrees," I barked back.

"You had your chance and you squandered it, Anjali. I'm not risking the future of Makaar on your misplaced judgment. Maybe with time, you'll be able to see them again but they're better off under my care."

"They're just as much my children as yours. They came from my body. You can't leave them and take them however you like!"

His guards lined up and saluted him; they pointedly

avoided my gaze. Damir turned his back to me, his travel cloak swaying in the morning breeze.

Without looking at me, he boarded his carriage.

"Goodbye, Queen Anjali."

"You bastard!" I cried. I made to slam my fist into the closed carriage door but the guards stood between us. Still, I screamed, "I'm their mother!"

My fury carried across the wind. Who was going to come to my aid?

Damir's carriage was in the middle of a line of many. His guards filled his carriage and when there was no room, they entered the nearby carriages to protect their king.

I felt a firm, comforting grip on my arm. Janitra was at my side; I could feel her tense support.

"Step away from the carriages, my queen," she muttered quietly.

As if on cue, we could hear Sanjana cry from Damir's carriage, "Mama? Mama!"

I struggled against Janitra's caution and protection. "No!"

I knew I had the strength to rip the door away and retrieve my children. Janitra still held me in place as a signal rippled through the carriage drivers and they urged their horses forward. The line lurched forward with the intention of leaving the palace grounds. Ushallavi soldiers dutifully opened the gates that would lead the entourage through a slightly more covert exit leading toward Makaar.

Breaking free from the carriage, I started to run a few paces, yelling at them to stop. Just as Damir's carriage reached the gates, three black arrows flew and embedded themselves into the carriage. A fourth arrow slammed into the driver's skull.

Without a pause, the carriage just in front of Damir's carriage exploded into flames.

"Sanjana! Devraj!" I screamed. A shiver of recognition and dread rolled down my spine like icy liquid. Frozen to the spot, Janitra came to my side and held me upright. She motioned to the remaining handmaidens and they sprang into action.

Clad in sleek armor, Pari and Dipa ran forward to get closer to the action with the hope of releasing the children from the carriage. Their breastplates, arm bracers, and full face masks glinted in the early sunlight as wood and gold moved with their powerful limbs.

My heart thundered in my chest. The arrows buried deep into the carriage reminded me of a similar carriage. The one that held my dead handmaidens—practically my sisters. The one I rode in my dreams when Abhijita visited me.

Carriages. Arrows. Death. Survival.

I sank to my knees and cried. Janitra lowered herself to hold me.

"They've got this," she whispered in my ear. "Just be patient, darling."

My sobs filled every space in my body and exploded out of every inch of skin. I howled in a way only a mother knows how.

I got to my feet and started making my way to the carriage.

As I ventured closer, other figures started to enter the stage. As if drawn by the smoke billowing up into the morning sky, people dressed as palace servants, gardeners, and farmers approached the space. Some of them turned to me and held their hands up.

"Your Highness, you needn't put yourself in danger—"

"Ushallav stands with you against tyranny!"

"Makaar will fall!"

Someone threw their arms around me and turned to direct me away from the flames and back inside the stables.

"Kavi?" I cried incredulously. How did he reach me so quickly? "Where is—?"

"I've got my best people going in to rescue the children. And I've got even better people to ensure Damir doesn't leave."

I couldn't tell by his spirited, passionate speech if he meant to suggest that Damir would die here. I shuddered and Kavi took it as a cue to hold me close in what I imagined he meant to be a comforting embrace. He kissed my brow before kissing my lips. I didn't kiss him back.

"We will ensure your victory, my queen."

I closed my eyes but I could feel his smile against my lips. I kept replaying the vision of those arrows making their mark—again.

"Black arrows," I muttered, almost letting the insanity take over.

"Yes, they're dipped in black paint," Kavi replied, a bit confused.

"There's no one in here!" We heard someone shout.

My eyes fluttered open and we looked to the line of carriages and the partially open gates now drawing close. The growing commotion drew us to our feet. Kavi guided me to a standing position as we peered out to whoever shouted.

I noticed Janitra was gone—likely joining my other handmaidens in their work.

"What do you mean?" someone else asked.

"There's no king or kids in here!" came the reply. "It's empty!"

"What?" Kavi sputtered incredulously. He tried to leave my side but I held him close and choked out a sob.

"What's going on? Where are my babies?"

A group of about ten people edged closer to the carriage marked with arrows. Their confusion and curiosity drew them close like flies to a carcass.

"Secure the queen!" someone yelled. I quickly released Kavi and took a step away.

"What's going on, Kavi?"

"You're not safe here," he replied. My tears dried on my cheeks and his affection for me soured. He tried to close the space between us but I took another step away.

"I'm not going anywhere. My children need me."

"Your kingdom needs you."

"I need you to back the fuck up," I seethed.

Shock rippled across his features but he recovered quickly. He took my casual morning clothing as an assumption that I wasn't ready and armed for such an encounter and lunged for me.

He tried to grab my robes so I swiped a forearm to block and slap his grasp away. I sent my other fist into his side before sweeping to the side and swinging my foot into his face. He reeled back from the quick combo as I held up my fists defensively.

"Did you not hear her? She said to back the fuck up," came Janitra's voice. Like a shadow, she materialized just behind me before stepping in front of me. She was now clad in handmaiden armor.

Kavi grimaced as he held the heel of his hand to his bleeding nose.

"You're not worthy of your station," he said, pointing a finger at her. "You failed her once. Her people will not let you fail again."

"Your people killed my handmaidens and nearly killed me," I seethed. "I know those arrows anywhere. The blood and guilt are on your hands, Kavi."

He gave me a look like he was disappointed but not surprised that I put the pieces together.

"Will you go quietly to face justice for your crimes?" I demanded of Kavi.

He gave a crooked smile as blood snaked down and over his upper lip. "We're not the only Black Wings that fly. You'll never fully clip our wings."

"You slaughtered my handmaidens and nearly took my life—all in the hopes of clipping my wings and making me your songbird. I'll take what I can get this day if it means that someone will face justice for what you've done to me and my family."

Janitra unsheathed a curved dagger—as long as her forearm from hilt to tip. Crouching in front of me in a defensive position, she growled, "Ushallav will be free of you—today and always."

Kavi growled as he feigned to lunge for the two of us before turning on his heel to retreat. He shouted something to the wind and attempted to jump into the billowing smoke so we'd lose sight of him.

For a moment, his choices distracted us from the fact that several archers with black arrows pointed at us approached me. I held up my hands defensively as Janitra still held up her weapon and assessed the line of attackers.

"Let the queen come with us and you won't get hurt," one warned.

Janitra crouched and made an attempt at slicing the closest assailant around their legs. In return, one of them shot her point blank in the head.

I shrieked in horror. She looked up at the arrow poised and hovering just between her eyes but not piercing her mask.

The air rippled like desert heat as Yeong-Gi's glamour fell away. Standing in full black armor, it was clear that a helmet protected his head. With the reveal, he stood at his full stature. He held his hands up defensively, but instead of curling them into fists, his fingers splayed out as if they were weapons enough.

The arrow fell harmlessly to the ground.

The archers looked dumbfounded at the prince of Haneul. Their strings slackened only a fraction as Yeong-Gi's appearance inspired action and confusion across the entire courtyard. Together, we used their surprise to our advantage as we systematically fought and disarmed the line of enemies.

Ushallavi and Haneulan soldiers rimmed the outer and lower walls, further boxing in our unwanted guests and the line of carriages. Haneulan soldiers poured out of the carriages where Makaarian soldiers were meant to be.

"They've got glamours!" A Black Wing member shrieked.

Across the fray, I locked eyes with Kavi. Any mask of a lover crumbled away as if *he* finally put the pieces together. I fixed my lips into a frown and raised my chin. I hoped he saw a fierce, fed-up queen instead of a weak plaything.

"Are you all right?"

Janitra, my Janitra, stood at my side. I gave her my best reassuring grin and said, "Probably not. It's good to have you here."

She smiled as her decoy left my side and began muttering something in a language I hadn't studied yet. He sent a gust of wind from his fingers and pulled an archer from the walls down to the ground.

Now that my ruse was complete, I removed my robe to reveal my own warrior's garb and armor. Like my handmaidens, I had a breastplate and arm bracers strapped over a sturdy cream tunic and trousers. The breastplate covered everything from the top of my neck to my navel.

The leather and wood armor made me felt strong like a sturdy tree trunk. I already felt fueled by rage and the mother bear strength in me; the armor gave me permission to soar into the fight.

Janitra silently handed me a strap of soft leather. I gratefully took it and pulled my long, unbound hair away from my face.

"Yeong-Gi's decoys are fine. Their armor and magic buffered the arrows. Damir and the children are safe and undiscovered where we hid them. Are you sure you're okay? That sobbing didn't sound fake."

"It's hard to say what was real and what was pretend. We can figure that out once all these people are out of my courtyard and lined up for questioning."

Despite the whorls of fighting, Janitra leaned in close and gave me a quick kiss. One that I happily returned.

"Yeong-Gi's glamour wasn't that bad," she tried to get me to crack a smile. And I did.

"He's a quick study," I conceded. "He really liked the lines you suggested. I almost forgot you were elsewhere."

"Well, now I'm here—right where I want to be."

And the defensive position she took, the one that partially separated me from the rest of the battle, reminded me of a parallel sparring situation. Only instead of a Gurpreet helping me test the mettle of my future handmaiden, we faced the Black Wings. United.

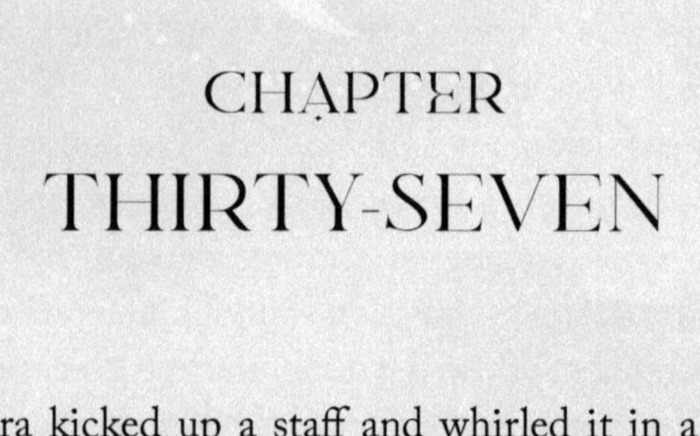

CHAPTER
THIRTY-SEVEN

Janitra kicked up a staff and whirled it in a striking stance. My hands and wrists, still wrapped, tightened as I held them defensively against the sides of my face. Light on our feet, we engaged with the Black Wings still on their feet.

Our guards, as well as the entourage of the northern princes, soon made light work of the Black Wing archers. They brought them down with arrows or got onto the walls and captured them.

When concocting our plan, we weren't sure how many Black Wings to expect. We were fairly matched in numbers but our attackers fought like they had nothing to lose. I half hoped that they would pull their punches at the sight of me—the queen they apparently fawned over and wanted to protect. Now, it seemed like they were striking first and seeking forgiveness much later.

I didn't like that I had to strike them down, and I didn't relish how easy it seemed to be. Abhijita's ways and wisdom guided me in the dance of protecting myself and my family without killing my people.

Bodies dropped to the ground. The nearest ally would secure them with rope or shackles. We agreed hours ago that outright killing anyone would prevent us from learning more about their true numbers, and the aggression could anger more Ushallavi people.

Hot pain shot through my left forearm and I swore loudly.

"Anjali!"

An arrow pierced my bracer and into my arm as I used it to shield my face. I was lucky that it wasn't severe but that didn't stop the panic and pain rippling through my whole arm.

"Search for the remaining archer!" Janitra called out.

"Anjali." Newen practically materialized at my side. His soldiers shielded us as he quickly pulled the arrow from my arm and quickly wrapped it before more of my blood seeped out. I hissed in pain as the prince pulled the material tightly and securely. My left arm now felt sluggish and useless in the fight but my right arm could still strike and defend.

As sweat started to dampen my face and hair, I steadied my breath and caught something moving in my eye. Kavi. He slipped from tree to tree and back into the palace. Newen seemed to sense what I had seen. I signed to him,

"I'm following that man inside. Send backup."

"Of course, Your Majesty," he signed.

"Thank you." I gave him a small hug and ran after Kavi alone before I lost his lying, conniving, betraying visage. I called for backup but didn't wait for it.

By the time I caught up, I had an idea of where Kavi was heading. I recognized the path to my brother's offices. As I observed Kavi's path, I couldn't help but roll my eyes. He had found ways to move just out of the Watchful Eye's path as they lined the walls.

He helped beautify them, so he knew how to avoid his own designs—his own creations. I guessed that he intended to do something that the gods would disapprove of.

Like a pest scuttling under the rugs and behind tapestries, Kavi swiftly slunk through the hallways. I practically ran at full speed to keep him in sight. He didn't seem to care that he could hear my feet not too far behind.

I swore he threw a smile over his shoulder before forcing open the door and slamming it behind him.

The door didn't fully click shut, so I threw it back open. "Kavi!"

My brother sat cross-legged on the floor and gave me a "don't act rashly" look in his eye. Three Black Wings trained their arrows at Ray's head; black scarves covered their heads from the nose down. Kavi sat coolly in my brother's chair like he hadn't just sprinted through the palace to get there.

"Right on time, darling," Kavi smiled.

"I am not your darling."

"There's plenty of time to discuss what you could be to me."

"You have no right and no cards to play with," I countered. "Even with a wounded arm, I won't have any issue dealing with you."

"Promise?" Kavi gave me what could've been a flirtatious grin and cock of his eyebrow. I scowled.

In a swift move, I threw up a teapot in the air and swiped it with my foot. With the kick, I sent it flying through the room and shattering against the wall. Kavi put a hand to his left ear, replacing his grin with a look of shock. Blood and cold tea dripped down his temple.

"I'm the trustworthy one here," I countered. "Underestimating me will be the last mistake you make."

"I wouldn't dare think less of you, dear Anjali." Kavi ripped away part of Ray's sash to staunch the bleeding. "In fact, I expected you would come. Your love for your family nearly outshines your love for Ushallav. Which is why I bought you here. We'll bargain with you so everyone will go to bed tonight happily and peacefully."

My patience felt razor thin with the reference to a bed. The slight upturn in his lip suggested that he meant to speak with a slight innuendo.

"If you think I'll go with you to fulfill your sick war fantasies to kill a bunch of Makaarians, you're wrong. That won't bring back the Ushallavi we lost. It won't bring my grandparents back, it won't bring my aunties, uncles, or cousins back. It won't bring back anyone you once loved."

"Are you willing to lose your children? The longer you talk, the sooner we'll find your hidden children and the

Makaarian king. Do you want to see any of them pierced with our arrows?”

I threw teacups and plates at him, creating a puddle of pottery shards around his person and across the wall.

“In my heart, I knew I was right to not let them around you. You’re sick to think that you can so blatantly threaten my family.”

“Your family? The only reason why you retain any of your power is because you bore the Makaarian heirs.”

I narrowed my eyes and didn’t break eye contact. Kavi’s eyes flickered and he gasped slightly. I felt like with each tick of time that I inhaled and exhaled, I grew in size and resiliency.

He was lying. And I was not going to argue with a liar.

I tilted my head to the side, challenging him to say anything else. In this brief window of time, I remembered that he and the Black Wings were only here because we had provoked them with what they wanted to hear.

For the first time in months—years—I felt more in control of my life and my worth as a person than ever. I was staring at archers threatening my brother but this was our trap.

“You—you,” Kavi struggled. “Were you seriously willing to watch your children ride away with Damir? Our chance of raising them in Ushallavi ways would leave with them. What is your play here?”

“My children are not pawns.”

“It won’t matter how you define it—we will find them and take them away if you don’t come with us. It’s the only way to show you how we want to shape Ushallav’s future.”

For effect, the archers flexed their bowstrings and we

could all hear the sounds of the strain. A careless move could slam an arrow into my brother. Ray did his best to look unbothered. Sweat beaded his forehead. Kavi gripped the armrests of Ray's chair, clearly vexed.

"You're willing to risk the death of your brother and king—why?"

"You are the ones holding weapons at him—not me. You're willing to risk murdering the king for your gains. This is how much I don't want to do what you say. I don't serve the Black Wings. I serve my people and the gods. Who do you serve?"

Kavi's face shook, unnerved.

"Despite what you may think, I want to help my people," I went on, "I know how much the wars with Makaar wounded the dead and the living. But throwing us back into the fighting will not serve you. Crippling our newest ally by threatening their future king—my son—will not serve Ushallav.

"Can you not see this from my perspective? I was serving my country in Ushallav. Your Black Wings killed my handmaidens and nearly killed me—nearly killed my unborn daughter. You think I want to listen to you and cower to your demands?

"You then try to worm your way into the palace, and I'm no fool to think that our meeting was just a 'chance.' It would be one thing if you or any of the Black Wings approached the palace with your petitions and concerns. But according to our archives—"

"Why would we? You weren't here to listen to us. Our king wouldn't listen to us!" Kavi sneered. I looked into the eyes of the archers, wondering if they would speak for themselves. Were they just as passionate as the likes of Kavi or were they sold a lie?

"According to our archives, no one has approached us about their concerns about Makaar. As citizens or a group, you haven't made a formal plea. My king didn't listen to you? We don't listen to violence. I understand that it's not easy to petition anyone to hear you. What I don't understand is why you would choose to stalk and harm my family instead of ever trying to be heard?"

Kavi rose from Ray's chair and made some sort of frustrated growl in his throat.

"This is taking too long," he muttered. "You royals wouldn't understand. You never have."

A flash of a blade reflected quickly in the light and suddenly a red line materialized across Ray's neck. Kavi had just wrapped an arm around Ray and swiped a small knife across his neck.

Ray finally spoke a few syllables as the line dribbled with blood. I couldn't understand—why was my brother speaking in Haneuli?

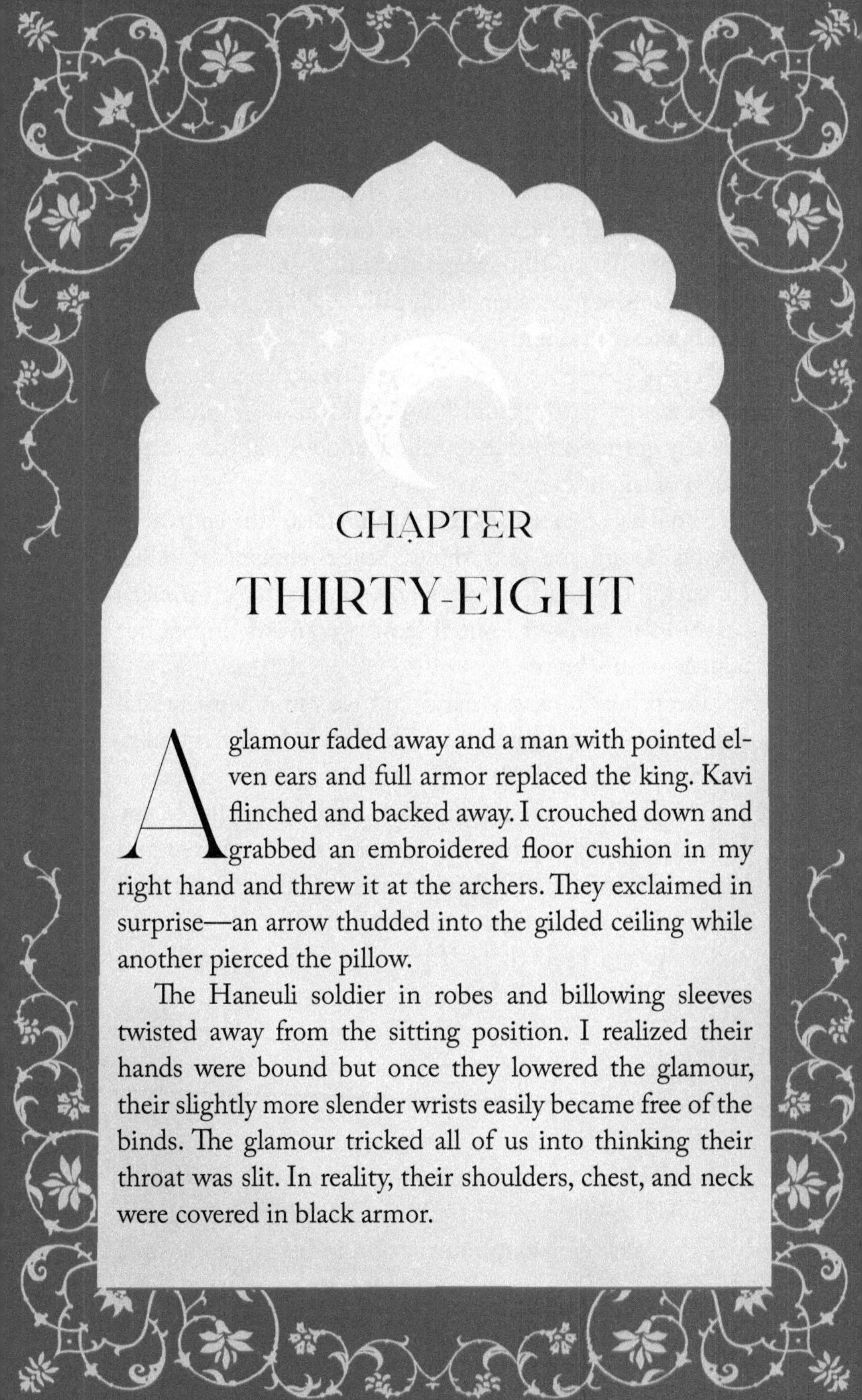

CHAPTER
THIRTY-EIGHT

A glamour faded away and a man with pointed elven ears and full armor replaced the king. Kavi flinched and backed away. I crouched down and grabbed an embroidered floor cushion in my right hand and threw it at the archers. They exclaimed in surprise—an arrow thudded into the gilded ceiling while another pierced the pillow.

The Haneuli soldier in robes and billowing sleeves twisted away from the sitting position. I realized their hands were bound but once they lowered the glamour, their slightly more slender wrists easily became free of the binds. The glamour tricked all of us into thinking their throat was slit. In reality, their shoulders, chest, and neck were covered in black armor.

They said something to me—I think?—but I didn't understand. I did understand their meaning as they broke down the door and sent precise strikes against two Black Wings members guarding the door. I followed, holding another thick pillow along my left side as a makeshift shield.

"Help!" I bellowed into the hallways. I heard several footfalls approaching, and I hoped it was more allies. My one ally gestured for me to follow and we ran toward the sound of thundering boots.

Shouting greeted us on both sides. The northern princes found me and signed some phrases of relief. Ekwueme threw a thick poncho—almost like a traveler's cloak—over me, and I felt at least two arrows impact but bounce off my body.

The prince took my hand and we ran down the hall as his retinue stayed behind. In broken Ushallavi, he said,

"Stay alive, Anjali!"

My arm throbbed with pain, reminding me of my current state of exhaustion. I shook the hand free and Ekwueme understood that he was prickling an injured arm. I used just my right hand to sign,

"Trap and bind them if you can. The man with the beard…he's the main threat."

As if summoning him with my signing, Kavi appeared in my peripheral. He sneered as he slunk through the hallway in the opposite direction. I was sure he hoped to slink away without consequence.

I pulled a knife from Ekwueme's belt and chucked it at Kavi. The blade caught him in the calf, which caused him to stumble. Enough disruption in his stride meant I could catch up with him and send my good fist into his right kidney.

A sputtered cough wheezed out expectedly as he doubled over. I grabbed a fistful of his tunic under leather pauldrons and shoved him into the wall. Several commands in different languages barraged my ears but it didn't stop me from punching him in the face. He crumpled to the floor and I picked up the knife.

Kavi curled into himself, inhaling and exhaling wetly.

"As long as I live, Ushallav will progress toward the future and it won't dwell in the past. And you won't come near me or my family again."

My chest heaved, full of adrenaline and righteous fury. If Abhijita guided me, I would continue to strike but my adversary wasn't getting up.

I honestly didn't know whether to subdue him for interrogating or kill him right here. I supposed that it wasn't for me to decide; Ray could choose. I'd made enough choices on a personal and political scale for a lifetime.

At my side, Gurpreet put a hand on my good arm.

"I've got this," they promised as they motioned to others behind me to apprehend Kavi. I knew this meant it was time to step back. Prince Ekwueme found me and ushered me to actually follow this time.

"Is it over?" I called out over my shoulder—to anyone.

Ekwueme, donned in a similar poncho, put a protective arm around me. After a minute of sprinting together, I saw Janitra. Something like an exhale and a warbled cry escaped me and she put a hand to her heart.

More soldiers and fighters flew past me in a blur as she took me in her arms.

"Are you okay?" I shakily asked. I patted her arms before cupping her face. In the space of an hour I thought that I'd watched her and my brother bleed—even if it was just a glamour.

"I am!" Janitra promised. Her hands, caked with dirt and blood, covered mine still over her cheeks. "My love—"

"We're not done yet!" I heard Kavi rise above the din. I didn't deign to look at him or reply.

I turned away from him to not let his challenge reach me. He wasn't going to call the shots—he never did.

"Gurpreet and the other handmaidens have him," Janitra said, observing for me. "I think he looks a bit embarrassed that he's been caught."

She tucked a strand of sweaty hair out of my face. "Next time you want to be a hero, don't leave me in the dust like that."

I sighed in her arms. "I know. I just didn't want him to get out of my sight. Everything went according to plan."

We embraced tightly. "Still, don't ever do that again," Janitra murmured in my hair.

"Okay. Promise."

<hr>

Pari and Dipa insisted I go to the infirmary with the others but I asked for a moment to myself. They did a lot more combat than me, so they had more cuts and broken bones to address. They gave me knowing smiles as they took their own advice and watched me delay reasonable action.

I just needed a moment with a warm drink and a view of the morning horizon. The sun glittering up, up, up, across the ocean and into a new day.

"I promise, I'm coming," I groaned to an oncoming figure. I leaned on the railing under an open-air archway and reveled in the beautiful breeze. The warmth of someone else at my good elbow was nice but suggested my moment of solace was ending.

"You pulled your punches, Anji," Gurpreet chuckled. I sighed, relieved.

"I know enough about Kavi. He can barely win an arm wrestling match. I didn't want to over-do it."

Gurpreet nodded and took in the view with me. I could tell the palace was starting to relax and ease into peace by the way the birds returned to the fruit trees and a cat resumed its sun tanning session.

"I shouldn't have wasted my time with him." I rolled my eyes.

"You and Janitra make a much more suitable couple," Gurpreet agreed. "I didn't want to sway you but the other sanctuary attendants are huge fans."

I smiled at the thought.

"I was talking about today's scuffle, but I'm sure both things can be true."

"I'm probably going to tease you about Kavi, but not today," Gurpreet said, nudging my right arm with her left. "The plan worked. When I get the all-clear, I've got a lot of questions. We'll get a full list of Black Wing members in no time."

I groaned. "There's still so much to be done."

"It's Ray's job. He'll call you in later. You've done so much. The sanctuary is still available if you need it. For a real break this time."

I bit back a quick retort. Her answer of "it's Ray's job" rubbed me the wrong way. Of course, it was his job. King Ray ought to handle this threat. But this threat was made against me in a deeply personal way. Could I trust that he'd do the job right? Or was this thinking what got me here in the first place?

"Ah, maybe. I think I'd prefer to vacation somewhere more child-friendly. It's been a long week. Did I tell you that Devraj has been missing his father? I'm sure Damir's sudden return is going to be…"

I couldn't even finish the thought. We rarely talked about parenting—there weren't many opportunities beyond our previous letter correspondence anyway. I wasn't about to overwhelm my child-free friend with the details—nor was I ready to try and find the words to explain Devraj's complicated feelings. Of course, he missed his father and wanted everything restored to the way things were before Sanjana's birth.

I had just apprehended the people responsible for many of the wrongs in our lives but I already prepared to feel like a bad mother explaining to him that I wouldn't be returning to Makaar, and it wasn't the agreed time to send the children there, either.

I felt a reassuring hand on my back and I returned to reality. A mixture of relief and shame twisted across my sore frame. I'd already learned so much in such a short time but I wasn't fully healed from unseen wounds. Something in Gurpreet's gesture told me that I had more time to learn how to combat my negative thoughts.

"Pari said as much. I'm sure with some breakfast and a nap, you'll know how to handle it today. This is why you're royalty and I'm not. You were born to sort this out—you and Ray and the rest of your family."

"And you don't think you'd make a good parent? Half of parenting is asking the kids if they are hungry or tired."

"I regularly attend to Abhijita's children. My hands are quite full." At that, we both laughed. I put a hand to my side as I felt a cramp bloom at my hip.

"Let's get going. We have a reservation at the infirmary." My friend coaxed me away from one of the most beautiful sunrises I'd witnessed and on to the rest of the day.

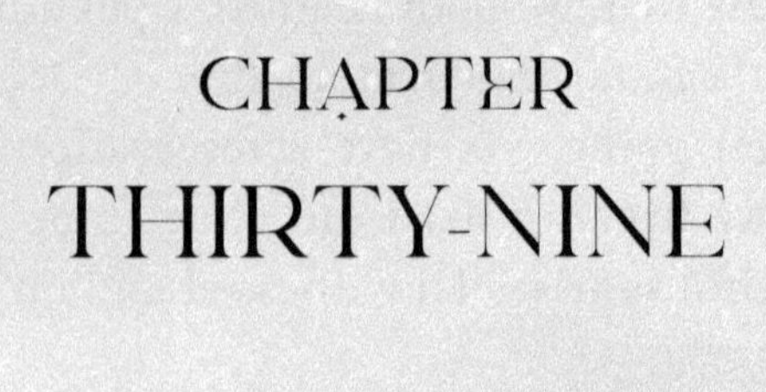

CHAPTER
THIRTY-NINE

Gurpreet and I lay in parallel beds as people in clean tunics and dupattas wrapped us with poultices and bandages. Despite our strength and stature, we meekly rested and followed instructions. I didn't ask for it but an attendant arrived with powders and lotions then dabbed carefully at my exposed skin.

"You already look like you got a full night's sleep," Gurpreet drawled, turning their head toward me.

"Everyone's doing their job and doing them well," I smiled. "Damir and the children will be here soon and I think we'll all feel better if I look a bit more refreshed."

What I really meant was that I didn't want to worry them beyond the bandaged arm.

Gurpreet nodded. Their brows arched, impressed.

Once the attendant removed their tools and bowed, I dismissed them and looked at my arms and hands. I appeared whole and clean. The attendants and healers felt excessive; all my remaining pain was inside my head and heart. A poultice couldn't reach those spaces.

I felt like Abhijita was using this moment to remind me that where a healing balm couldn't go, I had the power to enter and perform healing.

As I flexed my hands and felt this thought pound in my blood, little hands of a similar hue fell into my grasp.

"Mama!" Devraj cried. Without needing permission, he climbs into my embrace. I wrapped a left arm around him and pulled Sanjana up with a right arm. I all but crushed them in a hug.

"Come here. Come here," I murmured as I kissed their faces.

My eyes couldn't help but cry with happiness. I realized that all the strength I had and built up every day was not just for me but for them. No matter what would come, I will always be strong enough to protect them, gods willing. That is, until it was their turn to be strong for those they loved.

I looked up and smiled, perhaps a bit sheepishly, at Damir. He returned my gaze, and I could feel that he saw through the makeup and bandages. He kindly said nothing as he stood respectfully at the edge of the bed. Why did I want him to kiss my brow? And yet, I was relieved that he not only stood at a respectful distance but my brother joined his side. The room hushed as their king silently accepted their bows of respect.

I saw Gurpreet close their eyes in my peripheral vision.

At this moment, they apparently decided to pretend they were asleep.

"Is Gurpreet dead?" Devraj asked, aghast, in a hushed tone.

"They're sleeping, Devraj."

I didn't have to point out the obvious but it was easily felt: months ago, we were all in an eerily-similar situation where a tired king and his heirs came to visit their wounded queen after battle. I looked at Damir and hoped we wouldn't keep meeting like this in the future.

"It's good to see you both," I acknowledged the kings at the foot of my bed.

They looked at each other with tight grins before looking at me holding my children. Devraj wasn't waiting to recount the whole morning from his perspective while Sanjana held my hair in her hands and played with it.

"I thought it best to come tell you in person that our plan worked and the palace is once again secured and safe. The visiting royalty, including Damir here, are eager to see you back on your feet. I imagine we'll have more to discuss once you're healed—or at least until you convince us that 'you've been through worse' or something of that nature."

I opened my mouth to confirm that I most certainly have sustained worse injuries but chose to roll my eyes instead.

"Please come see me at your earliest convenience, sister," Ray said, giving me a meaningful look. "And pass on the good news to Gurpreet? They're at least getting in some good rest."

A small, innocent smile sat on my friend's face.

Once the healers said I could finally leave, I collected myself but didn't walk toward my brother's domain of politics and decision-making. I instead practically ran to the children's playroom.

Peals of laughter and screams greeted me.

"You're here, Mama!" Sanjana announced.

I wasn't sure which adults would be here with the children, but I wasn't expecting to see Damir and Janitra. My eyes flickered to them quickly before devoting my attention to Sanjana as she raised her arms and I picked her up. Devraj dropped a toy horse and joined us in greeting.

"Are you having fun? That toy looks new."

"Papa brought it! I have three horses now."

"Let's see them all lined up, Dev. It's a beautiful horse. Does it have a name?"

"Not yet," Devraj sounded a bit disappointed. He held his other cloth-stuffed horses with smudges of past stains of play and gestured to the one in his left hand. "This one's already called Horse."

"Ah," I laughed. "Give it some time. I'm sure the name will come to you after your next adventure."

I sat on a low couch and set Sanjana down as I felt her sink down my right hip and eagerly joined her brother. I finally looked up at Damir and Janitra observing us. I tried to determine what I'd missed before arriving.

I decided I didn't care. I practically leaped from the couch and embraced Janitra.

"Are you okay?"

I felt her shift and she murmured, "I'm still a bit sore but I'm fine." Her sari covered up most of her body so to my eyes, she looked tired at most. She looked lovely and perfect. She smiled reassuringly.

"You look victorious."

"Thank you."

I would've said something delicious and witty but we weren't alone. And my kids wouldn't hesitate to tell their grandparents a single thing.

I turned to Damir. "Have you had a chance to chat? Get acquainted?"

Janitra rose from her seat to hug me and slowly sunk back in her seat and I joined her. Damir, in his more casual tunic and trousers, sat up a bit straighter.

"She clarified a few things. Her Makaarian is very good, I might add," Damir replied in Makaarian. "She's traveled far to serve as a handmaiden but it's clear that she's no longer…in your service?"

I didn't want to sound sheepish or cowardly.

"I did choose her as a handmaiden but we are now courting. It's a bit of a new thing. But now that we've all dealt with the Black Wings, we can finally have some dinner and chat."

I tried not to blush but I couldn't help but smile. It had been a while since I felt so happy and hopeful.

"What does 'courting' mean?" Devraj piped up.

"It means that Janitra and I are spending time together because we love each other."

"Your list!" Devraj exclaimed, like it all clicked for him. A flicker of confusion crossed Damir's features.

To Damir, I explained, "When our parents decided we would marry, they made things quite easy for us. You made a list when you believed I was gone, right? The children helped me with my list."

Damir smiled sadly.

"I didn't really like the list, Papa," Devraj admitted.

"Why, Dev?" Damir chuckled at his son's honesty.

"I want to go home," Devraj replied, like that explained everything.

"You'll get to go home but you are already home. You have two wonderful homes. One with me and Einora and the other with your mother."

Devraj still wrinkled his nose with a pout. His chin sunk to his chest. But he still nodded as his eyes looked to the carpet. I wanted to reach out and say something but his father moved faster.

"We are happy, Dev. Things are going to be okay. Just because we have two different homes doesn't mean we're mad or sad. Einora makes me happy. I hope that Janitra makes your mother happy."

Janitra gave my hand a squeeze and I squeezed back.

Devraj looked up at the adults' faces as if trying to discern if his father was telling the truth.

"We love you, Dev. Come here." I reached out with both arms and he eagerly clambered into my chest. I pulled us up and swung him around to elicit a laugh.

I whispered, "We'll figure this out together." Whether anyone else heard me, it didn't matter.

After I spun us around a few times, I gently put him back on the ground and he giggled and tumbled.

"Mama, will Janitra play with us?"

"Of course, I will," Janitra affirmed.

"And tell stories?"

"Yes." Her confident, calm smile grew.

"And carry!" Sanjana added. As if to give the most satisfying answer, Janitra picked up Sanjana up and over her head and sat her on her shoulders. Sanjana giggled wildly as Janitra held her little legs for stability and ran a little circle around Devraj.

I smiled and locked eyes with Damir.

"She fits the bill," he murmured, as if to only reach my ears.

"Janitra is still sore from beating up bad guys this morning," I insisted, pulling Sanjana off Janitra's beautiful shoulders and back to the ground. As if on cue, Devraj and Sanjana began play-fighting—likely reenacting what they thought transpired this morning.

My children would probably broach this topic again and again. And I probably wouldn't be able to distract them so easily when they were more aware of the world and how our choices formed it. Yet, I felt a bit more prepared for those future moments.

I looked to Janitra and Damir. We were prepared.

CHAPTER
FORTY

I adjusted the waistband of my floor-length skirt and admired the embroidery. The skirt and blouse shimmered in my favorite shade of teal. The side parted as I moved, revealing a cream underskirt. I shrugged on a magenta embroidered dupatta that trailed behind me as I made my way to Ray's office.

There wasn't any reason to be nervous; this meeting was going to happen even if the Black Wings hadn't taken bold strikes against us. If anything, I was eager to see the princes after everything happened. Hopefully they weren't as wounded as I was. Maybe they were dolled up like me so Ray and I wouldn't feel as bad.

A guard opened the door for me and allowed me passage. I nodded at each prince before acknowledging

Ray. I was met with tired faces. I smiled wearily through my makeup.

Ekwueme gave a small wave to catch my attention. With speed, he signed, "You're a tough fighter. Can you teach me?"

I grinned and signed back in the affirmative.

"You held your own. We couldn't have done it without you."

"Prince Yeong-Gi was the star of the show," Bernadino added, giving a playful nudge to the stoic and politely smiling shapeshifter. It was an ability that many Haneuli can do. When he explained it to us, he told us that it was very difficult to do and therefore a rare, highly-prized talent. Many palace guards and actors alike got their roles based on these abilities.

I looked over to my brother. I knew it took quite a long time to convince him to let a glamoured soldier sit in his place. I was personally glad; thanks to the brave soldier, no one had to make any traumatizing decisions.

"Please send my deepest gratitude to your soldier, Prince Yeong-Gi," my brother signed solemnly. "My wife is particularly grateful."

Yeong-Gi placed both hands over his heart in a thankful gesture.

Newen signed, "That was a tense moment. I'm glad we all got out of it safely." During our brief scuffle, Newen and his entourage took control of security so no one else could be kidnapped or threatened. Due to their diligence, we avoided significant tragedy.

"I understand that you and your people deserve some rest and a victorious meal. We are working diligently to provide care. Along with that, I would like to know how Ushallav can further serve you," Ray signed. "Despite what a few of our people profess, we value our friendship and partnership. We are only as strong as our allies."

His words stirred the emotions of the room. Ekwueme said something in his language under his breath but it sounded affirmative and jovial. He transitioned to signing,

"It's been impressive to see how the Ushallavi and Makaarians have done their due diligence to retain peace after the wars of your grandparents. Thank you for ensuring that these Black Wings were addressed before they spread north. I'm honored that we could help in that effort."

"We'll definitely think of things that we need—like more of that lassi from the birthday celebration," Bernadino added. He referred to the yoghurty drink that suited anyone looking for a sweet, alcohol-free treat.

My heart raced and I couldn't meet anyone's eyes. They had first come to see me—so I could potentially court them. I didn't think I would find love so close to home. So quickly. So deeply. And yet it didn't make this situation less awkward.

I finally lifted my eyes to quickly measure the circle of royalty around me. I cleared my throat and straightened my posture. My hands formed the words before I lost my nerve.

"It means a lot that you would come all this way. I wish we had more time to catch up—and I hope there's more time to chat before you travel back north. After...everything that happened and divorcing King

Damir, I wanted to rekindle our friendships and potentially make a match. Something much deeper than just an allyship.

"But unfortunately—fortunately! Depends on how you view it—I have made a match with someone else."

During my shaky explanation, I noticed that Bernadino and Ekwueme were already holding hands and giving each other a "we have much to discuss" glances. I dare say Newen looked a bit sad but not surprised. Yeong-Gi smiled and asked,

"Could this possibly be the fierce woman who fought at your side? The epic poetry writes itself."

"Oh, I was hoping to hear about this from you directly," Ekwueme chimed in, signing with one hand so he could still hold Bernadino's with the other.

I laughed. "It's a lot, and it's sudden. But I'll tell you everything. And set up an introduction!"

After daring a look at Ray, I signed to everyone, "I'm sorry if I was misleading in any way. And I hope the party was worth the trip."

"You've been through so much, Princess Anjali," Newen signed. "It's good to see you well and smiling."

I signed, "Thank you. Now that the awkward part is out of the way—"

"Wait, what was the awkward part?" Bernadino joked.

"—I do have some ideas of how we can move forward as allies and friends."

"Let's hear them," Ray added, gesturing to his scribe. Periodically, I heard Ray muttering things to the scribe in Ushallavi so they could record the highlights of our discussion.

I dove into a speech and a plan. Arguably, there would always be dissenters like the Black Wings. But part of their stance hinged on the fact that Makaar and Ushallav were barely playing nice after a devastating war—and our neighbors to the north stayed out of it. What people knew about my princely friends bordered on myth rather than lived experience.

We could take Janitra's experiences of living in both countries and create opportunities for safe travel and exchanges across the Northern Sea to see these places and peoples for themselves. Even if Black Wing members continue to exist in the shadows, it would be their conspiracies, against lived wisdom.

And while I wasn't familiar with the numbers, I'm sure Ray and I could commission a report on how much in scholarships we could give to people to affordably make the journey. Maybe I was too optimistic but it only seemed fair. If I could help someone make the journey without fear of attack, I could continue to honor the ones I lost years ago.

I already knew I couldn't personally teach people that our country was stronger with allies but I wanted to open the door. The thought caught in my throat and I thought I might cry.

Could this be a way to honor my initial oaths when I married Damir? Bring people together for joint prosperity. My marriage was a symbol of that oath but I felt warmed knowing that I could still be this passionate, bold leader in other ways. My way.

"So does this mean we'll be seeing more of you in the future?" Ekwueme asked.

"I think so," I replied, charmed at the realization. With this as my project and responsibility, it opened up so many more ways to serve my people than to sit on someone's throne. I didn't care if I was still a queen, princess, or something else. I was still a mother—hopefully someone's wife someday. But I'd forever remain myself.

"What about your children? Sounds like you would be spread much too thin," Prince Newen asked. It didn't sound like judgment but more like a check-in.

Ray finished translating for his scribe and looked to me for my answer.

"This is really important to me," I replied, "and so is raising my children. I'm sure I can work with King Damir, Queen Einora, and my partner to find something suitable. I want my children to see the world and learn from it. But they're already split between kingdoms as it is."

"Not that it's our business—but we want to help where able," Prince Yeong-Gi added.

"It sounds like Princess Anjali needs more time to confer with the children about what they'd like to do," Ray interjected kindly. For the sake of his scribe, he spoke and signed simultaneously. "But I do look forward to what this change could mean for all of us."

After he looked around and garnered several satisfied smiles, he added, "Shall we eat? I'm starving."

Beloved People of Ushallav

It is with profound gratitude and pleasure that I can address you today, and with fortunate news. After much inves-

tigating and great sacrifice, our beloved Queen Anjali has yet again brought peace to Ushallav and honor to Abhijita's name.

In the background, a group called the Black Wings had held meetings and circulated information that would call for the capture and control of Queen Anjali in an attempt to usurp power in our fair kingdom. We have caught and interrogated many of their members but it is possible that many go free and anonymous.

This group did not consider Ushallav strong enough to hold our own, and did not see our current alliance with Makaar as satisfactory. If you or anyone you know has harbored such opinions, know this: our ties with our neighbors have never been stronger and have blessed our people more than we will ever know. The next time an enemy raises an arm to injure us, the might of five other kingdoms will rise to meet them.

Many Makaarians and Ushallavi have buried their fellows and lit incense for the souls lost far too soon. We work tirelessly with King Damir to ensure that Zayant sleeps soundly and Tamul is awake.

Queen Anjali fulfilled her duty as Abhijita's blessed daughter to sacrifice mind and body to apprehend the leaders of this group and deepen alliances with our northern friends. In so doing, I save the best news for last.

As a way to further the minds and talents of all interested Ushallavi, our court will sponsor any and all individuals who would like to travel and learn trades from any of our allies. They have much to share and we have much to offer. You may see many new faces come and go in the coming years. I sincerely hope that our culture and communities will leave a positive mark on our new friends.

Part of this program will involve the tireless service of Queen Anjali, who will retain her well-deserved title. She will travel to each country to measure the needs and successes of our new endeavors. With each step she takes, she continues to ensure safety and strength in her wake.

In the coming weeks, we will hold assemblies to hear your questions and suggestions. My scribes will record your impressions and bring them to me. May our generous honesty root out confusion and error.

The harvest season now settles in. My family and court wish you all a joyous festival season.

King Ray of Ushallav, son of Jagdish and Indali

"I guess this is why you're the king," I said, holding a copy of Ray's decree. My nose wrinkled. "You really laid it on thick."

"Dear sister, I'm king because Father said so—and I give credit where credit is due," Ray dared a smile in return.

"Well, I'm convinced that this is all going to work out well. This exchange program is going to work wonders."

"It was your idea."

"And I guess that's why I still get to be a queen, isn't it?"

"That's also because Father said so—and I'm inclined to agree. Your children will be heirs and a once-in-a-century royal divorce shouldn't change that."

I smiled. I already knew this but it didn't hurt to hear it repeated. One more thing Kavi and Leela couldn't take from me in the end.

"Shouldn't you be packing for your anniversary trip? Tejal said the southern mountains are very nice this time of year."

"Shouldn't you be preparing for your ex-husband's departure?"

I laughed. "I can't wait for this holiday to loosen you up, brother."

He dared yet another smile, just for me, before rolling his eyes and gesturing for both of us to exit his office. There would be much work to come but for now, our family could finally breathe a sigh of relief.

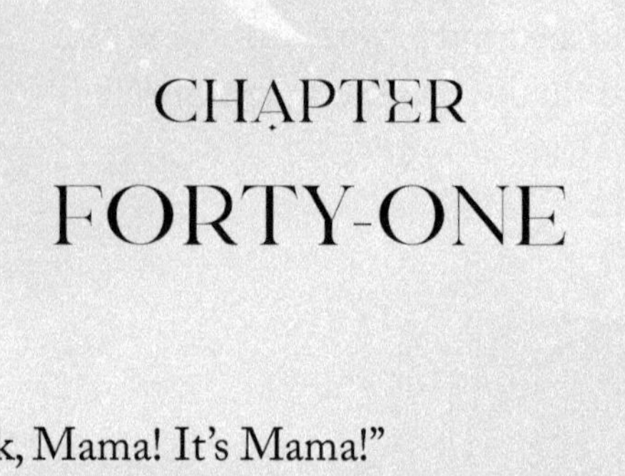

CHAPTER

FORTY-ONE

Look, Mama! It's Mama!"

Devraj waved as Einora's carriage came into view. We'd learned that it was easiest if our kids use the Makaarian word for "mother" for Einora and the Ushallavi word for me.

His hybrid use of Makaarian and Ushallav brought a sudden rush of pride. I smiled at my son's enthusiasm. It was still a good sign that he loved his stepmother.

As if on cue, Einora stuck her head out of the carriage and waved enthusiastically. It felt jarring to see such a jovial entrance in a place that had been littered with soldiers and Black Wings a couple of weeks ago.

We made sure that this reunion wouldn't create additional trauma for me or anyone else. We planted trees and flower bushes around the courtyard to encourage wonderful smells and more wildlife to the space.

Einora's entourage lined up, allowing a moment for the horses to catch their collective breath and be relieved of their duties.

Damir approached my side with Sanjana riding on his shoulders. He gripped her ankles tight and had a very triumphant grin on his face. There it was. Love. In a way that no longer devastated me, I knew that Damir had gracefully healed and moved forward. He enjoyed every second of this new chance at life and love. Good for him.

Approaching my other side, Janitra silently took my hand. I gave it a squeeze of happiness. We barely had a moment to relish this new phase of our relationship but we knew there was plenty of time to come for that.

Einora graciously received the assistance from her carriage driver and trotted as quickly as her shoes would allow to greet us. The plum-colored silk material of her skirts swished with her movements. Her v-neck travel dress covered her to the wrists and ankles and a matching travel coat covered the dress with a parallel neckline and a beaded belt and buttons to close the coat at the naval. Her blonde hair was styled in a braid crown with a matching plum ribbon interwoven with her curls.

She dove straight into her husband's arms.

"Hello, dear," she murmured into Damir's embrace. After giving him a meaningful extra squeeze, she turned her blue eyes to the children. "Hello Devraj and Sanjana! I heard you were the heroes yet again. Left me out entirely!"

She gave them quick hugs and kisses before taking Janitra in. Almost with reverence, she placed her hands on Janitra's biceps.

"I must learn everything there is to know about you," Einora beamed. I'd never heard her speak Ushallavi but here she was speaking slowly but determined. "Anjali has…oh, I just practiced that first part but nothing else, so I'll have to continue in Makaarian. But Anjali has been very cryptic about her love life and I have a feeling you won't keep anything from me."

"Your Highness, I would never," Janitra smiled, speaking in Makaarian. I nearly swooned. Einora pulled us both into a hug before returning to the rest of the group.

"Mama, Mama! I'll tell you about Janitra," Sanjana piped up from her tall perch. Einora leaned in as if to hear a secret but Sanjana didn't quite know how to properly whisper. Damir sneaked a quick kiss on the cheek as Einora leaned in. "She's very pretty."

Einora's mouth opened as if hearing quite the juicy piece of gossip.

"I've missed all the fun," she practically exclaimed.

"I've missed Gregori," Devraj answered. "Is he here?"

"Dear, he's spending time with his grandparents," Einora explained. "But I did bring a special surprise for you."

She offered her hand and Devraj took it. Together, they walked to the other carriages. Out spilled out several Makaarian children his age along with their parents. They had all traveled here to celebrate his sixth birthday.

Our visitors poked their heads out curiously but

broke into smiles once the rest of them heard greetings in Makaarian. Sanjana wriggled, itching to meet the children. Damir hoisted her over his head and placed her back on the ground. As soon as her feet touched the ground, she bounded over to the guests. Many of the adults bowed in acknowledgment of our presence.

One parent said to their child, "Thank the prince for inviting us to his party."

A boy slightly shorter than mine gave Devraj a hug and exclaimed, "Thank you for inviting us!"

"Thank you for coming!" Devraj squealed. I recognized many of the parents but that was the extent of our relationship. They must've really stepped in for us when I was surviving in the woods with Sanjana.

I could see a wild look in Devraj's eye. His little body was cramped and stuffed with so many emotions. I could feel something similar in my body. Before long, I blurted out, "Who's hungry?" A happy chorus replied. Food. Food solved a lot of problems.

Janitra and I led the way to the prepared lunch as attendants took luggage to the guest wings. Einora materialized in between and hooked her arms with me and Janitra. She immediately peppered us with questions— mostly about Janitra. We did our best to reply.

"Is it common for women to date each other in Ushallav? I hear it happens in Makaar but I clearly still have so much to learn. Anjali, I knew you had excellent taste."

I couldn't help but blush.

"Anjali invited some very attractive princes to her birthday party—this is before we officially began courting. But I think two of them might now be courting each other as well," Janitra added. "That last part is unconfirmed but fairly plain to the casual observer."

"Anjali!" Einora gasped. I thought she might faint from all the new gossip. "I knew I'd like Janitra. She tells me all the good stuff."

"I figured we would get to that but I didn't think that would be the first thing you'd want to know," I laughed.

With Damir and the children right behind us and my handmaidens surrounding us in silent protection, I imagined that our family entourage looked interesting to say the least.

It was a fleeting thought. After all, who cared what anyone had to say about my family? My children enjoyed limitless love and protection. When it was all said and done, I would do and say what must be done and said. I would become whoever I needed to be to ensure my children's happiness, Janitra's happiness, and my happiness.

I felt a vibration of happiness knowing that this second chance at life was precious and mine for the taking. This feeling bloomed up my spine and through every muscle in my body.

Once Einora left us and returned to Damir's side, Janitra took my hand. The bangles around our wrists rang merrily.

"Are you okay?" Janitra whispered in Ushallavi. I smiled at her and didn't care who noticed.

"Absolutely."

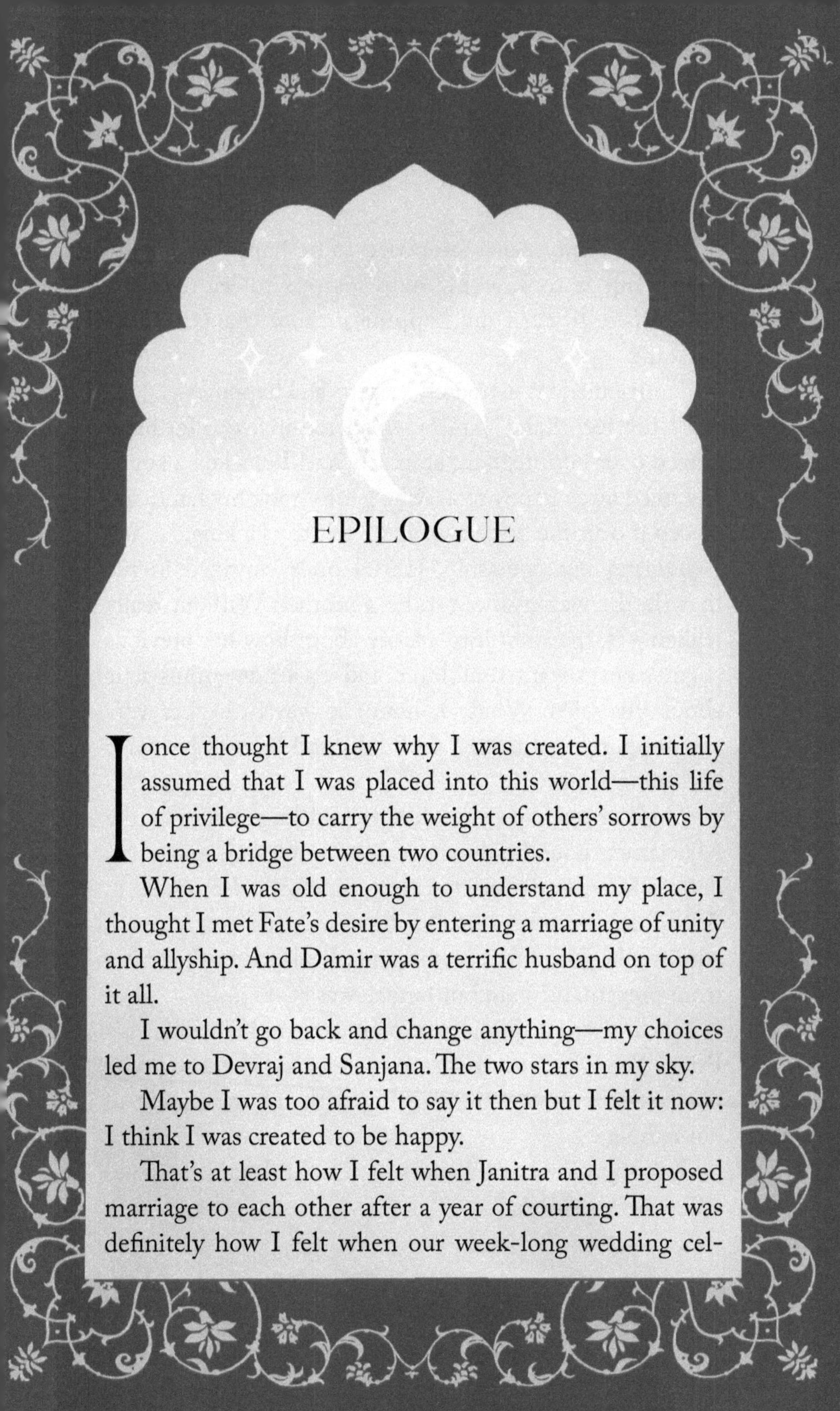

EPILOGUE

I once thought I knew why I was created. I initially assumed that I was placed into this world—this life of privilege—to carry the weight of others' sorrows by being a bridge between two countries.

When I was old enough to understand my place, I thought I met Fate's desire by entering a marriage of unity and allyship. And Damir was a terrific husband on top of it all.

I wouldn't go back and change anything—my choices led me to Devraj and Sanjana. The two stars in my sky.

Maybe I was too afraid to say it then but I felt it now: I think I was created to be happy.

That's at least how I felt when Janitra and I proposed marriage to each other after a year of courting. That was definitely how I felt when our week-long wedding celebration brought together all our familiar friends, allies, and loved ones.

Sure, everyone was supposed to be happy and enjoy peace. But it took a few hard lessons to learn that I didn't have to earn my happiness more than the next person.

Janitra made it extremely easy to feel happiness.

"I can feel them," Janitra whispered in awe. Her hand grazed over her pregnant stomach, and I cracked a smile. I blinked away happy tears. She gently took my hand and placed it over the same area and I felt the kicking.

During our courtship, Janitra once confided in me that she'd always wanted to be a mother. Without really realizing it, she went into a story about how her previous partner never wanted children and wasn't as enthusiastic about this wish. What an honor it was to be her wife and support her through the highs and lows of her wish becoming reality.

She'd never have to endure the stifling silence of the Makaarian household where I bore Devraj, and she'd definitely never endure the deep loneliness I endured in the wilderness after birthing Sanjana. This was where I, admittedly, got a little overbearing; I wanted to shield her from preventable pain but Janitra was strong.

She insisted on joining me on my trip to Haneul to visit Prince Yeong-Gi; my first stop on my journey through the north. So here we were, swaying with the movement of our carriage.

I gently moved my hand so I could rub Janitra's hand still over her stomach.

"You're handling this trip like a pro," I said before being lost in my thoughts again. "The bumps in the road can feel more intense when you're already not feeling your best."

"I'm feeling my best right now," she insisted. Her hand turned so it could take mine. Our wedding rings twinkle in a patch of sunshine. "Can you pass me something to eat?"

I reach under my seat and pull out a Makaarian pastry. The smell of strawberry made itself known and Janitra reached out gleefully.

"I do miss some of the food," she said between bites. I sat back and licked some stray jelly from my fingers.

We had just traveled to Makaar to ensure Devraj and Sanjana arrived safely at their second home. At this point, we were getting used to the change in seasons. When they were in Ushallav, I was there to educate, love, and raise them. When it was Damir and Einora's turn, that's when I traveled north and visited our allies.

Janitra wouldn't miss any of this; dropping off the children was harder than I expected. She was there to cry with me. And now she was helping me spearhead my new initiative: shepherding the first group of Ushallavi citizens to the north. I hoped they would explore what our allies had to offer and forever prove Kavi wrong.

"So, should we review the list of baby names or should we start designing the garden?"

She referred to the home my parents presented to us as a wedding gift. It wasn't too far away from the palace but enough to consider it a space all our own. Ray could have his space and I'd be happy to have mine.

As for the baby name list, that was a formality. We'd already fallen in love with the name Hira.

"Shouldn't you be resting?"

"All I do is rest, darling." Janitra affected a fake whine that sounded partially real. She took to life as royalty in stride. It was fun to watch.

"I like when you call me 'darling.'"

"Get used to it, darling."

I adjusted myself and then gently moved Janitra so she could use my lap as a pillow. She resisted for a moment but relented and settled in.

"You can tell me all about the seeds we ought to buy while we're traveling. We just need to ensure they're not toxic to animals."

"Are we getting a pet, too?" Janitra's eyes flew open. I laughed.

"Why not? And if we have guests, I'd rather be welcoming."

I poked my head out the window and observed the trail of carriages in our entourage. They were full of people—my people—ready to follow me north. Maybe they'd learn a trade, fall in love, or feel extremely homesick. Together, we'd chase after whatever the gods and life had in store for us.

For now, I trusted myself. There was no other way to say it. My happily ever after was in very good hands.

Reader,

Thank you so much for reading *The Vindicated Queen*. I think we can all agree that Queen Anjali more than deserved a delicious happily ever after. I'm so delighted that you now have her complete story in your hands.

If you have any thoughts about this book, please write an honest review on Amazon, Goodreads, Storygraph, Readerly, or wherever else you chat about or buy books.

To learn more about me, future books, or
my book editing services, please visit:

WITANDTRAVESTY.COM

Instagram: @whit2ney

Facebook: Wit & Travesty

Tiktok: @witandtravesty

ACKNOWLEDGMENTS

Another duology complete! With every book, I remind myself of how much I'm meant to tell stories that highlight under-the-radar perspectives while describing universal experiences. I proudly worked on all the writing and marketing, but now I get to give credit to the team and community that made this book possible.

First, you know I must thank Travis McGruder—husband and editor extraordinaire. We managed to move to Texas, publish this novel, adopt our first dog, and go through IVF in such a short amount of time. I relish any opportunity to tell you that I couldn't love this life without you.

Thank you, Karen Dunstan, for consistently serving as the president of my fan club. You got to read a very spicy scene that didn't fully make the final cut. Thank you for always being there—just a phone call away. I've admired how you've carved your own version of happiness, and it largely inspired Anjali's path.

Shoutout to my monthly author group chat for helping me navigate the publishing process. Thank you especially to Tori Nix for being more like a sister than just an author friend. Your readings and friendship have helped me balance my creative drive and my need for rest.

This book covers a lot of experiences that I hope are meaningful to my fellow romantasy fans. I feel more confident in sharing my work thanks to honest feedback from early readers. Special thanks to the following readers: Grace Melville, Maddy Bragg, Krissy Summers, Angel Curá, and Zena Wright. Special thanks to Amy Vogel, Kailey Bright, Rocio Carranza, and Kylie Wiggins for providing early author review blurbs.

Big thanks to Angie McGruder and Allison Acomb—you've helped me adjust to life in Texas and provide constant, much-needed support on my author journey. Whether you've joined me on my bookstore quest or attended my author events, thank you thank you thank you.

I must also thank Ana (@what_todo_about_reading) and Georgina Kamsika for serving as sensitivity readers for this book. While I created fictitious cultures for this book, much of Ushallav is inspired by Indian/South Asian culture. Thank you so much for providing honest feedback so I could confidently share a diverse cast that speaks to many non-fiction experiences.

If you're in love with the cover and the book layout like I am, please join me in thanking Naimly A. again for bringing this vision to life. And thank you again to Enchanted Ink Publishing who worked their layout and formatting magic yet again.

And of course, you know I have the thank those of you who are holding this book in your hands. Whether you've supported me since day one or learned about me through this release, I appreciate you! I'm grateful that you've bought/borrowed this book and shared it with others. I have more stories to share and characters to create; thank you for being a home to these creations.

WHITNEY MCGRUDER

is an author, editor, cosplayer, and self-proclaimed bookstore quest queen. While she's a bit too obsessed with books, she puts her experience to good use. McGruder strives to write, edit, spotlight, and indulge in inclusive stories.

Besides indulging in her fandoms, McGruder enjoys cross-stitching, building her dream library, hosting get-togethers, going on walks with Midna, and making her husband laugh. She's currently on a quest to visit every indie bookstore in Texas.

McGruder believes that book publishing should be about community—not competition. You can find her advice, books, and editing services over at witandtravesty.com.

www.ingramcontent.com/pod-product-compliance
Lightning Source LLC
Chambersburg PA
CBHW051246210726
48287CB00002B/367

9 781735 506494